2nd Last Chance

To ~~[redacted]~~ Thanks for the Help

Bill Wehtore

ISBN 1-886057-55-9

Manufactured in the United States of America

Warren Publishing, Inc.
19809 North Cove Road
Cornelius, North Carolina 28031

Dedication

This book is dedicated to my family and friends who gave me the encouragement to take this to a finished product, and especially to my wife Marie, whose faith and drive have been my confidence builder.

List of Characters

Slick - Lloyd Miller- Main Character
Jaw - Jarvis Alvin Wilson-Founder of Beverly Rehab Organization
Zipper - Francis Adam Zeigler - Aid to Jaw and 2nd in rank to Miller
Speed - Hal Townson - Loan officer with a competing bank
Beagle - Charles Mott - Attorney for Beverly organization
Flipper - Fred Clark - Owner of restaurant
Rock - Rocco DeAngelo - Bodyguard
Milker - Clyde Mills - Hotel Desk Clerk
Flower - Ronda Lewis - Flower shop owner
Typer - Nancy Tarka - Miller's secretary
New York - candidate in Beverly program
Mouse - worker at morgue
Driver - limo company owner
Pigeon - undercover operative
Rat - skid row bum
Fingers Brock - pickpocket
Dot-Com - computer whiz
Leggs - program members
Class - program member
Tipster - cab driver
Notes - Beverly organization accountant
Kid Gloves - Charter committee member
Briefcase - Charter committee member
Archer - Charter committee member
Stinger - Charter committee member
Writer - Charter committee member
Shoes - street person
Weeds - rescuer

Chapter 1

1st Day, Tuesday September 26, 1998, 9:00AM

If you chose to notice the little old man, it would have been obvious that he was homeless. He was around fifty, short, unshaven and a little overweight. He wore a dirty Charlotte Hornets cap, scraggly gray hair poking out all around it. A filthy tan raincoat carelessly hung over his blue University of North Carolina sweatshirt. His pant cuffs dragged on the ground behind dirty white and red tennis shoes. He hurried through the morning rush hour crowd. The warm sun caused rivulets to flow down his face and sparkled down his raincoat.

Finally reaching a phone booth, his fingers flew over the keypad. Passers-by would have overheard him sternly say, "Lady, just tell him Zipper's calling. If he doesn't want to talk to me, just cut me off."

Lloyd Miller recognized the grainy voice on the phone; "Zipper! Miller knew it had to be bad news. Zipper had never called his office.

"It's bad Slick. You're up. Read the obituaries. Later." The phone went dead. Lloyd Miller, known as "Slick" in the double life he led, dropped the phone onto the receiver.

Usually when Zipper talked to Miller, he made it a point to update him on recruits or the lack of them. An uneasiness began to over come Miller. In his mind's eye Miller could see the elfin-like man. He might have made a comical picture, if he was not one of the most sagacious men Miller had ever known.

By contrast, Miller in his mid-forties was one of those few men who naturally appeared neat and confident. Just under six feet, his frequent workouts kept him trim, his stomach flat and his body erect. Miller kept his mind sharp by reading every newspaper he could get. This morning, just as the unnerving call from Zipper reached him, he had finished the Wall Street Journal, USA Today, several papers from major Carolina cities and was about to start reading the business section of the Charlotte

1

Register. Now he flipped through the paper to find the obituary columns. Scanning the names, he found the reason for Zipper's urgent call. The name Jarvis Alvin Wilson leapt from the page and hit him like a fist in a fog. He took deep breaths to keep his heart from exploding.

> *"Jarvis Alvin Wilson, a.k.a. JAW, 64, of 801 N. Main Street, died Sept 25 at home. He settled here in the mid 1970s and worked as the manager of the Beverly Hotel until his death. A former marine officer and Vietnam Veteran, he was honorably discharged. He has no local family or survivors. Send memorials to the Beverly Trust in care of the hotel don't forget. The county has the remains."*

Remorse, shock and grief charged through Miller at once. In a burst of frustration he jumped to his feet and charged around his office. In a few moments he dropped into a chair facing his desk. At the front edge of his desk sat a plaque with his name on it. Under his name was the title "Commercial Loan Officer" and the logo for First Nation Bank. He had worked his way up from a small cubical to this resplendent office. It boasted a view of the Charlotte skyline that looked as if it could have graced a picture postcard. The burgundy carpet blended perfectly with the drapes and tasteful paintings.

Miller strained to remain calm. Holding his emotions at bay, he looked out the window without seeing the bright Carolina morning. Rising, he walked to the window. Looking down twenty-five floors, he could see tiny people going about their business as if nothing had happened.

"Jaw is dead! Don't you realize the impact?" he screamed inwardly, his voice thundering in his mind.

Jarvis Alvin Wilson, known on the street as Jaw, helped the down and out through a secret rehabilitation program. Jaw had no illusions about reclaiming those street people who had chosen their life style. Those he did work with were forced back into the mainstream of life with the help of street people, threats, intimidation, swindles, near slave labor and on occasion, physical violence.

Miller calmed only after the relief valve of tears broke loose and flooded his eyes. His sight blurred as he settled on the photo of his wife. He realized that if it hadn't been for Jaw, she would not be a part of his life now. Suddenly he broke into wrenching sobs.

It took some time and a little nose blowing before Miller thought he regained enough composure to summon his secretary. He pressed the intercom button, "Miss Tarka, put us in "Flap Condition" and come in here."

Nancy Tarka was exceptionally beautiful, tall and slender with shoulder length black hair. Surprised by the tone of Miller's voice, she entered his office unprepared for what she saw. Her boss of three months, who exuded confidence and self-esteem, was speaking into the phone, while tears rolled down his face as he fought to control his voice.

She sat hesitantly in her usual chair. The sun came over Miller's shoulder directly into her face. Being of Native American and Polish descent, her black velvet hair was edged by a silver halo. Tarka's face reflected a golden hue.

"Mrs. Mason please," he was saying, a pause then, "Pigeon, Slick here, bad news, Jaw went down." He paused to regain control as his chin quivered, "Your instructions are to go under and watch the back door. You'll be contacted when to surface."

Miller placed the phone in the receiver and spun his chair to look out the window. He noticed a billowing white cloud that looked like a dinosaur head. He studied it a few minutes while stabilizing his emotions and drying his eyes. Miller completed the circle, stopping to gaze at Tarka appearing to be in control. His eyes were like blue ice, his voice firm, "Ms. Tarka, I know you are dating a guy from 1st Securities Bank. A situation has come up and I need your assistance. Your 1st Securities guy can know nothing of it. You'll be exposed to knowledge that could destroy some very influential people. I'd not ask for your help if I were not

3

totally confident of your loyalty. That you help those people at a time they truly need assistance will not go unnoticed. I need to know if you are with me in the next five minutes."

"Hold on Mr. Miller, where did this come from? I can't give you an answer in five minutes. I need some answers from you. First, who or what is Jaw? And who's Pigeon and why are you calling yourself Slick? This sounds like gangster stuff. I'm into being a secretary who lives a long time. I don't want anything like the danger this is hinting at," said Tarka as she began to rise from her chair. Miller waved her down.

"The danger is only if you go public with the information you learn in the next two or three weeks," said Miller.

"How will anyone know it wasn't me?"

"I assure you false accusations are not an option. I would like you to accept. I know you have sound judgment and I can trust you to follow instructions."

"Is there any chance of getting fired over this?"

"None for you, as for myself, ruin would be a better choice of words."

Tarka thought a moment, "Mr. Miller, if you know about Bob, then you know about my family situation too. It took me over a year to get my Mother on my medical insurance. She must have the treatment she is getting without interruption. The doctor says, if treatment is interrupted, she could be bedridden the rest of her life, are you sure that won't happen?"

"If you lose your job, you'll have another the next day with at least equal benefits for you and your mother," said Miller flatly. "Now as for Jaw and Pigeon, they are members of an alliance of men and women who have been down and out and now have been helped up. The dues include dedicating your life to helping those who appreciate help."

Tarka thought a few minutes and said, "Okay, Mr. Miller, I'm in but please do not endanger my medical insurance."

Tarka knew she wanted in from the start. She was supposed to. The thought of something exciting as opposed to loan applications appealed to her but she could not sacrifice her Mother just to be adventurous.

"I promise. Thank you," said Miller, "now get a note pad. A paper one not electronic, and mark it "Beverly Hotel". I don't want anything left in short hand in the pad. When you are not using it, it must be in the bottom of your lowest desk drawer face down so I can find it in your absence. You will soon come to realize what information you get involves this flap. Keep copious notes."

When Tarka returned, Miller was standing in front of a wall safe hidden behind a mirror. "Ms Tarka, I can not give you the combination to this safe. However, the key under my calendar pad will unlock it if I do not spin the dial once it's open. Your "Beverly" pad must be put in the safe every night or any time both of us are absent from the office. Now write this message down, "Slick sends, code Beverly Flash, Jaw is down, standard precautions, Prime will contact." As he spoke, Miller reached into the safe and removed a phone pad. Handing it to Tarka, he instructed her to call each name with a blue star next to it. Each person must be contacted personally and list the names in the order they were contacted. He asked if she had any questions.

"Would you like the time of contact while I'm at it?"

"Yes good idea, I should have thought of it."

As Tarka walked out, Miller called his friend Hal Townsend, a.k.a. Speed, at 1st Securities Bank, "Speed, Slick here. Serious, Jaw is down."

"Aw shit," came the response. "Are you sure?"

"Yeah, Zipper called me and put me onto the obits in the morning paper."

"What can I do?" asked Speed.

"First launch that clown Bob I told you is seeing Tarka. We need about two weeks."

"Done, he'll be on a plane for San Juan this afternoon. We have a group going down to look over some potential investments. Hey! Keep that from your guys. Next?"

"New York is ready to blossom. Give him some bucks and have him get Malone Funeral Home to pick up Jaw. Tell New York not to spend more than five or six thousand. We don't want Jaw haunting us."

"Nice numbers if it includes the plot. That should be the style Jaw would want to go out in. Anything else?" asked Speed.

"No thanks, later," said Miller.

"Later," said Speed as the line went dead.

Now that the initial arrangements had been set into motion, Miller sat back in his chair clicking off the things he would have to do or should be doing now. First things first, inform his boss.

"Mr. Parkinson's office, may I help you?"

"Lloyd Miller here Ms Moore, is Mr. Parkinson in?"

"I'm sorry Mr. Miller, Mr. Parkinson is in conference right now. Would you like to leave a message?"

"Call in on line 4 Ms Moore, we have a Flap Condition."

"Yes Sir, Mr. Miller."

After a brief pause, "Parkinson here."

"Lloyd Miller sir, Jaw died yesterday. I just found out. I have to work it out. It should take about a week. I have nothing that can't be taken over right now. You should have my recommendation for the Talbot Industries Loan within the hour. I sent it yesterday via interoffice courier. I recommended against it. We probably wouldn't get hurt if you overrode me. We've been doing business with them a long time. Somehow a couple of zeros got added to the asset accounts and diverted from the liability accounts.

"Ed tried that one on me about ten years ago," said Parkinson, Miller could hear the smile in his voice, "He was a small company then. Ed got the loan as he probably will this time, but enough of this. Back to Jaw. Take care of him. Take a week; let me know if you need any help. You'll have what you need to settle." Parkinson trailed off as he broke the connection. A tiny spark went through Slick's mind. He thought the last word Parkinson said as he faded was "in".

6

Tarka passed a few calls to Miller while she contacted the blue star people in the phone pad. When finished she said to Miller, "I called 27 people and all twenty seven were already crying or cried when I passed the message. May I ask who Jaw was?"

"Jaw, Ms Tarka, was an eagle that dealt with turkeys. I've been thinking that I should tell you about our codes. I really can't give you all our codes, only because the words are common usage in street language. I would have to hear them to realize they are code. To us, it's like proper speech. When Zipper called he told me Jaw was "Down." Down by itself means dead. If a message gets passed to you on the street, never turn to see the messenger. If it requires an answer, wait for the messenger to say, "Clear." You will know when message passing is finished when they say "Later." That means, I still trust you, good-bye, I'll be there if you ever need me, or any other salutation you want it to mean. "How you holding?" means how's your mental state. You may hear that someone was "Eyeballed". It means one of us made it a point to be seen by some one we wanted to intimidate and make them aware we knew they were around. I'll give you more terms as the occasion arises. I can't tell you what the "Program" is so don't ask" said Miller.

He turned to the safe and replaced the phone pad Tarka gave back and withdrew another. "Do you recall how insistent Zipper was when he called? Well now it's your turn. Do not identify yourself. Say only that you have a message for these people from Slick. Give them and only them this message: "Beverly Code Flash Prime, Jaw is down. Malone's 8:00 PM, Slick sends."

"Sir, it's 11:45, if you want this done immediately, I can have lunch delivered," said Tarka.

"It would be best if you called out, and if you don't mind, order me a Reuben. I'll spring for lunch," said Miller as he reached for his wallet.

Tarka took the money and headed for the door but stopped short. She turned to Miller and asked, "Will there be much after hours work? The reason I ask is that Bob will try to find out what's going on if I'm late too often."

"If you mean 1st Securities Bob, he'll soon be on a plane to San Juan, helping on some investment evaluation," answered Miller.

"He didn't mention it," commented Tarka.

"He found out about it an hour ago. His plane leaves this afternoon."

Tarka looked at Miller in disbelief.

"Ms Tarka, you are playing with the big boys now."

Chapter 2

Tarka had long since delivered Lloyd his Reuben. Miller sat back in his chair to clear his mind. He stared across the room at the serene oil painting of a mountain lake. He imagined himself fly fishing for a moment. Miller blinked, shook his head and picked up the newspaper again. He re-read the obituary as he bit into his sandwich. Who wrote this he wondered? He read the last few sentences over and over, "He has no known local family or survivors. Send memorials to the Beverly Trust in care of the hotel don't forget. The county has the remains." It sounded like Jaw's words except for the mention of the trust. He wondered how Jaw could write his own obituary. Well, he thought, we are talking Jaw here. Why did the writer specify "local family" or even mention the trust? Miller called the Coroner's Office.

"I'd like to inquire about the remains of Jarvis Alvin Wilson please," said Miller.

"One moment please," said a female voice.

"May I help you?" asked a male voice.

"I'm calling about the remains of Jarvis Alvin Wilson."

"Mr. Wilson's body is at the Malone Funeral Home."

"I know. Can you tell me who wrote his obituary and who found him?"

"A strange thing about that, Jaw, I mean Mr. Wilson. . . . ."

"Beverly code?" inserted Miller rapidly.

"What?" a puzzled voice asked.

"Nothing, go on please."

"Mr. Wilson had a FAX machine set on a timer to FAX 911 central if he didn't turn it off by a certain time. I have a transcript of the FAX if you'd like me to read it?" asked the voice.

"Please."

"It reads, *This is Jarvis Wilson. If you receive this FAX it is because I am dead. I am at 801 South Main Street, in the*

Beverly Hotel, room 107. The night clerk left but a couple of the boys will be in the lobby. The key to my room is on the keyboard, one of them can show you where it is. I am already dead so no need to bust the door down or use sirens. I'm not going anywhere. You're doing a fine job, have a nice day.

"I made the run and found two envelopes on his nightstand. One was addressed to us. The other to someone called Zipper. The one to us had the obituary in it and instructions to pass it to the undertaker.

"The police found Zipper and had him open his envelope right then. All it said was to keep his death quiet until the obituary came out in the papers and something about a routine," the voice finished.

"Why do I get the feeling you knew Jaw?" asked Miller

"Maybe it was my slip. You're right, I did know him."

"How well?"

"Well enough to know about his attitude toward people," the voice answered.

"Thanks for your time and information. We will all miss him. If anything should come up on Jaw, I would appreciate a call. I'm..."

"I know who you are Mr. Miller," interrupted the voice. "Good luck," the line clicked and began to hum.

Miller, surprised by the recognition, had not thought to ask whom he was talking to. He didn't know anyone at the Coroner's Office. How did this guy know him, he wondered and why "good luck" and not a normal "good bye" or "good day". There was something else. Just then the intercom blinked and Tarka said, "Mr. Zipper is on line two." The thought left his mind.

"Talk," said Miller snatching up the phone.

"Jaw told me that if anything happened to him to check a certain shelf in the safe. I just did that and found an envelope that I'm supposed to give to you. I don't think we should be seen together and there is no way I can get to your office. Is there someone you can send down here?"

10

"Yeah, my secretary Ms. Tarka. Meet her outside the fourth door. She'll be wearing a green dress with a white collar. She's tall, beautiful and has black shoulder length hair. Ask her to buy a stick of gum for $5.00, she'll offer you a quarter."

"Got it, later."

Miller called Tarka into his office, "There is no way I can prepare you for Zipper except to say he looks like a street person. He will try to sell you a stick of gum for $5.00. You offer him a quarter. He will give you an envelope.

'I described you to him so he will approach you. When you get off the elevator, face Tryon Street and count four doors to your left. Exit through that door. He will meet you on the sidewalk. He's waiting for you now."

Tarka gathered up her purse on the way to the elevator. While she waited impatiently, she stared at a wall hanging of the Charlotte skyline. The elevator delivered her to street level. She counted the doors and walked out. Tarka paused after about ten paces and looked around as the afternoon sun blazed down on her.

There were a few street people wandering by, none paid her any attention. She felt a presence to her blind side and turned abruptly. There stood a filthy man in filthy clothes wearing round blue sunglasses.

"Got any money lady?" he groveled.

"No," she responded flatly.

"Just a buck or two is all I need," he persisted sticking out a hand cleaner then his face.

Tarka became angered, "Why don't you wash your whole body not just your hands?"

"Everybody likes ass lady, but nobody likes a smart ass. Give me some money. I'm hungry. Ya gotta have a buck or two."

Tarka was sure that this wasn't Zipper. He began advancing toward her. Tarka kept looking around and backing up toward the building.

11

"Hey you two, get the hell away from her!" came a stern yell from somewhere behind her. Tarka looked behind her and saw a policeman approaching, a short distance away.

"They had you surrounded lady, did they get anything from your purse?"

"They? But no, I put it under my arm. Thank you for helping me. I was starting to get scared," said Tarka.

The officer touched the visor of his hat, nodded and began to walk away.

A voice said, "Delivery made. Later"

Astonished, Tarka walked back into the building and directly to the elevators. When the doors closed, she checked her purse.

Tarka said, "I'd be willing to swear holding God's hand that nobody touched me or my purse before I put it under my arm," as she handed the envelope to Miller.

"Why do you think they call him Zipper? Look in your purse again, see if he was showing off," said Miller smiling.

She looked in her purse, "My God! There's gum in here. Is anything safe with him around?"

"Zipper couldn't make the delivery as we planned. A creep named Rat was near you. We don't allow Rat any knowledge of our operations," said Miller as he opened the envelope extracting a note. It read:

> *Dear Slick,*
>
> *I told you a few years back; you'd owe me even after I was dead. Well I'm going to cash in some markers with you now. I want you to tell my wife that I died. Her name is Mary Wilson. She lives in Binghamton, New York. Her phone number is 913-797-9744. I send her cards now and then but I don't want them to stop without her knowing why.*
>
> *I also told you that every man is a coward at least once in his life. My cowardice came in not facing Mary after I had wronged her so badly. Mott has my will. The*

$5,000.00 in this envelope is for Mary's expenses if she and or my son want to come to my funeral. If neither comes, use the money for legal expenses for my estate.

Lloyd, you were a substitute for my son. He has no use for me because I hurt his Mother. I hurt him also. I was the hero that went sour for him. I loved you as if you were my own and in many ways the two of you are alike. What I thought I did nineteen years ago was wrong. I never forgave myself, and then it got complicated. How can I expect my son to forgive me if I didn't face him?

My last shot Slick. I spoke to your Father again. He would be an asset to the program. Think about it Slick, call him.

Jaw

There was also a note folded in the letter. It said, *"Slick, again, have my body sent to Malone's. Also, ensure the place is secure until midnight every night I lay there."*

Miller walked to his desk while he read and sat down. When he finished the letter, he crumpled it and threw it at the wall. As he pounded his desk, he nastily said, "The rat shit bastard! Even dead, he's still on my ass about my Father."

Tarka, taken by surprise, jumped in astonishment. She could see Miller's eyes. They were full of tears. She quietly rose and left the room.

Miller sat in his office, tears flowing down his face again. I'm successful he thought. I have the world by the ass. All I have to do is work at a job I love and stay straight. Why the hell am I crying like a baby over the death of an old man, who isn't even related to me? He stayed on my ass for five years and damn near broke my spirit. He forced me to take a job that scared the hell out of me. He even had the brass to beat me half to death because I wouldn't give him my paychecks. Damn he was mean. I guess that's why I respected him so much. He was just mean enough.

After Miller gained control of himself, he went over and picked up the wadded notes. He smoothed them out and reread the letter. God, he thought, I don't want to call that woman, err lady. Jaw said if you don't know a woman, give her the benefit of the doubt and label her a lady. If she isn't a lady, she'll prove it soon enough. Miller glanced at his watch and pressed the intercom button.

"Ms Tarka, it's quarter to five, you can leave for the day. I'll call you at home if anything unusual comes up, otherwise, normal time tomorrow. You did a good job today."

As Miller dialed Mrs. Wilson's number, Tarka came into his office, laid her note pad on his desk and left. Just as she closed the door, an ageless female voice said, "Hello?"

Miller was speechless for a moment and finally blurted, "Mary Wilson please." As the words blurted from his mouth, anxiety suddenly built itself into a hard melon-sized knot in his stomach.

"Speaking."

"Mrs. Wilson, my name is Lloyd Miller. I'm afraid I have some bad news about Jarvis Wilson. Are you sitting down?"

It was then that Miller realized he should have rehearsed something to say to Mrs. Wilson. He also knew he used the wrong words. The knot in his stomach grew.

"Oh my God, Al is dead!" wailed Mrs. Wilson in what Miller took for true heart felt anguish. Miller's chin quivered at the sound. He wanted nothing more at this moment then to slam the phone down and get the hell out of his office.

"I'm sorry to say you are correct ma'am," the knot now cinched tight.

"How did he die? Where? What happened? Was he murdered?"

"He died peacefully in his sleep here in Charlotte, North Carolina. He died yesterday," answered Miller softly, the knot in his stomach easing as he spoke.

"Charlotte! How long has he been in Charlotte?" asked Mrs. Wilson incredulously.

"About nineteen years, you make it sound so unbelievable. Why is that?" asked Miller his stomach now at neutral."

"I'll tell you about that later. When is the funeral?"

"Final arrangements haven't been made yet. Are you planning to attend?"

"Of course! He was my husband. Our son James will be there also.

Miller asked, "Mrs. Wilson, what airport will you be using? I don't know a thing about your area."

"Binghamton has an airport, the Broome County Airport," Mrs. Wilson responded, and call me Mary, I insist. US Air used to have a flight from here to Charlotte daily, I'll check and see when we can get out of here."

"Don't bother Mrs.,ah, ah, Mary. I'll make the arrangements for you. Your husband left some money for your flight and accommodations if you chose to come down. Would you prefer a morning or afternoon flight and when?"

"The old bastard, he probably felt he wasn't worth the price of a ticket to come here. If you're going to handle it, get me down there as soon as possible," said Mary. Miller could hear her voice break again. He waited patiently.

"Was he well liked down there? What did he do?" asked Mary.

"Mary he was loved by a large circle of friends," said Miller avoiding any mention of the Beverly. He asked, "May I call you back and give you your flight information?"

"No Lloyd, I have to get off the line now. I need a few hours to deal with the shock of this and do some grieving. Make the flight arrangements and I'll call US Air between spasms. Just give me your phone number in case anything goes wrong," said Mary.

Lloyd confirmed James's last name and gave Mary several phone numbers, expressed his sympathy again and hung up. He immediately called the airlines and made arrangements for the Wilsons. Miller sat back in his chair thinking. The phone rang. He snapped it up saying, "Talk."

15

"Zipper here Slick, need any help?"

"Find a place to squat, let me tell you who I just got off the phone with. None other then Mrs. Jarvis Alvin Wilson, a.k.a. Mary Wilson of Binghamton New York, a.k.a. Mrs. Jaw."

"What! You mean the old bastard was married!"

"Yeah, remember the old joke, there's more? Well there is. Jaw's wife is bringing their son with her. I have them booked on flight 277 from Binghamton to Charlotte, arriving tomorrow afternoon. How about contacting Driver and tell him what we want?"

"His best from arrival to departure, twenty four hours, with one in reserve in case they want to go in separate directions," said Zipper.

There was silence for a few moments. Simultaneously they said, "Better alert the street."

"Who do you have at Malone's tonight?" asked Miller

"Rock will be at the door. I haven't heard from Pigeon yet, but I don't expect any problems. See you about eight. Later," answered Zipper.

"You're on, Later."

Miller hung up and had just gotten comfortable when a thought flashed in his mind. In his eagerness to get upright, he almost tipped his chair over. He glanced around the empty office sheepishly to ensure no one was watching. He grabbed the phone and dialed rapidly.

"Honey, I'm," was all he could get out to the immediately answered phone.

"I know about Jaw, Lloyd. I saw it in the paper late this morning. I'm sorry Honey. I was going to call you but I figured you had enough on your mind with arrangements and all. Don't worry about me. Do what you have to," said Suzanne Miller.

"Thanks Honey, by the way, I just talked to Jaw's wife, Mary."

"What! The old bastard was married all this time, or did he just get married?" asked Suzanne.

"Married all this time, but not only that, she's bringing their son along with her."

"God Lloyd, what else will surface?"

"I don't know. I really haven't had time to think about the trust and the program. I'm going to meet Zipper in about an hour at Malone's. Mott may be there and we can get together and get a handle on everything or part of it anyhow. Love you Honey, bye,"

Lloyd hung up with the picture of Suzanne Miller in his mind. She was a very pretty woman but not what you would call beautiful. Her short cut auburn hair blended with her petite body. She was only five feet three inches and complained of being overweight when she broke a hundred pounds.

Something she said kept Suzanne's image in his mind but what was it? Then Lloyd realized she assumed he would have to make all the arrangements for the funeral. She knew about Zipper, Charles Mott, known as Beagle and a few others, why would she assume he'd be in charge of arrangement? The question nagged at him some but he dismissed it to her confidence in him.

Chapter 3

Crime Boss Carlos Misota walked into his office feeling pretty good about how things were working out. In his late fifties, he was still in good shape. He stood 6 feet tall and kept his weight around 200 pounds, give or take a holiday. His black wavy hair was beginning to have that silver streak along the sides that he used to admire in older men. Now it was not so attractive.

His aide, Tony Deluca, followed him into the office. Tony let him sit down and arrange himself before he dropped the open newspaper on Misota's desk.

"What?" asked Carlos.

"Check out the last one sir."

Carlos scanned the Obituaries and found what Deluca knew would be interesting and said softly, "I'll be damned. The son of a bitch died."

Misota thought for a while and finally said, "Find Emile, he's probably shacked up with some whore. Find him and get him here, fast."

"Yes Sir," said Deluca as he spirited from the office.

Misota began to plan. He had two guys involved with the Beverly Hotel crowd on the hook. One owed him thousands in gambling debts the other bribed over kinky sex. He also had an Ace in the Hole that even Emile didn't know about. Carlos had strict instructions not to contact him for any reason. That really irked Carlos since this project was his brainchild.

A knock on the door brought Deluca back in, "I found Emile, he'll be here inside a half hour."

"Was he with some whore?"

There was a pause, Deluca answered, "Yes Sir."

"Tony, I'm not stupid, I caught that. I like it but remember, never try to serve two masters. Right now I'm the boss. Emil is my kid but he is also a soldier. By the time he takes over, he'll understand your value. Besides, I think they have better plans

18

for you up north."

"Thank you Sir. It does get tough when you have to rat on the Boss's kid knowing he's the next boss," said Tony.

Misota smiled and asked Deluca to get him a cup of coffee. Deluca delivered the coffee and left. The coffee odor had a calming affect on Carlos. He lit a cigar and slowly sipped the brew as he went over and over his plans.

As predicted, Emile walked into Carlo's office twenty-five minutes later. Carlos, deep in thought was startled. "Damn it Emile, I've told you a hundred times to knock before you come in here." Emile Misota was in his mid twenties. His auburn hair was from his Mother, his build, although a few inches shorter, was his Father's.

"Tony made it sound like you were in a hurry so I came right in."

"Never be in too much of a hurry to be courteous," said Carlos. "Sit down, that Wilson guy from the Beverly Hotel died. From what we can find out his heir apparent is a guy named Lloyd Miller who works for 1st Nation Bank. Everything we can get on Miller says he's a straight arrow and as smart as they come. We can't find any history on him but from the way he thinks, he must have lived on the streets for a while."

"Do you want him taken out?" asked Emile.

"Damn it Emile, dead bodies bring cops, live bodies bring information. If we can turn him, everything will be much easier. If we can't then we'll consider our options and don't interrupt," said Carlos. "I want you to put some people on the street. Find out what that Beverly Crowd is doing especially as far as Miller taking over."

"I'll send six or seven guys to the street and see what we turn up," said Emile

"That's good, we want to get information not give out information. Tell them to be quiet and listen. Oh, find that jerk Dot-Com. Tell him he's working for us now," said Carlos.

Emile left the room and Carlos thought about the situation more. With Wilson dead, there will be a time frame with no activity. The money in the trust and neither the stocks nor bonds would be touched until the funeral is taken care of. If one of his inside guys became the boss there would be no problems. If that guy Miller takes over then there could be a problem or two. Of course if Miller were taken out, it would give his insiders a better chance of taking the reigns.

Emile reported back around noon saying nothing big was going on and that not everyone knew Wilson was dead. He did find out that Wilson was at that cheap funeral home over on West Street called Malone's. Carlos told him to keep the guys out there something would come up.

Since his wife died, Carlos rarely ate at home. In fact, home was now a lavish apartment above his office. He preferred to eat out. This evening he was eating at the Golden Rose. His mouth watered as the aroma of the sizzling steak surrounded by three lobster tails was laid before him. He ate slowly enjoying the flavors of the steak slices followed by a piece of lobster tail dripping butter.

Emile sauntered up to Carlos' table and asked, "Why so late Pop? It's almost nine, you're usually home by now."

"I told you not to call me "Pop". I had a little trouble contacting the Don. I figured he should know about Wilson's death. I was right. He wants Notes to keep him up on anything that comes up. What've you got?"

"You won't believe this. Wilson has a wife and kid."

"What?" exclaimed Carlos. His frown indicated his concern.

"Yes Sir, they're going to be here for the funeral. We don't know where they live or how they're getting here," said Emile.

Carlos thought a few minutes. "It doesn't matter where or how. You can bet that someone from the Beverly contacted her. Wilson's obit said there was no one local. They have to stay somewhere. I doubt it will be at the Beverly but check it out just the same. Also check out the better hotels around town."

Emile proudly smiled, "I've already sent guys out but I don't think they will find anything until tomorrow, possibly late tonight."

20

"Why?"

"We didn't know Wilson was married and I don't think the Beverly guys did either. I think we all got some news and they're scrambling around making arrangements."

"That's good thinking Emile," said Carlos nodding his approval. "Keep hunting for her and check with our contact at US Air. Have him check to see if there are two Wilsons heading here from somewhere. If not, don't worry about it. They'll get here. What we really need to know is where they are staying. We may want to visit them."

Chapter 4

The late afternoon sun began laying geometric designs across streets, parking lots and the sides of buildings as workers streamed from office towers relieved to leave the burdens of the day. However, for the Charlotte Register's night staff, the day was just beginning.

Carl Gage was still recovering from his thirtieth birthday. It was a traumatic event for him even though he dressed like a seventy-year-old professor. At five foot ten, his medium frame was always covered in something beige, brown, and wrinkled.

Carl Gage sat at his desk in the News Room, checking early editions for the stories he had written. He found all three, none of which he was really proud of: a cabbie giving back a wallet full of money, a couple returning from Europe after being slightly injured by a terrorist bomb, and an elderly man who fought off a young thief to keep his Social Security Check. But, at least they had his by-line. He would consider selling his Mother for a good story. He slammed the paper down on his desk and walked over to look out the window. Nothing seemed to be happening in the city anymore. Yet he knew something had to be going on somewhere, he just had to find it.

He thought of going down to the police station, check out the arrest reports and see if he could get an excessive force story. They had a way of coming back at him. The last time he tried, the News Editor made two phone calls to check out a couple of the facts and threatened to assign him to rewrites on obituaries if he ever exaggerated a story like that again.

Still frustrated he returned to his desk and picked up the paper again. He turned pages until he came to the obituaries to see if anybody interesting had died. Jarvis Alvin Wilson, a.k.a. Jaw died. He had heard rumors about the man. He read the column. What is the Beverly Hotel Trust, he asked himself? He noted the wording, "Memorials will be sent. Don't forget." That's a demand he thought. He knew where the Beverly Hotel was located but could not remember hearing of any problems there. He decided to check out the hotel.

A cab took Gage through the bustling revitalized uptown area, down a side street to the Beverly Hotel. It was located in a part of town the street people referred to as "taint". It "taint" up town and it "taint" skid row. The hotel had seen better days but the area gave the impression that worse days could come. The building, to its very peak, was a replica of an eight-story wax paper milk carton. The lobby had the allure of a 1920 movie set from the paisley wallpapered walls, down to the stovepipe circular couch in the center. The furniture looked worn enough to be original décor.

The desk clerk wore a white short-sleeved tee shirt and red arm garters at his bare elbows. He was made to look more hawk-faced by the black eye shade he wore low over his eyes, his bald head shining above it. The clerk was an inch or two taller than Gage, thin, middle aged and seemed to be a still damp, but drying out wino. He wore a "Hi I'm" tag on his tee shirt with "Clyde" neatly printed in red. The other occupants of the lobby looked to be a drab, lost, lot.

Gage walked to the desk clerk and said, "I'm Carl Gage with the Register. I'd like to ask you a few questions about Jarvis Wilson."

"Don't know him," replied the clerk, "you wanna rent a room?"

"I meant to say Jaw."

"Only met him, didn't know him. Wanna rent a room?"

"How long have you worked here?" Gage asked.

Clyde fidgeted a bit, looked around the room, then at Gage and asked, "What time is it?"

Quickly Gage glanced at his watch. "Seven fifteen, but that doesn't answer my question." When the words were out of his mouth, Gage knew what kind of answer he would get.

"I've been working here for three hours and fifteen minutes, wanna rent a room or not?"

"Who hired you?"

"The manager, he came to me and asked, "Clyde, do you want a job? I say where? He says here. I say what do I have to do? He says rent rooms. I say I'll take it. He says you got it. You know fella, you're pretty good at asking questions but you sure as hell are lacking in answering them. Do you wanna rent a room or not?"

"How did you know he was the manager?"

"He had a plastic tag on his shirt that had manager written on it."

Gage persisted, "I want to talk to the manager."

"Why, I do something wrong?" asked Clyde.

"No, you haven't done anything wrong," answered Gage exasperated.

"Then why can't you rent a room from me?"

"I don't wanna - er - want a room. I want to talk to the manager."

"Hey, you a salesman?" asked Clyde slowly eyeing Gage suspiciously.

"No, I'm not a salesman, I'm a reporter."

"Is this an interview? Am I on TV? Hey, is that guy Funt out there somewhere?" asked Clyde excitedly looking out the front doors and windows on both sides of Gage.

Gage suddenly had an idea. He fished a twenty-dollar bill out of his wallet, laid it on the counter and pushed it toward Clyde.

"So finally, you wanna rent a room, but..."

"It's not for a room, its..." interrupted Gage.

"We don't make change," snapped Clyde

"It's not for change, it's for you."

"Oh thanks," responded Clyde as he put the twenty in his pocket. Clyde stood on his side of the counter looking at Gage blankly.

"Well?" asked Gage.

"Well what?" asked Clyde.

"Well, where's the manager?" asked Gage.

"Down to the parlor," said Clyde

Gage leaned back from the counter and looked through the lobby into the interior of the building. He finally asked, "Where's the parlor?"

"I don't know,' replied Clyde innocently.

"What the hell do you mean, you don't know where the parlor is?" asked Gage heatedly.

"Look pal, I've been in town three weeks, been a desk clerk for three hours, how the hell should I know where the parlor is?" answered Clyde sarcastically.

"What the hell does that have to do with it? How can you be the desk clerk and not know where a room in this hotel is?" asked Gage, now completely frustrated and not thinking clearly.

"I didn't say it was a hotel parlor. Hotels have lobbies; funeral homes have parlors. If you got out more kid, you'd know that. Now for the last time, you wanna rent a room or not?"

"No, I don't want a room in this rat infested dive!" yelled Gage.

"Aw don't worry about it, you seem like a nice guy, a little excitable but okay otherwise. The rats won't mind slumming one night if you don't snore or wet the bed," replied Clyde in a fatherly tone.

For the first time in many years, Gage lost his temper. He reached for Clyde, who was standing with his fingers resting on the counter top edge. In a flash, Clyde's right arm swung in an arc and came down on Gage's flying hand. Clyde slapped the hand to the counter and held it motionless despite Gage's efforts to extract it.

Through gritted teeth Clyde said, "make another grab for me and you'll use up all your medical benefits. The parlor you are looking for is at Malone's funeral home. Now, rent a room or get out. I'm through playing games with you."

Gage, both embarrassed and livid, looked into the man's cold eyes, turned and stomped out the front door. His rage carried him across the wide sidewalk to the curb. He stayed at the curb taking deep breaths while pacing back and forth, trying to calm down. He glanced over his shoulder into the lobby and did a double take. All the deadpan lobby dwellers were giving Clyde a standing ovation. Clyde stood in front of the Registration Desk waving his eyeshade in one hand and the twenty in the other while he took bows.

Gage walked back into the lobby. Everyone froze as he walked over to a man wearing a baseball cap and snatched it off his head. Gage put the cap on and turned to Clyde. Gage bowed sweeping the cap from his head gallantly.

"Here's to you Clyde. You are the best. I've never been jerked around by anyone with your skill and poise," said Gage. He straightened, replaced the cap on its owner's head and walked back out the door. Grudgingly, he enjoyed the applause from the loungers.

Gage took a taxi to Malone's Funeral Home. He knew of it as the least expensive funeral home in town by some article he read in a Register exposè on funeral homes. The location, also beyond the urban renewal boundary, probably had a lot to do with the fees. Gage had never been to Malone's and was pleasantly surprised by the neatness of the grounds and building. Once inside, he was even more impressed. The carpeting was a rich clean burgundy and cream color, accented with quality Victorian Furniture. Malone had three viewing parlors but only one seemed occupied. A huge man in a black suit was standing at the entrance to the parlor. He had just spoken for a moment to a visitor. He turned to Gage as he approached.

Gage walked up to him and asked, "Is this where Jaw is laying?"

"Yes sir, code please?" whispered the man softly.

Gage immediately had the impression that the giant was not very intelligent. However, his six foot, eight inch, three hundred plus pound body would probably negate any reference to his mental abilities.

"I don't understand what you mean by code," said Gage.

"Then please come back tomorrow, sir. This is a private viewing time," whispered the guard in a neutral tone.

"Who is allowed in?" asked Gage.

"Please sir," whispered the giant, as he seemed to grow larger. His whisper was now harsh and he began flexing the fingers of both hands, either of which would cover Gage's whole face, "come back tomorrow. Please leave now."

Defiantly, Gage looked at him and asked, "Why?"

"Because if you don't, I'm gonna hold the back of your head with one hand and punch out your lights with the other fast, hard and mercilessly, Sir," whispered the giant.

"Ah ha, you want privacy," said Gage lurching back a bit. "You got it."

As Gage backed away he said, "I must admit big fella, you have sparked my curiosity."

The guard's forehead wrinkled as though he was trying to understand Gage's words. His face seemed to light up, and then cloud back as he said, "Please fight it sir."

As Gage turned toward the door, it opened. A man rushed past him, walking directly to the guard. He could read the guard's lips as he asked his question. The visitor whispered something. The guard reached into his breast pocket and pulled out a paper. He checked what was probably a list, nodded and replaced the paper in his pocket, opened the door and allowed the visitor to pass.

As Gage walked down the front steps, two men approached. Their conversation stopped when they saw him. They seemed not interested in being seen or recognized. As they neared Gage on the dimly lit walkway, one man pointed to something and both men looked in that direction when they passed.

Gage stopped at the junction of the walkway and sidewalk and looked back at the building. As he stood trying to figure out what was going on, a taxi pulled up in front of him. The driver leaned out the window and said, "Mr. Gage, I'm the taxi you need."

"I don't need a Taxi."

27

"Why don't you get in anyhow and let the private viewing go on?" asked the driver in a friendly tone.

"What's going on here?" asked Gage.

"A simple private viewing of close friends of Mr. Wilson. Please sir, let's get going."

"I'm not going anywhere until I find out about this so called private viewing," said Gage.

The cabbie grimaced, shook his head and looked out the windshield of his cab. He noticed his turn signal on and shut it off. He leaned over to try again, "Please Mr. Gage, get in and let's see if I can satisfy some of your curiosity."

"Not until I get some answers."

"Please sir," came the recognizable voice of the giant guard, as a hand opened the cab door and another gripped Gage's neck. Try as he might, Gage could not resist the strength of the hand that guided him gently but directly into the back of the cab.

"Sir, my friends across the street pointed you out to the police officer talking to them. The cop is watching you leave. If something happens to you once you leave, any investigation will not include this place. If you come back here tonight, somebody will find your body after I work up a serious sweat," said the guard in a tone Gage believed.

The guard closed the door and the cab immediately drove off and turned right at the first corner. The cab maneuvered through the neighborhood until it came to a main cross-town street. The driver looked into his rear view mirror and asked, "Where to Mr. Gage?"

"Back to Malone's"

"You got a hundred bucks?" asked the cabbie.

Hopefully Gage answered, "Yes."

"So do I," said the driver. "I'll bet you a hundred you can't get within two blocks of Malone's tonight."

"I could go to the police and file assault or threat charges," said Gage.

"Yeah, you're on the cop's favorite reporters list. I'm sure they'll believe you. Besides that, you climbed in the cab yourself, I watched you," said the driver.

"Okay," said Gage. "You said you'd talk, now talk. Start with how you knew my name and thought I needed a cab, and go on from there."

"Simple, my dispatcher called and said to pick up Carl Gage in front of Malone's. You met Jaw at least three times, maybe more. You might not remember him. He was beginning to take an interest in you. That ended yesterday."

"What the hell are you talking about?" asked Gage.

"It's simple, Jaw helped a lot of people in this town. All you're interested in is sensationalism. You take any story and turn it into a scandal without lying; you imply things you can't prove. There are two sad things about that Mr. Gage, first you either don't realize or don't care about the impact of what you imply. Second, somehow Jaw's instincts said you could be a better reporter then that. I guess he thought he could help you meet your full potential."

Gage sat thinking a few moments. Who was this pompous ass to think he could improve my writing? He ran a second rate hotel for Christ sakes, and he's going to give me lessons on writing? Bull Shit. I'm going to have a good time getting this guy.

"Take me back to the Register," snapped Gage.

29

Chapter 5

Lloyd Miller sat in his office looking out the window. The sun now freely sending out its hues of yellows, orange and reds it saved for the end of a day. He turned back to his desk, leaned on his forearms and began mulling over the events of the day.

Miller's phone suddenly came to life, "Talk."

"Zipper here, we are set for a private viewing tonight, I've got Rock at the door."

"You mentioned that earlier. Has he come that far?

"Yeah," Zipper giggled, "Jaw used him on the front desk. Imagine all 6 feet 8 of Rock with a "Hi I'm ROCK" tag on his shirt and that silly visor Milker coned him into wearing. Someone would come in and Rock would be nice as pie until they got smart with him. He'd look over at Jaw, take a deep breath and keep on being nice. After a couple days, he seemed to get the hang of it. However, we do have a problem. Do you know who Carl Gage is?"

"Yeah, a trash writer for the Register."

"Right he went to the Bev. tonight, luckily we had Milker as desk clerk. I have to admit, Milker is good. He had Gage so mad; he stomped out of the place ready to eat nails. On the flip side, when Gage realized what happened, he went back in and gave Milker a "hat's off.""

"Where's the problem?"

"Milker let it drop where Jaw was laying but he didn't know it was private tonight. Then Pigeon called and said Gage took a cab to Malone's. We're probably better off with Gage showing up tonight because he will probably go straight in. Thing of it is, once Gage gets a taste of something, he doesn't let go. I think we should get over to Malone's now," said Zipper.

Miller sighed, "You're on. In five. Later."

If Miller had not seen Zipper dressed in civilian clothes before, he would not have recognized him. The transformation intrigued him. Francis Adam Zeigler looked as if he had just walked out of a boardroom. When he was Zipper, he looked as if he walked out of a dumpster.

"How you holding Francis?" asked Miller.

"I'm holding, but Gage is at Malone's. We better hurry. I don't know how good Rock will hold," answered Zeigler.

It was a short ride to the funeral parlor. Miller parked his car. Walking, they had just turned off the sidewalk to the walkway toward Malone's as Gage exited the building.

Miller recognized him immediately and said, "block me Francis, he doesn't need to know of me just yet."

As they approached Gage, Zipper ignored him and was pointing in front of Miller's face, commenting on the changing skyline. Inside, Rock was banging his fists together and pacing back and forth.

"Slick!" said Rock ignoring the stranger with him. "You gotta find Zipper and ask him if I can number that guy outside. He's gonna be trouble."

"Rock, you lighten up and tend to business in here," said Slick as he approached Rock.

"Lighten up my ass," said Rock, "you find Zipper and tell him what I gotta do!"

In one fluid movement, Slick grabbed Rock's lapels and pulled him to his own right. As Rock leaned, Slick braced Rock's knee. The huge man crashed to the floor, landing on his back. Slick immediately shot a measured blow to the throat causing Rock to choke.

"Jaw is lying in there dead, hardly cold, and you want to throw everything he did for you down the toilet before he's even in the ground? I should kill you right here and now!"

The two men's eyes locked. Relenting, Rock said hoarsely, "Yer right Slick. I guess I just gotta try harder. Please don't tell Zipper."

Slick helped Rock to his feet while Zipper stood behind him. In his Zipper voice he said, "Zipper already knows. Be glad that Slick got to you first. I would have killed ya."

Brushing himself off, Rock snapped to attention at the sound of Zipper's voice. Immediately, Slick got into Rock's face saying, "Here's what you're going to do Rock. You are going to act like a real man and do your job here. I'm going to call a cab to take Gage out of here. When it gets here, you stay put in here until the cab's turn signal stops blinking. Then you make sure Gage gets into the cab, but do it gently and don't break anything on Gage or the cab. If he comes within two blocks of this place before midnight, he's yours. Work up a good sweat but do not kill him. If you kill him, you're on your own."

Rock nodded his head in understanding but still stood frozen as Slick and Zipper walked into the viewing parlor. Rock, never having seen Zipper in civilian clothes, was not really sure who or even where Zipper was. As soon as he heard the door close, Rock walked to the front door to watch for the cab.

Slick nodded to Zipper. When Zipper returned from making the call he said, "Done, one of ours will get him. By the way, Rock really has come a long way hasn't he?"

"He sure has. As little as three months ago, I'd be dead now and he'd still be beating my body. What have you heard about the deal Jaw was working for him?"

"Jaw closed the deal the day before he died. We were going to surprise Rock on his birthday next week. He would be thinking it was only initiation," said Zipper.

We should still try the surprise contract on his birthday, but we need to get him initiated as fast as we can. Tomorrow at the latest," said Slick.

Zipper was nodding approval, "I see your point. How does 9:30, 10:00 tomorrow morning sound?" asked Zipper.

"No problem on my side. Just let me know for sure. By the way, do you know the numbers for Rock?"

"Yeah, how about thirty a year minimum for the first two years, forty five minimum after that, all guaranteed."

Slick was surprised but had too much on his mind to discuss it. He and Zipper moved back out to the hall. They watched through the window as Rock "gently" put Gage in the cab. Rock resumed his position checking everyone who entered.

Barely audible murmurs greeted Slick and Zipper as they reentered the parlor. The fragrance of mixed flowers gently touched their senses. Side by side, they solemnly moved to positions on each side of Jaw's coffin. The room was filled to capacity. A few latecomers were forced to line the walls.

Jaw lay in a dark bronze colored coffin, closed to the waist. Slick recognized the light gray suit Jaw wore as his "Sunday go to meeting suit" as he called it. The man looked at peace. A flower arrangement of white carnations and roses stood behind the casket. Slick and Zipper took a moment of silent prayer as they stood looking into the coffin. Slick scanned the room, found what he was checking for and cleared his throat while motioning upward with his chin.

All the seated men in the direction he motioned, began looking toward the wall nearest them. Four near the end of the rows got up and the four women standing along the wall took the vacated seats. Slick looked to Zipper and said, "You got it."

Zipper moved to the center of the coffin, paused a few moments facing Jaw and turned to the crowd, "If I may have your attention please. I have two things that I need to say to you as a group. But, before I start, I have a sealed letter from Jaw to all of you."

Zipper held up an envelope and tore it open. He removed the letter saying; "There is also a note in here."

Slick's head snapped to Zipper. Slick had been there when Jaw had sealed the envelope. Although he didn't know what was in it, no note had gone into the envelope that he had seen. Slick felt uneasy.

Zipper began reading

"Ladies and Gentlemen," "It has been the pleasure of my life to have known each of you. If my life meets approval with The Man, I will tell Him about each of you, if it didn't, I'll keep my mouth shut. I addressed you as ladies and gentlemen. You are not ladies or gentlemen because of breeding, money or luck. No*

one gets that title in that manner, regardless of what society thinks. There are ladies among you who thought it was a compliment to be called a pig. There are gentlemen among you who would be begging from a person, while being called scum. To the person, every one of you, the reader included, has pulled yourself up from some level in the lowest caste of our society to become a success again. You now have self worth and with label properly earned, you have the honor to be called, Lady or Gentleman. I again congratulate you.

You have all signed a contract with me that lasted until my death subject to payment of your debt. That contract required three things of you. First, that you pay your monetary debt to the trust in triple. Second, that you never discuss your time in the Beverly Hotel with anyone including your fellow guests. Third, that you never turn down a request of the Program so long as it is legal, and will not harm your family. I have been fortunate in my choice of each of you in that you have all responded to the trust's requests, not only to the letter of the contract but to the spirit of the contract as well.

If your debt is paid, you are now released from the first and third requirements of the contract. The second requirement of silence remains into perpetuity. I'm gone. That was the deal. But even now, I have a request of you. When I wrote the contracts, I was not sure I would find someone that I could be absolutely sure would operate the program and keep the same objective. I did find someone. He has been operating the program, for the most part, for the last two years. I ask you to renew your contract with the man who is reading this letter to you; Francis Adam Ziegler, known to you as Zipper. Yes ladies and gentlemen, this is what Zipper looks like when he is not under. Get used to it.

You will receive an envelope in the mail, containing two smaller envelopes and three cards. One card says "Yes", meaning you are still with us. Another card says "No" you are out now, but still bound to silence. A third card says, "I'm out". Use that card if you elect to stay and change your mind later. However, in, out, glad or mad, keep the secrets of the program.

God bless you all and stay strong. If weakness seeps in, call The Beverly.

Jaw

Zipper's voice was trembling as he finished reading. He looked to Slick for help with the other two announcements but Slick just waved his hand for Zipper to go on. Zipper took a deep breath, regained his composure and began to read, "The first note, hand written by Jaw says, "Slick is designated as my replacement to run the entire organization until a permanent head is appointed.

"Now the other two items. It's good news and bad news. First the bad. We already have the potential of serious trouble for the program. I don't know how many of you are familiar with Carl Gage; he's a reporter for the Register. All his articles are slanted to get the optimum coverage regardless of the truth of the matter. He has been snooping around the hotel. I do not see a problem for the majority of you, but those of you who cannot afford to be recognized or connected, beware. Now the good news, even if it is sad in a way. Jaw was married." The room erupted with mummers. Zipper raised his hands to quiet the room and went on. "His wife and son will be here tomorrow. The burial will be in two days, unless she has different desires. It would be nice if any of you could come back tomorrow and pay your respects to the family.

Last thing, I didn't know what the letter was about and obviously about the cards. Slick just passed me a note saying the cards will be in the mail next week. That's it ladies and gentlemen. Later."

Zipper walked over to Slick asking, "Why the hell didn't you tell me?" He reflected a moment, "Dumb question, right?"

Slick in the meantime was stunned. Jaw said if anything happened to him to take charge initially and things would work out. He shook his head and said, "I have no idea how he got that note in there but he sure shit in my mess kit. Who the hell is going to designate Jaw's replacement? This is too much. I'm going home. By the way, have you seen Mott?"

35

"No, he's probably hooked up with some legal stuff. How about a ride to the Hilton, I want to live like real people till this is over. I guess I'll have to get used to it. By the way, it's only ten o'clock, why did you restrict Gage even after the place is closed?" asked Zipper.

"A note in the envelope you delivered. Jaw said to secure the funeral home till Midnight. I don't know what he had in mind," answered Slick.

Chapter 6

Miller sat alone in his office sipping coffee. For the first time in years he wanted a cigarette. Jaw cured him of the habit by keeping him broke. He was surprised at how good he felt considering he had to stay up late filling Suzanne in on the days events. It was well after midnight before he had fallen asleep.

He called Tarka in and began going over the plans for the day. "Check with New York, make sure the funeral arrangements have all been made including the grave site. I want to be ready for the burial tomorrow. Who do we know at the Register?" asked Miller.

"I don't know right off hand, maybe Ted Holbrook. When I first began working for you, you had me familiarize myself by going through the files and spot checking records," said Tarka.

"Refresh me."

"When you were looking at a loan for Peca Electronics, you found that Ted Holbrook was a partner. You looked over the partnership agreement and found that he was the only partner personally liable for any new debts," said Tarka.

He found out about it when I started checking his financial statement and asked why. When I told him, he checked his copy of the agreement and that sentence was left out. He got pretty hot about that and made the other partners buy him out," said Miller.

"I heard he made a pretty good profit on that buy-out. It was either buy out at his price or jail for the other partners," said Tarka.

"How did you learn that?"

"I belong to a club called Admin Backup. A bunch of us girls with jobs like mine get together now and then. Sometimes a bit of juicy info gets dropped, especially when someone thinks they work for a jerk," said Tarka

Miller looked at her quizzically, with one eyebrow raised.

37

Tarka smiled, "No sir I don't. We also brag when our boss does something great."

"Do we have a number on Holbrook?"

"I'm sure we do. Do you want me to look now, or is there something else?"

"Yes, there's some late work tonight, any problem?" asked Miller.

"No."

"Good, we'll be picked up by a limo at four-fifty and driven to the airport. I found out that Jaw had a wife. She and his son are coming in at five thirty. In the meantime, after you talk with New York, see what you can find on a reporter named Carl Gage."

Tarka's look of surprise caught Miller's attention, "I take it, from your expression, that you know him or is it that you know of him?"

"I know him sir, we dated a while back."

"If you don't mind my asking, was it good times or bad?"

"Both." replied Tarka, "He's sort of a free spirit. He is very insecure and wants desperately to be the best. He has no idea how good he is. If you tell him how good he is, he gets irate and thinks you're mocking him."

"Tarka, he could be real trouble for the whole organization. I get the impression you still have feelings for Mr. Gage. Trust me on this; I need control. Later, we may be able to give him a story that will make him."

Tarka left the room, returning in a few minutes with Holbrook's phone number. Miller called him immediately. When a familiar male voice answered, Miller said, "Ted Holbrook, how are you doing? Lloyd Miller here."

"Hey Lloyd, okay, thought about you yesterday and figured I'd be hearing from you."

"Why did you think that?" asked Miller suddenly on guard.

"I read Jaw's obituary yesterday."

The immediate reference to Jaw caught Miller by surprise. Miller was barely successful in keeping the surprise out of his voice when he asked, "Did you know Jaw?"

"Yeah, I knew him. I've gotten little bits and pieces every now and then about him. It seems he ran some kind of halfway house or something in that hotel, but I never broke it."

"Why would a story like that interest you?" asked Lloyd.

"Don't be naïve Lloyd. If someone in town is running a successful rehab program, that's news. I understand once in the program the only way out is to graduate."

"Ted, we need to have lunch,"

"Have I hit on something?" asked Holbrook. "I can't today, I…"

Miller cut him off, "You have to!" immediately angry with himself for the response.

"I don't "have to" do a damn thing Lloyd."

"Meet me at Clark's, say 12:15," stated Miller.

"First you demand that I break an appointment I've had for a week. Then you tell me we are going to have a stand-up lunch to discuss something you make sound like the next thing to a national security crisis. What do you take me for, an idiot?"

"No, a good reporter," said Miller. "We'll have a booth."

"Damn you Miller, now I almost have to come just to see how you can get a private booth in a place that doesn't even have chairs. Note I said almost."

"Be there Ted. Call it a favor returned."

Miller hung up before Holbrook could respond. He was disturbed at Holbrook's knowledge. Sketchy as it was, it was on target. He had to find a hold on Holbrook. Zipper would know if there was any dirt.

Miller called the Hilton and asked for Mr. Ziegler's room. "Zeigler here," came the answering voice with authority. "Damn Zipper, I hardly recognize your voice in a normal tone."

"Funny Slick, what's your problem?"

"I contacted Ted Holbrook at the Register in hopes to get him to chain Gage down. He knows the system's basics."

"I know. He tried several times to break the news on the program. He hasn't made it yet so don't give him anything he can use," said Zipper.

"Grab it Slick. You're the man now grab it. It's very important that you handle Holbrook right or the program and the whole concept is down the toilet," said Zipper.

The line was silent while Slick fought for calm. He understood the gravity of the situation and that was what worried him. If he was up against a businessman, he could grab it and deal with it. But, this was different. This was the program at stake. Real people were unknowingly depending on him for their security. This was not just some parchment called an Incorporation Declaration. He was now responsible for the anonymity of the organization.

"Grab it Slick," said Zipper again. "Put this in your pocket. Holbrook knows the street is aware of the program. During a few of his attempts to get a guy drunk enough to talk, he got drunk himself. On those occasions, he availed himself of the services of a lady of the evening. The same one both times, a hooker named Vera."

"Yeah, I remember somebody, probably Jaw, telling me about that. He snooped for a while and suddenly quit. We have to put off Rock until this afternoon. Later."

Miller asked Tarka to come into his office. She began speaking as she approached her chair, "Driver called and said everything was on. I called New York, he said everything would be ready for the burial tomorrow."

Miller smiled, "Call Flower and give her the info on the Wilson's arrival and hotel, stuff like that. Tell her flowers, fruit and snack tray. I'm meeting Ted Holbrook for lunch at Clark's at 12:15. I plan to leave here about 11:50. You go to lunch at noon and be back by 1:30."

Miller walked out into the bright late morning sun. Even tinged with auto exhaust, the air smelled fresh and invigorating. He was at his best in the office now. Although he still loved the street and missed the old days. He remembered being hungry but not for more then a couple days and never when he was in a city this size. He could talk a man out of a few bucks and usually parlay that few bucks into a couple hundred. That was back when he was dealing with strangers and all he had to worry about was himself. When it came to being responsible for others, Miller turned to worms.

Jaw had seen something in him. Jaw pulled, tugged and beat it out of him whether Miller wanted it out or not. As always, Jaw had been right. He was happier now then ever before in his life.

As Miller walked toward Clark's he studied the street with a trained eye. He spotted Rat first. It was an appropriate street name for him. He looked like a rat, acted like a rat, lived like a rat and smelled like one. Rat had no class. Slick was surprised when he spotted Zipper, especially because he was in his "Zipper" regalia. Miller spotted more of the Beverly crowd spread up and down the street. They all tried to look inconspicuous, which in itself was no small task. Looking up and down the street, Miller noticed a pattern. The Beverly crowd was about evenly spaced up and down the street, but Rat had disappeared.

Miller checked his watch. If his timing were right, he would arrive at Clark's five minutes before Holbrook. Turning to walk into Clark's, Miller glanced toward an approaching Zipper. Zipper had his fists clinched, down in front of him. It was a Beverly warning of danger.

Now wary, Miller entered Clark's. Fred "Flipper" Clark was behind the serving counter. When he saw Miller, he motioned with his head toward the door at the end of the counter. It opened to a narrow hall ending at the back exit. Several feet before the exit, a door stood open to the left. In the room was a round booth. Seated in the booth was Ted Holbrook.

Holbrook looked up and smiled at Miller, "Have a seat Lloyd."

"How did you get in here?" asked Miller, taken aback.

"Not hard to figure out Lloyd. There are no seats out front, so there had to be a table or something in the back. Why walk all the way around when I could come in the back door? So I did. You should tell Clark to keep the door locked," said Holbrook.

"Well Lloyd, are you going to sit there studying my wrinkles or are we going to talk?" You know, I divorced my wife for looking at me just that way."

There goes the Hooker ploy thought Miller and said, "Ted do you know that Peca got some guy in South Carolina to sign on as a partner like you did?"

"Yeah, so I heard."

"They did a number on that guy by swapping pages in the contract after it was signed. Now he gets to tote the note for two million while he and the cops hunt for those guys. That could have been you."

"I know Lloyd. I also remember that you set me straight. I got out of that with a little profit. I owe you for that too. Obviously it's payback time. What favor can I do a dead man?"

"No favor for a dead man, how about a favor for a widow and her son?"

"Widow? Whose widow? Jaw's widow and his son?" asked Holbrook.

"Yes, Jaw's."

"When did he have the time to get married? He was at that damn hotel most of the time."

Miller, surprised by Holbrook's comments, paused a moment and said, "First my favor. I need you to keep that clown Gage away from the Malone Funeral Home. Jaw had a lot of friends. They would like to pay their respects to his widow and son. They don't need to be hounded at a time like this by a reporter who only writes trash."

"So the old bastard finally wised up," muttered Holbrook softly to himself.

"What do you mean by that?" asked Miller immediately picking up on Holbrook's fascination with Jaw having a wife.

Still preoccupied, Holbrook asked, "By what?"

42

"The old bastard finally wised up." quoted Miller.

Miller saw Holbrook shake his head as if coming back to reality, suddenly realizing where he was and what he was saying. Holbrook stammered and said, "Hell, he almost never left that hotel or his room for more then two or three hours and usually at night. I never heard of him vacationing," answered Holbrook.

"Well will you give Jaw his just due?" asked Miller.

"Where does Mrs. Wilson live?"

"New York."

"In the City?"

"No. What difference does it make?" Miller asked, pausing. "Unless maybe you're thinking of doing some kind of a story on Jaw. Something like 'Local Hotel Owner Abandons Wife.' " That would put you on a par with Gage."

"Watch your mouth Lloyd. I'll debate with you all day long but you get insulting, I'll knock you on your ass," said Holbrook coldly.

"That, my dear sir, would be one of the most painful failures you would ever have," said Lloyd staring unblinking into Holbrook's eyes.

Both men sat staring at each other for a full minute. Miller finally broke the silence saying, "All I'm asking is that you and Gage lay off Jaw and his so-called organization."

Holbrook snorted, "No way. I'm going to break this Trust thing."

An alarm went off in Miller's head. If Holbrook knew about the trust, how much more did he know? Miller couldn't concern himself with that right now. He needed time to get Mary Wilson and her son in and out of Charlotte before the shit hit the fan.

"Break the damn story, that's not my point.

Last night some of Jaw's closest friends were having a private viewing. Gage showed up and tried to bust it. All I'm asking is to let the funeral and viewing go. No interview, no cameras, no video taping."

"Why," asked Holbrook?

"That smut merchant, Gage turns everything into garbage. I don't know who will show up for the viewing. We don't need Gage's caliber of writing turning it into a comic opera."

"I think you're paranoid about Gage. I can control what stories he is assigned. I can't control what he does in his free time. I'll try to give you what you're asking for Lloyd. And just so it's clear, you want no coverage of Jaw's funeral, such as interviews, photos or video tape, is that right?"

"No it's not Ted and you know it's not. What I'm asking for is to be left completely alone by the Register for the time being."

"What does that mean, how long are you talking about?" asked Holbrook.

"Until Mrs. Wilson leaves town, or five days, which ever is least," said Miller.

"You're not asking me to lay off the Trust story?"

"What Trust?" asked Miller.

"The Trust that funds a rehab program out of the Beverly Hotel. The Trust that funds a program that the mere mention of got me this demand for lunch. The Trust that lined the street with Beverly Hotel tenants from my office to here. The Trust that kept this sparing contest going through an entire lunch hour. That's the Trust I'm talking about."

Miller smiled and said, "Must be a hell of a Trust. You want me to have a sandwich packed for you or do you really have time to eat?"

"What the hell, I'll eat here. Tell them my usual."

Miller went up front to order and was back almost immediately, Flipper having made both he and Holbrook's usual sandwich. Back at the table, Miller sat and began eating. After a second bite he asked casually, "Assuming what you said is true, why are you so interested in this trust thing?"

"It's news and that's what I do. Besides, did it ever dawn on anyone that if you didn't have me coming at you all the time, your security might get lax? Actually, I'm counting on you guys getting a little cocky."

"You talk about it like I'm involved," said Miller.

"You must be, or you wouldn't be here on the Wilson family's behalf. I think your street name is Zipper, Speed or Slick. I'm pretty sure you're not Zipper because I understand he stays undercover most of the time. That leaves Speed or Slick. I would be inclined to think of you more as slick as opposed to speedy, although your rise in the banking business was fairly speedy. But, all in all, I would guess you are Slick."

"If you're right, what good would that information do you?"

Holbrook finished his bite and said, "Actually, it would raise more questions than it would answer. For instance, why a particular name like that as opposed to something like Dragon or Orion which depicts no particular personal skill or endeavor. If the name is chosen because of some ability such as a guy slick enough to fleece someone out of their money, then maybe there are some criminal charges pending somewhere."

"What happens if you don't approve of the past of some of these people?"

"It doesn't matter whether I approve or not. The public has a right to know if someone has a shady past. In your case, you have no past. We looked into you sometime back and we couldn't find anything on you prior to your appearing at the Beverly Hotel."

That shook Miller, "What the hell do you mean, you looked into my past? Why me?"

"Face it Lloyd, you're a rising star in this town. Your rise in First Nation has been fairly astounding. The Business Editor tried several times to do a story on you and couldn't get to first base. Where were you educated? Where were you born? Where were you raised? All we know is that you weren't in the military. There isn't a thing available on you."

Miller could not take any more of Holbrook's high and mighty reporter self-righteousness. He glanced at his watch and said, "Sorry Ted, I have another appointment. Thanks for helping the widow. The check is taken care of," said Lloyd as he stood up. Miller left the way he came in.

Holbrook sat smiling to himself. In a few minutes a man came in through the back entrance and sat down. . .

"From the day I met Jaw, I was always amazed at how he could talk to a man for a few minutes and get his measure and know whether he was worth a damn or not. He sure has a winner in Slick," said Holbrook.

"I still think Jaw should have given him more insight on the entire organization. We still would be able to test him. Well, I guess it would be harder," said the newcomer.

"I hope you know, controlling Gage isn't going to be easy," said Holbrook.

"I believe that. Jaw approached him three times. Each time, he came away empty. He told me Gage had the talent to be the best writer this town ever had, if only he wasn't so scared. Jaw sent out some kind of feeler on him. I haven't been able to get to his file yet to see if any answers came back," said the newcomer.

"Let me know what you get back from Slick. It will be interesting to hear his reaction to our conversation."

"He was shook up before he came here. This will be a better test than I thought. I'll let you know this evening. Later," said the newcomer.

"Later," said Holbrook. He turned and walked out the back door.

Zipper waited a few minutes then hurried out the back door so he could catch Miller before he got to his office building.

When Rat noticed all the Beverly people along the street he realized he had better become scarce. He hurried down the alley next to Clarks. He caught sight of the dumpster and immediately checked it out. He found a bag lunch someone had failed to pick up and sat behind the dumpster eating a cold hamburger and fries. He heard someone walk past. Later he saw Zipper entering the back door of Clarks. A few minutes later he saw Holbrook leave and then Zipper. Maybe this was worth a little something thought Rat. Who was that reporter that was asking around this morning?

Chapter 7

2nd Day September 27,1998 9:30 AM

When Carlos Misota walked into his office, he was surprised to find his son waiting for him. Emile sat in an armchair with a leg hung over the arm. The smug grin on his face told Carlos his son had news.

"Well spit it out," he said. He walked around his desk and sat down with a sigh.

"The Wilson's will be staying at the Queen Charlotte and they are coming in on USAir from Binghamton, New York. We also found Dot Com," said Emile proudly.

"Emile, you sit there like you did something special. You did your job. That alone is something to be proud of but it isn't more than I expected. Can you tell me what time their flight will arrive or what room the Wilsons have reserved?"

"They'll arrive at 5:30 today. I'm not sure of the room number,"

"Considering that the Queen Charlotte has 200 rooms, that information would help," said Carlos softly.

Emile straightened in his chair and grimaced, "I think my men have that info, I'll get it. Dot-Com will be here tomorrow morning. I told him to make noises like he was leaving town."

"Now that was good thinking," said Carlos.

Emile smiled weakly wishing that just once he could do everything right for a whole day, one time was all he asked.

"You know we've been watching that reporter Holbrook. I think he is in with the Beverly crowd. I think they turned him. He stopped nosing around too suddenly. I told Benny and Frank to follow him and find a place to ruff him up a bit that wasn't an obvious hit.

We'll pay him a visit at home. He'll open up once we get his attention."

"I think we should keep our people out there nosing

around," said Emile.

"You're right about that. Also, find a couple places to stash someone if that becomes necessary," replied Carlos.

Emile left the office. Carlos thought about Holbrook. The more he thought about him the more sure he was that Holbrook was turned by Wilson. Carlos was inclined to let Holbrook lay. He could be hit later. The fewer people he had banged up the fewer the chances for screw-ups.

Carlos began to go over his plans. Phase 1 and 2 were interchangeable, that was beauty of it. He could grab the assets, which could be as much as 15 million if those jerks he owned were right. On the other hand he could grab the organization. It would take longer, but he would still get the assets. What was that old saying: "A bird in the hand is worth two in the bush? "

Well, I don't like birds, thought Carlos. That parakeet Emile had as a kid, shit on me and bushes have all kinds of crawly things in them that usually bite when disturbed and you didn't know what's behind a big bush. I'll grab the money and worry about the organization later.

The organization was an extra anyway. There might be some good shakedown material there but he had reservations about using the street people as runners. He'd probably have to take some losses and kill of few of them before the word got out that making the deliveries was mandatory or else. He would probably have to stick to winos. Druggies were to unpredictable.

Carlos thought about the 15 million. His cut would be half. The Don would get the other half, which was okay. The Don gave him this territory and half of everything was payment for it.

Carlos decided to go for his workout and be patient, it would all come his way.

Chapter 8

Miller was deeply shaken as he walked out of Clark's. His mind felt muddled and his palms sweaty. The sunlight felt as if someone had stuck fingers in his eyes. He stepped away from the door and put the edge of his hand across his brow. He stood there a moment wishing he could just keep his eyes shut and see no one or no one see him. He stood there long enough that he heard a voice ask, "You okay mister?" Miller nodded yes before Pigeon could say, "Clear". He dropped his hand and began walking toward his office building. He tried to put things into perspective. Slowly he began to feel calm as he walked.

Holbrook had more suspicions than he had facts. What bothered Miller was Holbrook's logic about himself, the names and the trust. Was Holbrook helping the trust or after the trust? That led to two more lines of thought. First, if Holbrook was after the trust, then he knew more than he was saying and would be watching for activity in certain areas. If that activity happened, he would have them. Secondly, if he was helping the trust, he would have to be a member. Miller had never heard Jaw or anyone else mention a street name that he could not put a face to.

"How we doing?" came the interrupting voice of Zipper from just behind him. There was a slight pause Zipper said, "Clear."

"He says he's going to help us somewhat," replied Miller.

"What does that mean?" asked Zipper "Clear."

"I'm going to hold him to keeping the Register off us for five days."

"Did he agree to that?" asked Zipper. "Clear."

"I asked to hold the Register off until after the widow left town or five days, which ever came first. He said he would try. That's good enough for me," said Miller.

"Will that be enough?" asked Zipper. He paused a few moments to let people pass and said, "Clear."

49

"Yes."

"Later."

Tarka was at her desk talking on the phone as he entered the outer office. She looked up expectantly. Miller waved his hand, palm down in the signal for "don't tell them I'm here."

In a few minutes Tarka walked into Miller's office, "Do you want your messages?"

"Hell no, but you might as well give them to me."

"Mr. Mott called and said Gage was checking the trust at the court house. Pigeon called and said Gage was hitting the street asking questions about the Beverly Hotel and the Trust. She also said she had Rock eyeball Rat. I was talking to Flower when you came in. She said the deliveries were made. She's going to water down."

"What?" asked Miller leaping from a relaxed chair back position to sitting straight up. "Were those her exact words?"

"Yes sir," responded Tarka, surprised at the reaction.

Miller grabbed his phone and rapidly punched in a number. He listened a moment and said, "New York, a water down. Get Bottle to Flower, now...ten minutes ago.... I don't give a damn what he's doing, get him to her. Later."

Tarka let Miller gather himself then said, "Mr. Miller, you looked so down when you came in, I wondered if I should even bother you with these messages. I'm glad I did now. You need to tell me more of your codes as you think of them so I'll know what is important enough to tell you about immediately. What was the big deal about Flower watering down?" asked Tarka. It seems a simple thing to me. She is going somewhere and relax."

"Flower is an Alcoholic. When she waters down, that means she is going to get dead drunk. If she does, it means she forfeits the loan on her business. She is still under contract for the loan."

"You mean she signed a loan contract that said she couldn't get drunk and it's legal?"

"For the most part, yes."

"I don't understand."

Miller cut her off, "Ms Tarka, there is a lot about how the trust and the program operates that is not readily understandable, but that is not a concern of the public. If the situation presents itself, I'll fill you in on what you need to know, until that time, please."

"Yes sir," said Tarka. She sighed, rose and left the room.

Miller glanced at his watch. It was three ten. He'd have time to call Beagle. Miller punched in the numbers.

"Cha-Cha-Charles Mott here," said Beagle, almost a physical clone of a younger Mickey Rooney.

"Beagle, Slick here, how you holding?"

"I'm ha-ha-holding S-S-Slick, but it isn't easy. I'm really too busy to deal with e-e-e-emotions and I feel a bit ashamed," answered Beagle, his slight stutter indicating tension.

"Tell me about it," said Slick. "I'm about ready to run. Jaw could have done a better job preparing us for this."

Slick's statement seemed to put new life in Beagle. "That's ka-ka-crap Slick. None of us would be where we are today if we weren't able to make it without him ba-ba-badgering us like he did in the beginning."

"I can deal with his death alone, but it's really the trust and the program that concerns me the most. And now, we have the "Register" on our back again. If they get next to someone that tried to get in the program and failed, God knows what they'll print," said Miller.

"I know. That smut jockey, Gage was at the court house this morning checking on the trust," said Beagle.

"He was at the Beverly and Malone's last night," said Slick.

"Is that what Ra- Ra -Rock was all worked up about? He was still cranked up when I saw him after eleven," said Mott, the tension seeming to have left his voice.

"What were you doing there so late?" asked Slick, noticing Mott calming.

"I couldn't make the regular viewing. I went down there after I finished. The place was all but sealed. Rock was pacing in front of the door, grumbling about wanting to number some guy."

" He was all worked up over Gage coming in and not leaving right away. I had to down him to get his attention. I let Rock put Gage in a cab. What I called about was the trust, are you sure it isn't traceable?" asked Lloyd.

"I'm sure. All anybody can determine is that the trust was established to help the homeless find a place to stay for a week or two while they find work. Jaw contributed two thirds of the hotel's profits to the trust. The so-called contributions the participants made were all cash. I put them in through the back door in a sub fund under a different name. When the board makes a decision to make a loan, it looks like my firm made the decision."

"What board?"

"S-S-S-Sorry Slick, legal talk. It takes a ba-ba-board of directors to operate these things. Actually, it's Jaw, Zipper, you, s-s-s sometimes me making the decision of the board," said Mott, the tension returning to his voice.

I never made any decisions on loans. How many of those are out besides, Flower, Flipper and Driver?"

"Yes you did. It was p- p- probably in ca- ca- casual conversation with Jaw confirming someone was ready for a loan. We'll talk about the ta,-ta-trust after the funeral. Zipper told me Jaw's wife was on her way down here. She could spell a lot of trouble for the estate. If she has a pa-pa-problem with this thing, we may be at the end of the line, like it or not."

"My impression of her is that she'll go along with Jaw's work here."

"God Slick, I hope so. We have so much in the works right now. It's like making waves when the water is at your nose. Waves could kill about six or seven careers."

"Six or seven? All I knew about was Rock and New York. That reminds me, Zipper will be contacting you. We need to do Rock in a hurry."

"N-N-N-N-No problem with Rock and as far as the rest goes, I'll crank you in when the funeral is over. You are going to be a busy man, if you make it."

"What do you mean, if I make it?" asked Miller.

There was a slight pause, then Beagle said, "L-L-L-L-Lighten up S-S-S-Slick, you and I both know how you were in the p-p-p-p-past. You just told me you were ready to run. Then you came on with your concern over the program and trust. You're sounding like the whole thing is on your sh-sh-shoulders. I have to admit most of this phase is. Let me give you a bit of advice. Don't try to do it all yourself. Use the right people for the right job. When I was a kid, my Dad made my brothers and me help him put an addition on our house. We always held our hammers near the head so it took fifty hits to drive a nail in. My old man taught us to hold the hammer at the end of the handle and let the tool do the work. You perfected your talents hanging around the Beverly, use them."

"You're right Beagle. Later."

Miller slowly cradled the phone. He felt as if he didn't understand everything that was going on around him. He sat trying to recall key conversations. The guy at the Corner's Office, Holbrook, Zipper and now Beagle, all said things that surprised him. Possibly even Parkinson and Suzanne. It was not so much their words as much as their innuendo.

Tarka walked into Miller's office and asked, "It's four o'clock. Is there anything we need to take with us to the airport or any last minute arrangements?"

"No, just help me with the small talk once we pick up Mrs. Wilson."

A limousine was waiting at the curb as Miller and Tarka walked out of the Executive Entrance door. The chauffeur stepped out smiling as soon as Miller came into view. He was in his forties, of medium height and well proportioned. His bright red hair streaked with silver, showed around the edge of his cap and gave him a distinguished look. Tarka was impressed. Miller smiled as he approached the limousine and asked, "How've you been Driver? I didn't think we'd be getting the boss."

"Fine sir, I hope you're doing as well as the day permits. You didn't think I'd miss the chance to see Mrs. Wilson did you?" responded Driver, as he helped Tarka into the cabin.

Miller entered, Driver closed the door and took his position. Driver spoke into a microphone as he pulled into traffic. Once underway, Driver picked up a phone and said into the cabin, "Mr. Miller, there's a bourbon on the rocks for you and chilled white wine in the rack for the lady."

Miller nodded and smiled. Before he could reach for the drinks, Tarka reached up and grabbed Miller's drink, held it up to the glass divider and asked, "Any more like him at home?"

"Sorry Miss, the makings are there but you'll have to mix your own."

"Been there, done that, got the tee shirt" said Tarka smiling as she handed Miller his drink and began to mix her own saying, "I could get hooked on a ride like this. I'll bet a trip to Columbia and back is all it would take."

"It can be arranged," said Driver.

Tarka elected to ignore the statement. They rode in silence. Miller was lost in thought over the day's events. He was beginning to get a vague impression as they arrived at the airport. It was 5:15 P.M. Driver dropped them off at the US Air entrance. After checking the arrival board, Miller and Tarka headed down the concourse to meet the deplaning passengers.

As the passengers began exiting the boarding gate, Miller suddenly realized he did not know what Mary Wilson looked like. How could he have let such a major detail elude him? He looked at Tarka and asked, "How will we know them?"

Tarka looked at him and smiled. Then she turned to a trim lady, with a medium build and platinum hair. She had an air about her that gave the impression of self-confidence, however at this moment, she looked a little lost.

"Mrs. Wilson?" asked Tarka.

"Yes. I hope you aren't Lloyd," said Mrs. Wilson, smiling.

Miller stepped up, extending his hand, "I'm Lloyd, Mary. This is Nancy Tarka."

"Nice to meet you both," said Mary Wilson. Over her shoulder Mary said, "Come here Jimmy."

A sullen man in his late twenties, rangy build with a ponytail came toward them dressed in a beige sports jacket, jeans and tennis shoes. His face bore an expression of contempt.

"My son James."

Lloyd extended his hand but James looked at him with disgust, keeping his hands in his pockets. Mary Wilson elbowed him in the ribs with enough force to rock him.

"I'm here because you made me come Mother. I do not have to acknowledge the sort of trash your husband would have associated with."

"My husband was your father!" Mary snapped trying to keep her composure.

"Are you speaking of the so called man that deserted us?" asked James.

In less then a spark, Lloyd moved nose to nose with James looking straight across, eye to eye. He gristly said, "Out of respect for your dead father and your mother, I'll let that pass. But if you don't watch your mouth, I'll drop you like a used tampon."

Instantly James hands flew out of his pockets. His expression became one of challenge. He returned Lloyd's stare, as he coldly stated, "Not in your finest hour."

"But you'd be taking on a load," said Mary stepping between the men. "Let's get out of here before I'm tempted to tell you to try anyhow."

Mary turned to Tarka and they began to walk down the concourse. Lloyd could hear Mary say to Tarka, "Drop him like a used tampon. Sounds like something my Al would say, gross, but to the point. I'm really surprised with Jimmy. Lloyd really caught him off guard."

As they rode into the city, Mary asked about the funeral arrangements. Lloyd explained that all the arrangements had been made from casket selection to burial plot as per Jaw's instructions. He assured Mary that any changes she wanted would be taken care of immediately, including shipping Jaw's body to Binghamton or anywhere else if she so desired.

Mary's chin quivered and her eyes filled with tears as she asked, "When can I see him?"

"We can go directly to the funeral home if you like, or we can stop by your suite and let you freshen up first if you prefer," said Lloyd.

"He's dead. He doesn't care how I look. Take us to the funeral parlor," said Mary.

"Drop me off at the hotel," said James.

Mary Wilson suddenly twisted in her seat and slapped James smartly across his face. James, sitting between his mother and Tarka, could not move freely enough to avoid the blow.

"You self righteous ass! I loved your father. He made two mistakes in his life. He made one drunk and the other sober when he didn't drown you when you were a pup. This time you're going to listen to the truth. Your father is not guilty of what he thought he did. He was having drinks with some friends he came to know in Binghamton. A woman thought your father was some kind of retired rich guy. She drugged his drink and took him home with her. In the morning she told him she was going to report him for having sex with her thirteen-year-old daughter. Your father couldn't face me with that accusation.

The woman pulled that trick one too many times and the police arrested her. In her confession she mentioned your father. The police came to see him but he was already gone. As the cops tell it, none of the men, including your father could have sex because of the drug she used.

"You not only look like your father, you act just like him. We are talking simple forgiveness here," said Mary Wilson sobbing as she finished.

Miller and Tarka sat quietly, visibly uncomfortable at being exposed to family trauma. Miller picked up the intercom and told Driver to go to Malone's. The four rode the rest of the way in silence.

At Malone's, Driver pulled to the side entrance. When the limousine stopped, Rock opened the car door and led the way into the building to the viewing parlor. Mary Wilson walked the last few yards alone.

"Oh Al," she sobbed, "you look so young, so good."

Mary looked back at Lloyd, tears running down her cheeks and asked, "Does he really look like himself Lloyd? Did he really look that good?"

"Yes, he really did," said Miller, through a lump in his throat that nearly choked him.

"Look Jimmy, look how good your father looks!" said Mary, pulling Jimmy Wilson to the front of the casket. Jimmy stood looking at his dead Father, glassy eyed but no tears flowed.

The viewing room was dim except for the soft light over Jaw's torso. On the black drapes behind the casket were scattered tiny reflective dots of some kind giving the impression of the void of space. Lloyd looked around the room and noticed Ted Holbrook sitting near the back of the room. Lloyd immediately stiffened with tension. Mary felt the stiffening and looked around at Holbrook sitting alone.

"Something wrong Lloyd?" asked Mary.

Uh-h-h, No, I just didn't expect to see anyone here."

"There is only one man in here. Who is he?" asked Mary.

"I guess he's an old friend," answered Miller. He and Mary turned back to Jaw's casket. He wondered what Holbrook was doing here.

Chapter 9

Nancy Tarka stood to the side, out of Miller's view. She was wide-eyed with shock as she looked down at the man she heard called Jaw. She had known him as Mr. Wilson. Now things were coming together. What a difference Wilson, and one night as a hooker, made in her life.

On that night in 1996, her first on the corner, a big elderly man approached her from a black hooker just up the street.

"Jolene tells me she hasn't seen you before. What are your prices?" he asked.

Tarka was taken aback by the blunt question. The man didn't even ask if she was a hooker. Then she realized the man was no fool, why else would she be standing out here?

"What are you interested in?" asked Tarka.

"You know, a fuck, some head, butt banging. What's your specialty?" he asked again.

Mental pictures of each act mentioned flashed through Tarka's mind. She had been in place as a hooker for ten minutes and knew she would go broke. There was no way she was going to do most of those things with a stranger.

"Well kid, what the hell is your specialty? I ain't got all night," the man persisted.

Tarka's eyes filled with tears as she realized how she was considering degrading herself. She had to have some money. She couldn't steal, refused to sell drugs, and the possibility of an honest loan was out of the question. Hooking was her only alternative and she couldn't go through with it. She knew that now.

"I'm glad I was the first one," said the man gently. He moved to her and put his arm around her shoulder saying, "Let's go before you change your mind. I can help you."

58

The fatherly tone the man used seemed to be sincere. As they passed the hooker, Tarka thought was Jolene, the hooker said, "trust him kid, he really will help you."

They took a cab to an all night diner. The man ordered coffee for both. When the waitress was gone he asked her name and Tarka told him.

"Tell me Nancy Tarka, why you are trying to become a street whore when it is obvious your Mama taught you better?"

"You don't know anything about me. You don't know what my Mother taught me," she answered angrily.

"I know your Mama taught you not to do what you were about to do tonight, or you wouldn't have filled your eyes that way."

"I don't know what kind of a pervert you are mister, but if you get off by seeing women cry, I want my money up front."

"That's what it's all about, isn't it? Money."

Amazingly fast, the man grabbed her left arm and roughly pushed her sleeve up. Then, just as suddenly checked her right arm. He sat back saying, you aren't shooting, your eyes are clear and you aren't shaking, so it isn't drug use. What are you doing imitating a hooker?"

"It's none of your damn business," said Tarka as the waitress brought their coffee. The waitress obviously overheard Tarka.

"Honey, if he is willing to help you, you're in good hands. This job isn't much but it pays well. I ain't out there licking dicks for a living and getting beat up a couple times a month. He got me out of that and he can help you too," said the waitress.

Tarka thought a moment and said, "Okay mister what the hell ever your name is."

"Wilson."

"Okay Wilson, I need more then a waitress job. I need four or five hundred a week and medical insurance that will cover my Mother. Do you have anything like that in your stock of second rate jobs?" she asked sarcastically.

"I can help you to the limits of your experience and knowledge, Miss Smart Ass. What are you qualified to do?" asked Wilson.

"I graduated from the community college with a 3.8 grade average in office sciences. I can take dictation, type 90 words a minute and I am 10 key efficient. I do not put out for interviewers which disqualified me at my last three interviews, one of which was with a woman," said Tarka nastily.

"If you aren't lying to me, you'll have a job by week's end," replied Wilson.

Tarka was stunned. She wanted to believe this man, but it was too much to hope for and she didn't know what the catch was. The promise of a job did not solve her immediate problem.

"You are talking two weeks minimum before a pay check. I was out there because I need money now. I have to find the courage to go back out there,"she said, her voice trailing off.

"What is so pressing that you have to give up your pride?" asked Wilson.

"My Mother's life if you must know. She has a heart condition. Our rent, the power bill, the gas bill, Mom's prescriptions, all of them, overdue now, I have two days to get $268. to the insurance company to keep Mom's health insurance up. Don't Miss Smart Ass me Wilson. I'm willing to be an organ donor if it will save my Mother."

"Okay kid, you made your point, don't grind me into dust. I can help you. Write your name, address, phone number and landlord on this paper," he said as he tore a sheet from a small spiral notebook. "Tomorrow I want you to come to the Beverly Hotel in jeans and sneakers. Be there in the morning by 7:30.

"Now I have to leave," he said standing and taking the paper Tarka filled out. "Take care of the bill with this and keep the change." Wilson threw a fifty on the table and walked out.

Tarka sat stunned. The waitress walked up and asked, "Did he leave a fifty?"

Tarka dumbly nodded yes.

"Take a word of advice from an old ex-street creep, kid. Do everything he tells you. Trust him completely and agree to any deal he wants. You will never be treated as fairly in all your life. The coffee's on me."

The following morning, a sleepy Nancy Tarka rushed from her apartment five minutes before her bus was due. As she waited for the bus, she realized she had not dressed warmly enough. She stood, arms across her chest shivering, in the morning haze. She wished now she had put on that T-shirt she decided against under her gray sweatshirt. By the time the bus arrived, Tarka felt frozen to the bone. What little enthusiasm she had for what faced her that morning was all but frozen out.

However, right on time, though a bit winded, she walked into the lobby of the Beverly Hotel and immediately thought of old western movies. The lobby was an almost perfect replica of hotel scenes she remembered. She asked for Wilson and was sent to room 107. As she approached the door, she began to worry, wondering what was about to happen.

Taking a deep breath, she knocked and almost immediately Wilson opened the door. He smiled at her and motioned for her to follow as he started toward the elevator while he sipped his coffee. Slurping his coffee, Wilson hit the button for the seventh floor. When the elevator doors opened he locked the elevator in place and walked to the end of the hall. Wilson unlocked a door marked "Staff."

Reaching in, he pulled a ball chain that had a tiny glowing plastic street lamp at the end. A light clicked on, Tarka could see a little room filled with cleaning supplies. Wilson fished in his pocket and pulled out a key and said, "This pass key will get you into all these rooms. Don't let anyone into a room; send them to the front desk. If they get feisty, you go to the front desk and let the duty manager know what is going on.

"I want you to clean all the rooms on this floor. Sweep, mop, change the sheets and pillowcases, make sure there are two bath and two face towels, soap, shampoo and an extra roll of toilet paper in each room. When you finish the rooms, vacuum the hall and you're done."

"What the hell do you think I am?" asked Tarka.

"I think, dear lady, that you are going to clean the rooms on this floor or you may choose to be the bitch who wants to share her crotch with me. Which is it, lady or bitch?" asked Wilson.

Tarka had too much pride to answer. She began to pull the cleaning supplies out of the storage room. As she cleaned, she reasoned. I can do this right, get paid for it and never come back or he may want to hire me, at which point he can kiss my ass. He may also want to see if I will work. Maybe the guy wants to get these rooms cleaned for free and get laid to boot. She really didn't see Wilson like that. He'll probably tell me the fifty from last night was payment and get the hell out!

Around noon, the desk clerk brought her a bag lunch and by three she went down the elevator. Wilson was at the front desk, as Tarka approached he asked if she was finished. She gave him her one raised eyebrow look; he smiled and took her back up to the seventh floor. His inspection resulted in a series of grunts, harrumphs and damns as he inspected every room. He led her to the elevator and back to room 107.

"Well Nancy Tarka, I'm still batting a thousand. I picked you as a winner and I won, your work was fantastic. I do not think the thought of you and I naked in bed together can make it through sixteen rooms of cleaning. Somewhere around eight or nine rooms, a scum bag would have said, "The hell with it, I'll lay the old shit and walk." All the rooms were equally cleaned which shows pride in yourself and your work. That is what I was looking for today.

First things first, I have a contract for you to sign. What it says is that you will repay in triple all the money you are given. If you equate it to a mortgage, it isn't quite so bad. It gets you a new life immediately," said Wilson.

Tarka recalled the sincerity of the waitress from the night before and the hooker, "Okay."

Immediately after Tarka signed the contract, Wilson began to overwhelm her saying, "Here are your receipts for your rent for this month and next. Here are the receipts for your utility bills, with a two hundred-dollar credit on your power and gas. Here is one thousand dollars cash for food, medicine and maybe a new dress for Mom and yourself. This is your appointment for your interview with personnel at First Nations Bank tomorrow."

"You're kidding!" replied Tarka almost breathless.

"No, the total comes to two thousand seven hundred twenty dollars even. The contract will say you owe the Beverly Trust eight thousand one hundred sixty dollars. You worked seven hours today at seven dollars an hour so you can deduct forty-nine dollars from that total. I'm going to throw in the meal this time, next time you pay for it. Your payment day is Thursday and your first payment is due the first Thursday of next month. You make the trust a minimum payment of fifty dollars per week for four weeks. If there are five Thursdays in a month, that payment is optional," said Wilson.

"I don't have a job, how can you be sure I can pay that?" asked Tarka.

"Were you paying attention to what I just said about First Nations Bank?" he asked.

"Of course I did, I have an interview tomorrow. That doesn't mean I'll get hired," responded Nancy.

"I may have to slap you around yet," said Wilson. "They think it's an interview, you are not going there to be interviewed, you're going there to get hired, so get hired!"

Chapter 10

Tarka was roused from her memories as Mary Wilson asked, "What time is the viewing?"

"Viewing is seven thirty to nine, we should get you to your suite. You can freshen up and have dinner. I have to ask, will you be coming to the viewing?" asked Lloyd.

"Of course we are!' answered Mary, punching Lloyd lightly in the chest.

On the way to the Queen Charlotte Hotel, Lloyd told Mary and James not to worry about meals, transportation and such. All they had to do was call Room Service or sign the check in the dinning room and bar. Everything will be taken care of.

"This place looks like something out of an upbeat travel magazine," said Mary as they walked into the hotel lobby. "Where the hell do we check in?"

"That's taken care of," said Lloyd as he nodded toward the Bell Captain who had the key card. The Bell Captain led them to their suite. Miller and Tarka left after a few minutes. Miller was dropped off at the Beverly and Tarka taken back to the office.

Shortly after Miller's arrival at the Beverly Hotel, he, Zipper and Beagle stood waiting for Rock in a large, darkened room in the basement. Each of the three men stood under a focused spot light. The beams formed a small white circle around each man. The brightness of the lights distorted the color of their clothing and made their faces appear phenomenally white and grotesquely shadowed.

Centered in front of the three men was a podium encircled in a fourth beam of light. The podium was a simple affair with four feet in an X shape. A single vertical rod, covered with a nine by nine inch table with green felt on its surface. The entire podium, except the very top was painted white. The four lights

64

were the only light in the room except for a slit of light from under a door directly in front of the men and podium.

The shadow of two feet appeared at the bottom of the door. Suddenly the silence was shattered by five distinct knocks on the door. All three men stepped on their foot switch, killing their respective lights. The door opened and the silhouette of Rock appeared framed by the exterior light. Rock was guided five steps into the room and stopped. The door slammed shut with a loud bang startling Rock. He and his guide were barely visible

While the lights were still out, Slick, standing in the center of the three men, asked, "What is your business here?"

"Zipper told me to be here to get lighted," answered Rock.

The three men could hear whispering. Rock finally said, "I have been told... that I may come here...and ask to be brought into the light..., in the light I can be a better man."

On the cue "man" all three men stepped on their foot switch and Zipper said, "Let your guide bring you forward."

Slick, in a commanding voice, asked, "Rocco DeAngelo, do you wish to come to the light?"

Rock shifted on his feet and said, "Yeah."

There was the hiss of whispered words and mumbling from Rock. Then he said, "Yes Sir, I want, a-a- wish to come to the light."

"Who has forced or influenced you to make your decision?" asked Beagle.

After more whispered words and mumbling from Rock, he said, "Nobody makes me do anything."

"Who has promised you worldly gain, monies, riches or fame?" asked Slick.

After more whispering Rock said, "Nobody said anything about that stuff."

"Then what gain will you achieve by coming to the light?" asked Zipper.

"The light will help me be a good guy and not beat up people all the time. I don't like to be in jail and I don't like everybody to be a scared of me. I want to have some real friends."

65

There was silence while the three men in the lights looked and nodded at each other. Then Beagle asked, "Rocco DeAngelo, do you know that if you come to the light under the guise of lies, deceit or dishonorable agenda, that the punishment can be as severe as death?"

There was an extended period of whispering and guttural noises between Rock and his guide. Finally Rock looked at the three men and said, "I ain't here telling lies or doing a rip off."

"Rocco DeAngelo, proceed to the podium surrounded in the circle of light, " said Slick.

Rock stepped forward, alone. He stopped at the podium. He looked down and saw five coins, one of each silver denomination.

Slick began, "Rocco DeAngelo, before you are five silver coins sealed in plastic. They represent all the riches you can expect from the brotherhood you are about to join. You must now answer 'yes' or 'no'. Will these riches be enough to see you through the rest of your life?"

"Yes," answered Rock after momentarily turning to his guide .

Slick went on, "You have answered affirmatively to the most important question you have ever been asked. By answering in the affirmative, you have committed the rest of your life to helping those in need of inspiration to regain their place in society. You will not push them forward, but will pull them with you as you are now committed to advance yourself.'

'Your coins will represent the progress you are now committed to forge for yourself. You are now at the first coin. Its value has no relationship to your value to society, your self worth, or your value in assisting others of lesser position. You will periodically be given a copper coin that you have earned through your personal achievement. To reach the next level, you must earn enough copper coins that when added to the value of your current level, they equal the value of the next silver coin."

"Huh?" said Rock. There was whispering between Rock and his guide. Rock turned back o Slick and said, "Oh, okay."

"As of this moment Rocco DeAngelo, you are no longer allowed to think of yourself as a nothing to society, no longer a homeless derelict. The title Mister seems insignificant to most but it is not. Mr. DeAngelo will help those in need who are tying to help themselves. Mr. DeAngelo will never use or allow the use of illegal drugs in his presence. Mr. DeAngelo will act as a man of honor and distinction. Welcome to the fold Rock, you are more then deserving," said Slick.

More lights came on and the three men walked over to Rock and congratulated him, Miller first. After a few moments of small talk, Miller excused himself and remained in the room. He turned out the podium light and started toward the semi-circle he and the other two men formed. He stepped on the first two but for some reason paused at the third, looking into the darkened room. Lloyd reflected back to the day he stood asking for "Light". Indiscriminately events passed through his mind until somehow he settled on the events of the day. Everything was going smoothly but he had that nagging feeling in the back of his mind that there were events about to occur that he could not anticipate.

Chapter 11

Miller returned to his office. He was glad to be back in his own comfort zone.

"Miss Tarka, I only ask that you bring me one cup of coffee in the morning but, I wonder if I could prevail upon you to break a precedent?" asked Miller nodding toward the wall cabinet.

"No problem sir, I could use a drink myself."

"What do you think of the Wilsons?" asked Miller once they were both seated.

"Mary is a feisty little lady but it seems as though the right mourning isn't there."

"I don't understand."

"I don't either," replied Tarka. "I know she hasn't seen Jaw in many years. It seems as though she's expecting her son to accept his father at a time when it really makes no difference. I could see her eyes as she was giving James hell. I can't be sure if it was anger or desperation I saw. She's had a long time to spring that revelation on James, why now?" asked Tarka.

"I asked myself the same question. I don't know what to expect of a woman who has been separated from her husband as long as she has. I guess it would be hell to wait as long as she has and when the waiting is over, she sees him in his casket. It just doesn't feel right Tarka, but I don't know what right should feel like. I caught an innuendo when she started on James. It could be this was the first time James couldn't get up and walk out," said Miller. He paused a moment or two and said, "You really don't have to stay Tarka."

"Mr. Miller, I have to call you 'Mr. Miller.' Even though I like the way you say my name, please call me Nancy for the duration of this assignment. As for staying late, I didn't know the man as Jaw. I did know him as Mr. Wilson. I didn't put it together until I saw him in the casket."

"You did! How did you meet him?" asked Miller.

"That, my dear sir, is none of your business. You can stay here or leave now. I went home during lunch and picked up another dress to wear this evening. I'm going to change in the outer office," said Tarka walking toward the door carrying her drink.

"Make it quick, I'm going to have a pizza delivered," said Miller laughing.

Miller called the pizzeria, the front door guard and his wife.

"Hi Honey."

"Hey stud, you holding?"

"Yeah, you planning on going to the viewing this evening?"

"I sure am. Will Mrs..... Jaw be there? Have you eaten this evening?"

"Yes and I have a pizza coming for Tarka and me."

"Oh the old fluorescent light, garlic and wine ploy, huh?"

"No, actually, I'm going to use bourbon on her."

"Let me know in detail if you score. I would like us both to have the same mental images during the last moments of your life," said Suzanne Miller jauntily.

"Yes Ma'am, I'll be good. Later."

When Tarka re-entered Miller's office she had the deliveryman in tow. The smell of Pizza filled the room. Miller paid and they got down to the business of devouring the pizza. As Miller began his third slice, the phone rang. It was Mary Wilson.

"You don't have to escort us Lloyd, Jimmy and I are headed to the funeral home now."

Before Miller could respond, Mary hung up. With complete surprise written all over his face he looked at Tarka and said, "The Wilson's are on their way to Malone's."

Tarka glanced at her watch as she finished chewing her bite of pizza and asked, "What's wrong with that? Its only thirty minutes early."

Miller thought a bit and said, "Nothing I guess. I have everyone in place and Driver is with them. It's just a surprise and I don't like surprises."

Miller sat thoughtfully for a while wondering why it bothered him that the Wilsons were going to Malone's. He had a mental flash of all kinds of street people coming up and giving their condolences to Mrs. Wilson. The mixture of street people and suits should confuse her enough so as not to have the slightest idea of what Jaw had been up to. Then Holbrook and Gage popped into his mind and he flustered. That is what bothered him, protection. Miller looked at Tarka and said, "We have to get over there, that was Holbrook there this afternoon."

Miller and Tarka arrived by taxi and were surprised that their cab was fifth in line waiting to drop off passengers. There were several groups of people standing out front and a steady stream of people going into the funeral home.

Inside, it was elbow to elbow. They jostled their way through the crowd and looked into the viewing room. There stood Mary and James accepting consoling words from people exactly as Miller imagined. It seemed not to matter to Mary, or for that matter to James what the mourners looked like. Each person appeared to receive a sincere reply in return.

Miller and Tarka scanned the room. It was filled with suits and rags, all talking to each other. As they began to look closer at the faces, a familiar voice came from behind them.

"You two are blocking the door." They turned to see a distinguished looking man. His silver hair impeccably styled. His expensive dark suit fit his trim six-foot body perfectly. Squeezing past them was their boss, Stanley Parkinson, Bank President.

"Good evening Lloyd, Miss Tarka, quite a crowd isn't it?" They were both too surprised to answer anything but a mumbled, "Yes Sir" in unison.

Miller regained his composure and said, "I'm sorry sir, I must have looked rather foolish. I had no idea that you knew Jaw this well."

Parkinson leaned forward between them and whispered. "There's a lot you don't know yet Slick." He smiled as he walked toward Jaw's casket.

Miller was puzzled by Parkinson's comment but before he could fully recover, he noticed a serious looking Zipper approaching.

"Slick, I'm glad you and Typer are here. Holbrook and Gage talked to Jaw's family before anyone could get to them. I don't know what the hell passed between them."

"Damn it Zipper, why didn't you have Rock take care of them?" asked Slick.

"He was busy. We caught Rat and Fingers Brock trying to pull wallets. We caught them before they got the first one. Rock knocked them out and threw their bodies in the dumpster. He should get a coin for that one. He only hit Rat once and you could tell it was controlled. He is taking his vows seriously."

"Christ, when it rains, it pours. Where are Holbrook and Gage now?" asked Slick.

Before Zipper could answer, Tarka asked, "Are you Zipper?"

"I sure am Typer, don't you recognize me or my voice?"

"Actually, I swear I have never seen you before in my life. Why are you calling me Typer?" asked Tarka, looking surprised

"Well we figured you'd end up deep enough in this thing that you'll never want out. So we gave you a street name."

"What makes you think I'll let myself get in that deep?"

"You're half way there now. Before this thing is over, you'll be in," said Zipper. Then turning to Slick he nodded toward the corner of the room and said, "The spies are over there."

Slick felt the anger of betrayal building up in him but he kept it at bay. It was a large room but it seemed he arrived in front of the two men as if ported there.

"Good evening Lloyd, nice crowd" said Holbrook.

"It is, isn't it," answered Miller testily. "You aren't here on a story are you Ted?"

"No," Carl said. The two men shook hands but Gage seemed preoccupied. Holbrook continued, "Carl said he was run out of here last night and wanted to come back to see what all the to do was about. Since I knew Wilson, fleetingly, I thought I'd come along with him."

Miller kept glancing at Gage who was constantly scanning the crowd, his mouth agape.

Holbrook went on, "We talked to Mary and Jim Wilson when we first arrived. It's amazing how much they still admire Jarvis even after he stayed out of touch for so long."

"My Father left home like Wilson did," said Gage. "I know I couldn't have that deep a feeling for him if I found him dead or alive. We were among the first four or five here. The Wilsons couldn't have known his mixture of friends. They are greeting everyone with the same warmth, regardless of how they are dressed. You can actually feel their admiration for the man radiate from them. It is sort of awesome," Gage said.

Slick studied Gage's eyes for a moment, turned to Holbrook and extended his hand. As they shook hands, Slick said, "The closer you were to Wilson the deeper the grief. I congratulate your honorable attention to detail."Slick then shook Gage's hand and walked off.

"What did that mean?" asked Gage.

"It means he's taking hold," replied Holbrook with a rueful smile. "Let's get out of here."

Gage wasn't really ready to leave but he followed Holbrook toward the door, still looking at the crowd. He spotted Nancy Tarka and made a mental note to call her. Gage did prevail on Holbrook to hang around in the foyer for some time afterward.

During the course of the evening, Miller met his wife. The two of them mingled with the crowd but somehow they became separated. At one point, he saw her talking to Tarka behind the Wilsons. In a few minutes, they drifted back together. Suzanne Miller left as she came, alone.

As she walked through the foyer to the front door, a voice behind her asked, "Message, can you be at Latta Park at ten AM tomorrow? Clear."

"Yes," she responded without a glance or hesitation in her stride.

Viewing hours were extended an extra half-hour on Mary Wilson's insistence. Finally, viewing was coming to a close. Mary and James both looked fatigued. Tarka stayed with them the entire evening giving them support and answering what few questions she could.

Tarka found Miller and said, "I don't know what happened but both of those people are the proudest, most loving family I have ever seen. Even junior there has come around completely. I can see it in their eyes, they aren't faking."

"I didn't think they were faking. That of course, brings up the question of what happened? I talked to Carl Gage. He was touched by their sincerity. I can understand Mary, but I'm sure one slap in the mouth didn't do that much good for James," said Slick.

"I'm sure it didn't. We may find out something this evening. They invited us to their suite for a nightcap. You do know the Wilson's want the burial at six tomorrow evening, don't you?" asked Tarka.

"They can't do that!" exclaimed Slick, loud enough to draw the attention of a few people.

"I guess I should have asked you. You already made the arrangements," said Typer.

Lloyd looked at Typer and asked, "Just what the hell arrangements did I make?"

"You let Malone know through New York. Malone is making arrangements to have a preacher here for the service. Zipper called Grey Hound and arranged for busses to be here at six. I told Driver. I can tell that nobody bothered to tell you. The new time for the service will be in the Register tomorrow."

Slick didn't know whether to be mad, glad, or proud. Just as he was about to speak, Zipper came up and asked, "Is there anything we missed boss?"

"Nothing but the feed afterwards, if the Wilson's want one," answered Slick.

"Typer asked and they decided against it," said Zipper.

Miller began to perceive what had taken place with pride. "If only Jaw could see what he spawned," said Slick sarcastically.

As they talked, the last of the viewers cleared the room. The Wilsons prepared to leave. Slick watched as they picked up their coats and talked. Mary walked directly to Slick. Smiling she said, "I can't believe how many people Al knew. It didn't matter whether they were rich or poor. They all loved Al, I mean Jaw, as you called him. You were right Lloyd."

"There is a large chunk of respect mixed in with the love, Mary. I'm glad they all turned out, said Slick. I wasn't too sure if anyone would be here." He smiled and wondered where the hell they had all come from.

Mary Wilson offered Miller, Tarka and Zipper a ride to the hotel. In the hotel room, a bar was already set up. Mary told everyone to help themselves and excused James and herself. They were both back in a few minutes, Mary dressed in slacks and a fresh blouse, James having shed his tie and jacket.

Mary refused all offers to make her a drink and mixed her own. She took a sip and said; "Smoke if you like, I'm sorry if they bother you but I do," and she lit a cigarette.

Once everyone was seated comfortably, Mary dropped the bomb by asking, "Who will tell me what kind of organization Al ran out of the Beverly Hotel?"

Miller almost choked on his drink. Zipper paled and looked at Miller. Tarka's eyes automatically shot to Miller.

"Well Lloyd, all eyes go to the preacher. What's going on at the Hotel?" Mary demanded.

74

Lloyd smiled, for her benefit and his own. He was holding. "Well Mary, I guess it's as good a time as any. Jaw sort of helped a few of his hotel guests get their lives back in shape."

"How?"

"In different ways, some he'd give a little guidance to, others he'd dry out. Still others he'd find out what they were good at and pump them up. He would find them jobs and keep an eye on them until they settled in."

"What did he do for you Lloyd?"

"Just about all of the above."

"What about the trust," asked Mary?

He didn't want to answer any questions about the trust, "Well Mary, it's hard to explain."

"I really asked one that time," said Mary with a sparkle in her eyes.

"Yes you did, in its simplest terms, the people that Jaw helped, contribute to the trust and it in turn, is used to help candidates get started in their own business. However, I was not privy to the actual inner working of the trust. You will have to talk to Jaw's attorney, Charles Mott about how it really works." Lloyd surprised himself with calm answers. He waited for her to respond.

"I have no intention of upsetting the apple cart, but I really would like to know what my husband was up to while he was gone," said Mary. Then as an after thought, she asked, "Will this Mott fella know about Al's estate and will and things like that?"

"I'm sure he would," said Lloyd. "I spoke with him today and he assured me that everything was in order. Whatever that means in lawyer talk."

"Well, let's talk about something else," said Mary.

Lloyd asked, "Why were you so surprised that Jaw settled in Charlotte?"

Mary smiled and said, "The obituary I read on Al said he was honorably discharged from the Marine Corps. Actually he retired. It was his retirement I lived off all these years along with some cards he sent every few months with money in them. We were stationed at Cherry Point on the coast, and used to come to Charlotte quite often to go shopping. Near the end, we began looking for a house to buy and settle here.

About two months before Al retired, my Father, a very active man, had a stroke. My Mother could not cope with my Father being bed ridden. I ended up going back to Binghamton to help my Mother get over the trauma. She never did adjust, Dad lingered on a little over a year and Mom died about three years later.

While she was alive, we tried getting my Mother to sell out and move to Charlotte with us but she didn't want to leave Dad. So we stayed in Binghamton. We vacationed on the North Carolina coast and arranged our route to pass through Charlotte either coming or going.

When Al left, about six months before Mom died, I waited about a year and began looking for him. We both loved Charlotte so it was the only place I thought to look. I checked with the police, ran ads in the paper and showed his picture around in shopping centers but nobody admitted knowing him. The occasional cards I received were from all over the country. I have no idea how he did that."

Everyone sat in silence thinking of Jaw, finally Zeigler said, "Well it's getting late. I guess we had better get going."

"Yes you're right. I didn't realize how tired I was until I relaxed," said Lloyd.

"Lloyd, would you have Mr. Mott contact me tomorrow, early? I'd like to get things settled as soon as possible and get back home no later then the day after tomorrow," requested Mary.

Lloyd nodded and the three of them walked out to the elevator. When the elevator doors opened in the lobby, a worried looking Ted Holbrook was sitting across the way.

He jumped up and hurried to them and said, "Lloyd, we have a problem. Gage is going to do an in depth story on Jaw. He let it slip that he had an inside source."

Slick looked at Holbrook with ice in his eyes saying, "You gave me the time and I expect you to keep your word Ted."

Holbrook was shocked, "Lloyd, I told you what I'd try to do, no guarantees."

Without a change in expression Slick said, "I don't need any guarantee from you. When you said I could have the time that was good enough for me. To me, it's an automatic. I have the time. That's the power of your word to me Mr. Holbrook." Lloyd took Tarka by the arm and headed toward the waiting limousine, leaving Zipper and Holbrook standing with mouths agape.

"He isn't holding any more. He's got a grip on the handle and is pumping it," smiled Zipper. "When is Gage going to submit the story or any idea about the slant?"

"None at all, he was pretty emotional at the viewing. It was as if something personal happened inside him."

"I'm going to try to get Slick to hit on Gage, one on one. I'm impressed on how he just handled you. Let's see how good he is on his feet," said Zipper.

"He was pretty good on me wasn't he," said Holbrook smiling.

Miller led Tarka to the limousine just outside the glass doors. In the reflection of the glass, he could see Zipper and Holbrook in conversation. Miller asked Tarka where she wanted to be dropped off and told Driver as he entered the cabin."

As they rode, Miller asked Tarka for information on how to deal with Carl Gage.

"I've been giving him a little thought since I noticed him at the viewing tonight. He is going to do his story no matter what anybody thinks or tells him. Once he gets it in his head to do something, he is going to do it."

"We need to stall him so that he doesn't submit his story to the editors until day after tomorrow's late edition goes to press," said Miller, half to himself. Then he asked, "Do you think there is anything you can do?"

Tarka gave Miller the raised eyebrow, "What do you think I am?" look.

Miller flushed, "No, No, not that.

Tarka smiled, saying, "I know." She paused a few moments in thought, and then said, "I don't even know how to get in touch with him anymore. He was thrown out of the apartment he lived in when I knew him. I helped him pack."

"You did?" asked Miller excitedly. "Tell me everything you saw, pictures, mementoes, souvenirs, anything. Is he a Mason, Elk, Moose, anything?"

"Just a second here Mr. Miller. I just had a novel idea. Why don't you ask him to run his story after Mrs. Wilson leaves town?" asked Tarka.

"Thanks Nancy, you can let go of the chain now."

"What does that mean?" asked Tarka.

"It means that you just flushed my toilet and got the junk out of my head. Now let go of the chain and let it fill back up," said Miller.

Still puzzled, Tarka asked, "How do I do that?"

"Quit looking at me like I'm some kind of idiot."

They arrived at the parking deck that held Tarka's car. Miller got out of the limousine with her and looked around. All seemed clear. As she started toward her car, Tarka stopped and said to Miller, "Goodnight sir, keep a clean bowl."

Miller grunted as he climbed back into the cabin and closed the door. As the limousine turned to the descent ramp, Miller glanced back at Tarka. He thought he saw a shadow move but was uncertain. The limousine continued on.

Chapter 12

Tarka walked to her car. As she inserted her key into the door lock, she glanced to the left and right. To her right, she saw the limousine silently rolling away. To her left was the hood of her car, which seemed to be different. In the gloom of the parking deck, it was difficult to ascertain what the illusion was but her hood appeared to be extended on one side. A warning signal flashed in her mind as the door lock clicked open. Tarka yanked her key out of the slot and leaped into her vehicle as the hood extension straightened vertically. A man ran to grab her door. He was ever so slightly faster then Tarka. She slammed the door shut but as she tried to hit the lock, to her horror, the door swung open and a hand flew to her throat.

"Make a sound and you're dead," said the man coldly as he dragged her out of the car.

Tarka made no sound but held the man's wrist with both hands, afraid to do anything. He was not choking her, but he did have a strong hold on her neck. He was not an ugly looking man Tarka had always pictured rapists as sweaty, ugly, fat, unshaven men with dirty hands and green teeth. The man who held her at arm's length was far from ugly. Actually he was rather handsome, tall, trim and in his mid forties. He had the tell tale wrinkles of having been a heavy drinker, but his smile was very warm. He was trying to use it on her now to stop her struggling.

"Calm down," he said. "I'm not here to kill or hurt you. I just want to talk. If you have any doubt that I won't kill you, you're wrong." He then cupped one of Tarka's breasts in his hand and twisted it enough to run sharp pains through her chest.

"Okay, you have my attention, keep your hands to yourself," croaked Tarka, her eyes filling with tears.

"Don't tell me about keeping my hands to myself, or I'll give you a damn wedgie," he said forcefully. He trailed off saying, "I don't know if it hurts women like it does men."

The statement was like cold water in Tarka's face. "A wedgie! You're going to give me a wedgie?" Her eyes sparkled and she giggled. "You were going to attack me and get my attention by giving me a wedgie? Are you new at this line of work? You don't get out much do you." Then her anger took over. She slapped him across the upper cheek and ear.

The man let go of Tarka's throat. As soon as his hand was clear of Tarka's throat, he flew in a long arc upwards and back. He landed flat on his back. A large black man in some type of long overcoat loomed over the attacker.

"What're you doing easing in on my turf?" asked the black giant.

Tarka sighed under her breath, "Oh Shit."

"Tell' um Miss Tarka that Slick said this is my ground and I've gotta be sure you are safe on your ground," said Butch as he stood with one foot on the man's throat.

Tarka, relieved and surprised, was not slow on the uptake, "That's right Butch."

"Want I throw him over the rail, he ain't much a-tall?"

"No, I want to know what he was up to," said Tarka.

Butch grabbed the man's shirt, yanked up him and turned him around. Butch twisted the man's arm into a hammerlock and grabbed his throat from behind.

"You said you didn't want to hurt me. You scared the living hell out of me and copped a cheap feel. That hurt. Who the hell are you and what do you want?" screamed Tarka.

"I'm Dot-Com!"

"Well I wondered what happened to you," came a voice from the shadows.

Tarka spun around and almost bumped into Miller. She immediately started, "This son of a bitch had me by the throat and twisted my tit. He said he was going to give me a wedgie!"

80

"A wedgie?" Miller chuckled. "What do you expect from a middle aged Nerd?"

Tarka grunted and said, "He still scared the hell out of me and copped a feel!"

"He's yours," said Miller to Tarka.

Tarka continued her circle till she was lined up with Dot-Com. Butch's pressure on his arm kept Dot-Com on his toes. She took a step toward Dot-Com and punched him in the stomach putting all her weight behind the punch. The man woofed in pain and was in the fetal position before he hit the ground. Butch and Miller were impressed with the blow.

Dot-Com rolled on the ground gasping. The three onlookers stood passively watching.

Slick asked, "What's your play Dot-Com?"

"I heard something was going on between the Beverly and the Misota's. The Misota's approached me to be their hacker. They told me to report in the morning. You'll have a man inside but you can't contact me. If you do anything by computer, I'll do my best to get it through. They will probably have a man on my back all the time. So if it is computer action, make it smooth," said Dot-Com in a raspy voice as he wiped his face and winced in pain.

"What do you know that I don't?" asked Slick.

"The street has it that the Misotas are going to try a take over. They want the Beverly's operations especially the street network and the trust," said Dot-Com.

"What the hell are you talking about? What are the Misotas up to?" asked Miller.

"I don't know for sure, I think it will involve computer money transfers," said Dot-Com.

Tarka asked, "What do I have to do with all this? Why did you grab me?"

Dot-Com, startled that Tarka spoke to him, answered immediately, "I really didn't know if you were Tarka or not. If you weren't, I would be in trouble. Then I was going to make you pass out and leave you locked in your car."

"Why the hell didn't you just ask?" asked Tarka.

"The Misotas, you never know who they own," said Dot-Com.

"I know one thing for sure, I do not want Miss Tarka mad at me,"said Butch.

Tarka looked at Butch frowning, "I should have guessed. Nobody talks with the accent you used. Who are you really Butch?"

"Isaac Thorn," said Butch softly

A memory flashed in Tarka's mind. "Isaac Thorn, are you the Isaac Thorn who beat up four cops a few years back?"

"Yes ma'am. I'm not like that anymore," said Butch in the same soft vice.

"Did Mr. Wilson, ugh Jaw help you too?" asked Tarka.

Butch only nodded but Miller spoke up, "Butch defended himself in court and almost won. Jaw was so impressed with his defense that he took Butch under his wing. Butch has completed three years of education at J. C. Smith in two years and has been accepted into UNC's law school."

"That's great Butch, keep up the good work," said Tarka. Then she looked to Miller and asked, "What's a Misota?"

"Carlos Misota is the crime king pin in Charlotte and most of North Carolina," Miller answered and turned to Dot-Com and asked, "What else have you got on Misota?"

"All I know is that that is the word on the street and the Misotas came after me to do some computer work for them. They still haven't told me what I'm supposed to do," said Dot-Com as he rose to his feet.

Tarka, not at all interested in Misota, asked Miller what made him come back.

"I thought I saw some movement. I didn't see Butch so I came up the stairs," said Miller. "It's over now, anyone need a ride?"

Tarka took a step toward Dot-Com, who immediately leaned forward for more protection.

"You really pissed me off," said Tarka as she gave Dot-Com a right cross to the chin. Dot-Com spun around in most of a circle as he fell to the concrete floor.

Tarka turned and headed for her car. Miller stepped back to make way for her. He was smiling broadly and shaking his head. Tarka winked as she passed.

As Tarka drove away, Miller realized that Butch had slipped away. Miller stood looking down at Dot-Com for a few minutes. Then he said, "Dot-Com I don't know if I can trust you. My first inclination is to kill you but you just may be of some help to the program from the inside. I want you to understand that if you turn on us, you will not leave Charlotte alive. I am probably being overly cautious. I never met a mistake of Jaw's so don't take offense, but do keep in mind that I am not, I repeat, not, lying."

"I know I screwed this up tonight," moaned Dot-Com, "but I really am on your side. Just don't send that woman after me if I can't control my end and screw up."

When Miller arrived at ground level, he found Zipper sitting in the limousine grinning.

"Damn Zipper, how did you get here so fast?" asked Miller.

"I know a short cut."

Slick told Zipper about the incident at Tarka's car. They both laughed until Slick brought up the Misotas. Zipper became grim. "Jaw told me about them a couple days before he died. He said to keep it quiet until he checked out a few more things. He wasn't sure but Jaw thought they were about to put a contract on him. Jaw thought if he were dead that Misota's inside guys would take over," said Zipper.

"Inside guys? What inside guys? Inside what, us? Did he say 'guy' or 'guys'?"

"He said 'guys'. He didn't let on if he knew who any of them were."

"Well that's about as good as diarrhea," said Slick. "Now I have the mob to deal with. By the way, Tarka came up with a novel idea about dealing with Gage. She suggested that we ask him to hold off until Mary Wilson leaves town."

"You're right, that is novel. Do you think he would go for it?" asked Zipper.

"No, not really, Tarka says he is head strong but I'll give it a try just for reaction's sake. Maybe it will give me an idea of where he is coming from and how strong his feelings really are."

"The way I see it Slick, Gage is the key to getting the program and the trust back into anonymity so we can begin to operate again. Right now we're dead in the water and must stay that way. The effect on New York could be disastrous. Legs and Class can be held in training a couple more weeks."

Miller thought a moment and said, "Rock's contract is signed, he can go on. I'll handle the payments. You really know how to keep the heat on a guy. What about you, why can't you deal with Gage?"

"One reason is I can't approach him under or out and be able to deal as fast as it may take. You are the only one who has known ties with Jaw. But, the best reason I have is that I don't want to," said Zipper, eyes twinkling.

"All that old bastard asked me to do was call his wife. He didn't mention the program or the trust in his letter. The note in my letter only talked about his body. Then he slips that damn note in with your designation and suddenly this whole thing is on my back. Now I find out we could be targets of the local mob."

"Slick we knew he was a sly old bastard. Maybe this is his way of telling you something. You can be sure he knew the implications of contacting his wife."

"Yeah, everybody began to look to me for instructions, but he made you head of the program. What does that leave me doing? Am I supposed to replace you and go under? I doubt I could live like that again. Aw hell Zipper, I'm going home and get some rest."

Chapter 13

On his way home, Miller made sure his route took him past the Beverly Hotel. He looked in as he waited at the traffic light. There seemed to be little activity in the lobby. A few turns later, he was on the interstate, headed for his lakeside home.

He parked at the side of the house and walked to the backyard. As he wandered down to the pier the fresh smell of the lake grew stronger. The serenity of the evening sky filled with moon and stars, had a calming effect. In his mind's eye he pictured himself out on the water, driving his boat.

"Hey stud, mind a little company? My husband isn't home yet," said a female voice, bringing Miller back to reality.

Miller turned to see Suzanne's silhouette against the houselights. She was wearing a thin dress with no slip. It was obvious she wore nothing underneath. Her auburn hair had a glow around it. She stood cocked on one hip. Miller grinned saying, "If only the boys on the corner could see you now. You'd probably be able to double your price and not carry quarters."

"Hey Stud Ant, if you had as much of everything else as you have mouth, you'd be able to handle it well enough that I wouldn't have to go out for some real stuff," she said as she shifted to the other hip and bounced on it a couple times.

Miller laughed and walked toward her saying, "Since you haven't doubled your price, I'll pay it. Do you have change for a dollar or do I have to have exact change?"

They were two steps apart. Suzanne adjusted her approach so that she was able step beside Lloyd, sweep one of his legs with hers and drive him to the ground with a thud. Suzanne held on to his arm to break his fall.

"What do you say to that Bug Stud?"

"Stop payment on the checks to Karate School!"

He looked up at the nakedness under her dress, sighed and said, "Since I'm down here and you're up there, how about

85

stepping over? The moon is in my eyes."

"Moon or Mooned, you still haven't had enough smart ass," she said as she stepped back and fell to her knees, crawled over and squatted on his chest. Her knees were up and Miller raised his head to peek between her thighs.

"Damn woman, it looks to me like you busted a seam in there."

"Smart ass!" said Suzanne as she scurried back and began to tickle him. They wrestled in the grass until Miller finally had her pinned to the ground with her arms over her head. He leaned forward and kissed her softly once, a littler harder the second time. He let go of her arms and scooped her head up and kissed her passionately. They rolled several times ignoring the cool dampness of the grass. They stopped with him on top. She slid her hand down between them and freed him. He immediately entered her with a hard thrust. They both sighed. Neither of them needed much movement. The climactic moment shuddered through their bodies, marred only by their conscious effort for silence. They did not want to alert their neighbors with moans and groans. They laid in silent bliss savoring the glow of their lovemaking. Reluctantly, they separated and walked arm and arm to the house.

Later Miller had drinks poured when Suzanne walked into the living room. He handed her a glass of wine as the phone rang. Miller hurried to it. It was Tarka.

"I'm going to be late in the morning Mr. Miller. I have been invited to breakfast."

"Okay, do you have any idea how late you'll be?"

"Aren't you interested in who I'm going to breakfast with?"

"Of course I am. I'm sure you will let me know when you come in. It has to be with someone we're interested in or you wouldn't go," said Miller, thinking either Holbrook or Gage. "Carl Gage called about ten minutes ago. He saw me at the funeral home this evening. He said I'd been on his mind lately. I should be in about nine fifteen or so. Later."

Miller smiled to himself. Tarka had heard him use the term

"Later" when ending a conversation. So Gage was trying to back door him, interesting. Miller walked back to the couch saying, "That was Tarka. She's having breakfast with Carl Gage tomorrow. He could be trouble if he writes the kind of article about the Beverly the way he usually writes."

"I assume Nancy knows him?"

Miller told the story, as Tarka had related it to him, prefaced by the conversations in the office. He went on about Tarka and her adoption by the organization. "She was easy to work with. There were no sex games, as played by some secretaries in the secretary pool. She just did one hell of a good job."

"I already figured that," said Suzanne. "I talked to her tonight. She is really happy working for you. She has a lot of respect for you."

'I did tell her not to get any ideas. You were lousy in bed and didn't know how to use the little that you have," said Suzanne.

"Obviously, she had bitten her tongue and didn't tell you she knew better."

"Is she alive? Seriously Lloyd, Tarka will be good for you. You can trust her. I do."

Miller leaned back on the couch and realized how relaxed he was. No matter how uptight he was when he got home, Suzanne always found a way to remove every vestige of tension.

As Miller laid his head on the pillow, Jaw crossed his mind. He recalled when he had met Jaw. Lloyd had walked into the Beverly Hotel, looking for a room he could afford. There were a few people who looked down or were out sitting in the lobby. He had just arrived in Charlotte and money had been short. He'd take care of that later that evening. At the desk was a middle-aged man. Lloyd had signed the register and had decided to pull the change flim-flam. He had done it very smoothly. The desk clerk had pulled the key from its hook and faced Lloyd.

"That was as smooth as I've ever seen the switch pulled. Now, you have a room here. Use it or not, but you're going to pay me thirty bucks for it," said the clerk.

"What are you talking about old man?"

"You're going to give me back my money and pay an extra ten for the room for trying to flim-flam me. If you call me 'old man' again, I'll show you what an 'old man' can do. Now pay up."

Lloyd had not been able to resist the challenge. He had leaned over the counter and, in the man's face, said, "You talk big Old Man."

That was all Lloyd got out of his mouth before, he swore to God he was a snot nosed kid in a man's body, and had agreed to pay. He had been yanked from his feet and jammed across the old man's shoulders. The old man had begun pulling Miller's neck in one direction and his leg in the other. Lloyd had been thrown on the counter with enough force that he had slid off the end of it and on to the floor. He had heard muted laughter in the background.

Miller was never sure which had been damaged the most, his body or his pride. He had paid the thirty dollars and had limped off to his room deciding to take the night off. A nature call awakened Miller around 3AM. He decided to go to the lobby for a pack of smokes. As he had walked out of the little canteen area, the desk clerk had come through the front door with a girl that looked to be about sixteen. When the clerk had seen Lloyd his face had brightened. As he had walked past Lloyd, he invited him along for a good time, saying, "She only charges five bucks."

Although this hadn't been Lloyd's style, the expression on the clerk's face made him go along. What happened in the next hour had changed Lloyd's life forever. They had gone into a room. The clerk grotesquely described positions, and sex acts, to the girl and demanded she participate in at least one of them with him. When the kid finally broke down in tears, he offered her a sandwich and a coke, letting her settle down. Then the clerk enticed Lloyd to try. The girl panicked, grabbed the sandwich and sprang for the locked door.

It had been then, that the clerk had called the whole thing off. He and Lloyd had left the room leaving the girl with the key and telling her she had a job in the morning. The old clerk had leaned against the wall sighing, his eyes full of tears.

"Damn if they don't get younger all the time," he said softly.

"How do you know she will work? What about management?" Miller asked.

"I am the management, and the sandwich was the key. If she had left it, I would have let her out," said the old man over his shoulder. Then he had stopped and turned to Lloyd saying," I'm known as Jaw." He had stuck his hand out to Lloyd and continued as they shook hands. "From now on you're known as Slick. Don't use your real name around here unless I tell you to. Be down here in the morning at seven thirty and I'll fill you in."

"Slick huh? What do you propose to call the kid in the room?" asked Lloyd.

"I decided that before I brought her here. Haven't you noticed her walk? She'll be Pigeon," said Jaw.

Miller awoke that morning feeling unresolved. The aroma of coffee drifted to his nostrils. He was sitting on the edge of the bed when Suzanne walked in. "I'll tell you what Honey, I don't know if I woke naturally or if the smell of that coffee woke me. Damn it smells righteous. I have to have a cup of that stuff," he said.

Suzanne took her shaking on one hip stance and said, "Open your eyes big time. You can start with the cup on your night stand."

Miller cocked an eye toward the nightstand. There sat a cup of coffee. Miller grunted approvingly and took a sip, immediately burning his lip and howling.

"Lloyd baby," Suzanne said, as if talking to an infant, "Mommy sends you to school and you eat the books. I've told you a hundred times, wake up before you drink your coffee. Coffee is hot."

"Thanks Honey, I needed that. It's so wonderful waking up

to a thoughtful loving wife who thinks first aid is rubbing salt into a wound."

Sitting at the breakfast table, Lloyd looked out over the lake. The placid scene was in direct conflict with the day he faced. He took strength from the sight, drawing from the serenity. Suddenly a fish jumped from the water creating concentric circles of tiny waves that spread until they were no more. At that moment Lloyd knew he could calm the waters. Lloyd bid Suzanne good-bye with a kiss.

"Grab hold Slick, you can do it," said Suzanne.

Lloyd very seriously said, "In the words of the great intergalactic philosopher, Hans Solo, 'Hey! It's me!'

As Miller drove away, Suzanne's thoughts turned to her rendezvous in the park.

Chapter 14

As Miller walked through his office door his phone began buzzing. He snatched the receiver, "Miller."

"Hi Slick, Pigeon here. This morning was a watcher's nightmare."

"What's going on?"

"You won't believe it. You've heard of lover's triangles. I was in a watcher's triangle. I spotted Gage at seven thirty this morning. He picked up a woman I couldn't see. I followed them to the Copal Grill on Wilkinson Boulevard. On the way, I spot Ted Holbrook and he's watching Gage. When I finally get in position, it turns out that Gage is with Typer. In the meantime, Holbrook spots me watching him watching Gage who is busy with Typer."

"Kill the connection but keep talking three more minutes! Call back later," ordered Miller.

Less than two minutes later, the phone rang again. He answered it on the first ring, "Lloyd Miller here."

"Uh,uh, sorry wrong number," a muffled voice said and hung up. Miller thought the voice sounded like Holbrook's but being muffled, he couldn't be sure. If it was Holbrook, and he could see Pigeon still on the phone, that should stall him. He felt himself beginning to get too wrapped up in this. Pigeon was going to give him history. He called Beagle for Mrs. Wilson.

Miller realized he was looking at the newspaper. He wanted to see the notice about Jaw's funeral and found the local section. On the second page, the black bordered notice read, "Burial Scheduled for Tonight." The notice went on to say that services for Jaw's funeral would began at 6 PM at Malone's Chapel. It also said that busses would be available for those who wanted to go on to the graveside service. As he finished reading, Tarka came walking in and flopped down in a chair, appearing to be worn out already.

"That tough huh?" asked Miller.

"I don't know if I'm compromising a friendship or a cause that I really don't know the truth about. I'm in this deep. Slick; please tell me what I'm into. Maybe I can feel better about myself if I know what it is I'm protecting," said Tarka re-adjusting herself in her chair.

"Slick eh, I guess I do have to help you out somewhat. There is an organization in this city that helps certain people who lost their perspective. The people who get involved in this rehab program are taken through a series of steps leading them back to full self-esteem and productivity. There are no failures. If they start the program, they finish it. No dropouts are allowed. Understand that's how they got in the position to need help in the first place. Someone allowed them to drop out instead of helping."

"What happens if someone wants to drop out?" asked Tarka leaning forward.

"They are forced to stay and forced to progress."

"How can you force someone to stay in a program they want out of?" she asked.

Miller paused for a long moment then replied, his voice soft but firm. "You don't need any more than what I've told you to make your decision. You've been pointing that purse at me long enough. It is time for you to decide whether you're going to give that tape to Gage or give it to me."

Tarka stiffened at his words. Her face reddened. She tried to look Miller in the eye but could not hold the gaze. She slowly got up and walked out the door.

In a few minutes she knocked on his door and walked into his office. Tarka walked straight to Miller's desk, laid her steno pad and a small roll of recording tape on it and said, "Thank you Mr. Miller for allowing me insight to the program. I hope it helps many more people. I apologize for what I did. I never thought you would see through me so easily. I assure you, I will never reveal anything about your program. I called the Secretary Pool to send up someone to replace me."

"Are you going out the front door or back to the pool?"

"Back to the pool, if you'll let me."

"I'm sorry Ms. Tarka, but I can't allow that. It has to be out the front door."

"I understand," replied Tarka, so soft it was barely audible and began to turn to the door.

"However, I will give you the option of staying and finishing this with me, if you wish." Tarka froze as he began to speak, and turned back toward him, her mouth agape. "You mean you think you can still trust me after I taped our conversation for Carl?" she asked incredulously.

"I believe you were going to make up your mind after we talked. It was evident that you had some kind of burden when you came in here. I didn't realize you had the recorder until you became persistent at aiming your purse at me. It was very amateurish. I'd like you to stay Tarka but only if you're sure, with absolutely no doubt, that your loyalty is with the program and me."

"I want to stay, and yes, I know where my loyalties lie," said Tarka smiling misty eyed.

"Good, now brief me on your meeting with Gage."

Chapter 15

Suzanne Miller arrived at Latta Park as scheduled. She followed the paved paths to a junction and veered off on a dirt trail that led to a secluded point. A man who seemed entranced with the ripples of the lake occupied the single bench at the overlook. As Suzanne passed him, she uttered, "Clear." She received the same response.

"How are you Uncle Tee?" she asked, using the name she had used since infancy.

He got up and they embraced as he asked, "Just fine, how's my favorite niece?"

"Doing okay except for the loss of Jaw."

"How is that husband of yours? Did he have any great problems last night?"

"If he did, he didn't show it. I was a little concerned this morning when he got up. He seemed tense, but when he left the house, he was a different man."

"What do you mean, a different man?"

"He came down to breakfast a little groggy. I caught him staring out the window but I didn't say anything. When he got up to leave, he seemed more self confident or determined. Oh, I don't know. He seemed to have grabbed it all of a sudden."

"Suzanne, we have to be sure about him. Jaw was sure Slick could handle the management side. He insisted that we test him on the judgment under pressure side," said Uncle Tee.

"Do you think he can deal with the Chair?" asked Suzanne.

"It is not for me to say."

"Come on Uncle Tee, Mom told me, that when a Holbrook had something to say, they said it."

"My sister thought of the Holbrook's as the American Royal Family," replied Ted Holbrook.

"That doesn't answer my question," insisted Suzanne.

"I'm not going to answer your question."

94

"Then tell me who's on the board that decides," she persisted.

"I know you don't really expect me to do that. Suzanne, the only reason we brought you in the back door is to give us a truthful insight on Lloyd's reactions at home. He has no idea that I'm involved in the trust or with Jaw. I am not a board of one. There are a-a- many of us. Probably clout wise, I'm the low man on the totem pole. They are good people who have put their professional reputations on the line by accepting membership on the board. If Lloyd blows the trust, all of these people will lose their standing in the community."

"If Lloyd makes it through the next couple of days, the way he made it through the last few, there should be no problem naming him chairman and you will meet all the members of the board. As I told you before, Suzanne, Lloyd doesn't know the board exists."

"In the meantime, I'm supposed to, what's the term, 'rat' on my husband behind his back, to a board that wants him as its chairman but is putting up all kinds of obstacles to disqualify him," grumbled Suzanne.

"I'd say you summed it up pretty good."

"Damn it Uncle Tee, he's my husband! I'm supposed to be supportive and loving and, and up front with him! I feel like I'm some kind of gutter scum," wailed Suzanne.

Holbrook stood and extended his hand to her. When she stood, he hugged her and began to guide her back to the trail. As they strolled toward the parking area he said, "Honey, if Lloyd doesn't make it, he will never know unless you tell him. If he was appointed and failed, well, who knows what effect it would have on him or the trust?"

"Damn it! That's my point. You keep saying if, and I keep saying he can handle it."

"Honey, if."

"See, there you go again, if!" Suzanne interrupted.

"All right! There are too many other people involved to allow someone who has not dealt under pressure for a while, to assume that position without being tested. That's what we are doing."

Suzanne could not argue with that logic, but it did not rid her of the feeling that she was being disloyal to Lloyd. She wanted to be honest with the man she loved.

They strolled along the trail, each lost in their own thoughts. Holbrook caught color in the corner of his eye and looked to his left and saw a stag. He gently stopped Suzanne and nodded toward the deer. They stood fascinated in silence, the animal frozen in its stance. A beautiful rack of antlers crowned its head. A loud explosion suddenly startled them. Before they could turn to the sound, the deer staggered, in an awkward manner, and fell to its side. It rocked oddly a moment and then lay motionless.

"I got him!" yelled a man, as he came running out of the brush about twenty yards up the trail from the two stunned walkers.

"What the hell do you think you are doing? This is a public park for Christ sakes," yelled Holbrook.

"You two seen too much. I'm going to have to convince you that you saw nothing," said the man menacingly, his face covered with camouflage paint.

"The hell you say," said a livid Holbrook as he strode toward the man. "Give me that God damn gun, you stupid son of a bitch!"

Holbrook, in his rage, walked right up to the hunter and reached for the barrel of the gun. The hunter swung the butt of the gun at Holbrook, hitting him on the side of his head. Holbrook staggered sideways a few steps, knocking Suzanne to the ground. The hunter followed Holbrook as he staggered and hit him in the chest with the gun butt. The blow drove Holbrook backward to the ground.

Suzanne scrambled on her knees to reach Holbrook's bleeding head. "Oh my God, He's dead! He's dead!" she screamed, as she held Holbrook's head.

"He ain't dead Lady, I only knocked him out," said the hunter, who was leaning over Suzanne's shoulder.

Suzanne felt the touch of the hunter's leg against her shoulder. Without thinking, she rammed her elbow into the man's crotch shouting, "How the hell do you know?"

The hunter, already bending over, immediately grabbed himself in reflex action. He fell into the grit of the trail, hitting his forehead and nose. He hovered there a second and Suzanne pushed him away from the moaning Holbrook.

She tried to awaken Holbrook. She sensed more then saw a presence behind her. As she turned, the shadow of a man loomed over her, and a fist came straight at her cheek, followed by an explosion of color and then blackness.

Chapter 16

3rd Day 10:00 AM

Tarka set two cups of coffee on Miller's desk. He had already gotten the steno pad out of the safe and gave it to her saying, "I want you to make notes of what you are telling me. I'll let you do them in short hand if you promise to translate them immediately."

"That would be easier," she said. "Well, Carl called almost as soon as I walked through the door. He sort of hemmed and hawed around for a while, but finally got to the reason for the call. He was half drunk from the sound of him. He said he saw me at Jaw's wake and wondered what I was doing there. I told him I was a friend of the family. He insisted that Jaw had no family and that the Wilsons were actors that had been hired for the occasion. I asked him why he felt that way, but I couldn't get a direct answer from him. He did keep stressing the point that the Wilsons were imposters. After we argued a while, it seemed as though his voice began to crack a little, as though he were about to cry or was crying. Then he cut the conversation short and asked me to breakfast.

"We went to the Copal on Wilkinson Boulevard. At first he came on as his old self. As the conversation wore on, I could feel a distinct change in his mood. He even became a bit glassy eyed when we discussed the wake and the Wilsons. He had the impression that Jaw forced people to work for him and others, but kept the money they were paid. I asked him if the people were maybe working off a debt. He seemed to accept that possibility out of a desperation to have some kind of an answer.

"The conversation stalled and I glanced at the Register and commented on the headline about the Viet Nam Veteran who had shot himself. Carl said he could relate to the story because he was a Desert Storm Vet and had very few good memories. He seemed lost in thought and to break the silence I asked where his hometown was. He's from Elmira New York. In

98

conversation, it turns out that Elmira is not very far from Binghamton. Then his mood really turned glum and he broke off and we went outside."

"When did he convince you to do the taping?" asked Miller.

"When we walked outside, he asked if I was still in the First Nation's pool. I told him, yes. He asked if I knew you. I told him I did, and was working for you now. For some reason, he thinks you are a Jaw graduate, but can't prove it. He says he knows you and Holbrook had lunch at Clarke's yesterday. He saw your name on Holbrook's calendar pad, 'Miller, lunch at Clarke's, 12:15, back door.' It stood out because he had no appointments that day. Carl insisted that you were bribing Holbrook not to let him print anything about the Wilson funeral. I told Carl that was ridiculous and I guess I got a little testy with him. Before I knew what I was saying, I agreed to ask you all the questions he gave me. It was my idea to tape it so he would know I wasn't lying. I had the option of letting him hear the tape, or telling him to go to hell," said Tarka.

"Are you sure you are not adding things in or changing anything around? What you've just told me is a quagmire of assumptions. It could throw a new light on everything," said Miller, who was almost lost in thought as he spoke.

"I'm telling you everything exactly as it was said and as it happened. I'm not finished. All that conversation took place just outside the front door. Carl asked me to wait a second and went back inside. As I stood outside waiting, a female voice behind me asked, 'Are you working? Clear.' I said that I was and she said, 'You are being watched by outsiders, gone, later.'

"Carl came out a few seconds later and we walked toward the car. Suddenly he sprinted forward at a car that was trying to get into traffic. He kept yelling, 'Come here you bastard,' but the car made it into traffic before Carl could get to it. He came back ranting and raving about Holbrook trying to kill or steal his story. What he didn't pay attention to was the bag lady driving an XKE that, I think Holbrook was after. Carl turned to Worms, made excuses for his behavior, and left. He just had to get out of there to be alone to think. He gave me a twenty and told me to take a cab back," she ended saying the last sentence with disgust.

"Do you think he is losing it?" asked Miller.

"I don't think so. He is really into this story and what he is finding is tearing him apart."

Miller thought about what Tarka had told him. He had better read the transcript before taking it apart. He had to keep an open mind on this one for sure. He looked at Tarka who was busily writing in the note pad.

In a few minutes she finished transcribing the shorthand and gave it to Miller. He read it over and laid the pad down. He sat silently looking at Tarka for a long time. She began to get uncomfortable at his stare. They finally settled into a staring contest.

Miller broke the silence saying, "Nancy, uh, Typer, there's something wrong here. There are things happening before their time and things going on in one place that are known to people elsewhere who should not have the knowledge. Typer, I want you to answer the next two questions with either yes or no. Typer, are you a member of the Beverly Hotel Stand-up Association?"

Typer raised one eyebrow, "No."

Miller walked around the desk to Typer. He pulled some change from his pocket. He took Typer's left hand and dropped five coins in it, one at a time saying, "These are five coins I had in my pocket, almost any five will do. There are things you can do with five coins that you cannot do with three coins, unless you have done good with the two missing coins." With that, Miller picked up two coins from her left hand and put them in her right hand. "You now have three coins in your left hand. I now give them to you to use wisely. Do you have an obligation to someone who has fewer coins?"

"No," said Typer and asked for some change.

Surprised, Miller emptied his change on the desk and looked away. Typer added two pennies to the coins she had and dropped some in Miller's left hand.

Miller looked at his hand astonished. There were two silver and two copper coins in his hand. He walked around his desk and sat heavily.

"I can't believe this," he said shaking his head, "I am the acting head of this organization and you are working for me, and you are Zipper's man."

"No, I am not Zipper's person," said Tarka.

"Who the hell's 'person' are you?" asked Miller in frustration.

"I'm sorry, I can't tell you that," replied Tarka in a whisper, "You know I can't"

"Why have you been assigned to me like this?"

"To help you. The program and the trust are in danger and you are supposed to be the one who can get it through this period safely. Hell I got roped into this assignment without knowing there was any kind of organization out there," said Tarka.

"Who roped you in?"

"I can't tell you that right now."

"Damn it Typer! The only one it can be is Zipper. He's Jaw's selection as successor to the program and the trust."

"Slick, you told me about Zipper's letter and read it to me yourself. You still didn't understand what was there. Jaw gave Zipper the program, not the trust."

"The trust is run by Beagle," injected Slick.

"I don't know about that, but someone has to give him orders," said Typer.

"Well, I'll be damned. You mean there is something my secretary doesn't know, about the clandestine organization I enticed her to help me with?" asked Miller, getting more frustrated.

"Mr. Miller, I have no inside knowledge about anything that is going on that would be of any benefit to you. Jaw set up everything on one premise... trust. Now is not the time to start questioning Jaw, the trust and the organization. You can do that once you get the transition taken care of. Jaw was the least help in all of this. It was his obituary that mentioned the trust. Concentrate on getting the story turned, the hotel operating and the trust back under. That is the kind of work you do best, so do it and later roll whatever heads you want to roll."

Chapter 17

Suzanne became aware of the cold ice pack on the side of her face. It hurt but also felt so good against the burning. She could hear herself moan, but seemed to have no control over the sound. Her vision was blurred. She thought she was focusing but wasn't sure. She was either looking at a faded brown coat, with the most ridiculous design on it, or she was still coming into proper focus. The coat moved and produced a woman dressed in so many layers of rags that, despite the frailties of her hand, she looked overweight. The ice pack turned out to be a cold can of coke.

"Pigeon, where did you come from?" asked Suzanne.

"I was following this guy named Gage. Then that guy," she nodded at Holbrook, who was sitting on the ground holding a coke to his jaw, "started to follow me. I lost him and then followed him and here we are."

"What happened to the guy who did this?" asked Holbrook.

"Guys," said Suzanne and Pigeon.

Pigeon went on, "I started yelling for the cops. They grabbed their deer, threw it in a pickup and got the hell out of here."

"Are you alright Suzanne?" asked Holbrook.

"Yes Uncle Tee. I thought he had killed you. How are you doing?"

"Uncle Tee?" asked Pigeon.

"Come here Pigeon," said Holbrook, who pulled some coins out of his pocket as she approached him. "I'm too foggy to tell it right, but this is where I stand." He opened his hand, showed Pigeon the coins and removed one. He spoke seriously to Pigeon saying, "Your loyalty and friendship to the program, trust and Slick will be best served if you tell him nothing of this. You will know I'm telling you right in a couple days."

Pigeon looked at Holbrook in awe, "You were one of my assignments. What am I supposed to tell Slick and Zipper?"

"Report to Zipper. He will give you your cover story. By the way, how did you follow me here?" asked Holbrook.

An immediate twinkle rose in Pigeon's eyes, "I'll tell you that in a couple days."

Holbrook endured the pain of a smile and said to Suzanne, "You're going to be our biggest problem. What the hell are we going to tell Lloyd about your shiner?"

"Shiner," exclaimed Suzanne! She tore into her purse for her compact mirror. She looked at herself in the mirror and cried, "Oh my God! Look at my face! That son of a bitch! I'll feed him to Lloyd! I'll be damned if that hemorrhoid is going to get away with this!"

"Wait a minute honey, how do you explain me?" asked Holbrook.

"I see you as some guy who got smacked in the head and still would not get involved. I don't know who you are, or what you look like!" yelled Suzanne getting madder and madder. "Uncle Tee, get the hell out of here. Pigeon, what kind of pickup did they have and what was the tag number?"

Holbrook knew his sister's daughter was all but a clone of her. He knew better then to argue. He sighed and said, "If this is the way you want to handle it, it's yours. I'll call the police."

Suzanne didn't know what her uncle told the police, but there were three cars there in ten minutes. Pigeon was gone, but she had given Suzanne a good description of the pickup and the tag number. Unknown to Suzanne, Pigeon had also given the tag number to Holbrook.

Suzanne told the police that she had stopped at the park on her way to visit a friend. She had some personal things to think about and had decided on a walk in the park. While walking, she had met an older gentleman. They had walked along together discussing nature and things.

Suzanne explained, "The man happened to notice a deer in the little meadow back there. A shot rang out and the deer fell.

A hunter appeared and the man had become enraged. He started yelling at the hunter. The hunter hit the man with the end of his gun, knocking the old man to the ground. As I bent over to tend to the man, the hunter came close and I elbowed him in the groin. Someone else came up behind me and as I turned to him, he punched me in the face. I was dazed, but was able to stagger to the parking lot and saw the pickup the men loaded the deer's body in and I got the truck's number. I fell and passed out for a few minutes. When I came to again, I staggered to my car. A fisherman came by and I asked him to call the police. As soon as the fisherman had left, the old man came staggering out of the forest. He got into his car and left without saying a word. He might be crashed down the road somewhere."

The questions came and Suzanne answered, "No there were not sexual liberties taken.

"No, I didn't see the man that hit me."

"Yes I think I can identify the man with the gun, but he did have paint on his face.

"I understand you can't do anything about the man who was hit without him but what about the man who hit me?"

She showed the police where it had happened. They found no blood where the deer had died. The officer taking the report read over his notes while Suzanne looked around and insisted this was where it had happened. The officer looked a little puzzled.

"Ma'am, exactly what did you tell the fisherman, when you asked him to call us?"

"I told him to call the police and get me some help."

"Did you tell him what happened?"

"I don't remember," answered Suzanne, not knowing what had been said to the 911 operator.

"Ma'am, you described the hunter, gave me the tag number of the getaway truck and the description. Now you're telling me you don't remember what you told the guy who was going to call for help?" the officer asked, incredulously.

"Officer Crandle, would you step over here for a moment please?"

Suzanne and Crandle looked toward the voice. Suzanne only saw another officer. Crandle stiffened noticeably. He responded with, "Yes Sir Captain."

The two policemen spoke for a few minutes in low tones. All Suzanne could hear of the conversation was the end when Crandle said, "Yes sir, not a problem." The captain turned and walked off, Crandle returned to Suzanne.

"Thank you for your cooperation. If you will stop by the station tomorrow afternoon and ask for the Watch Commander, he'll have your statement typed and ready for you to sign. By the way, both men are in custody, and the deer was a fake, a target. It's like the incident was a set up."

Suzanne could not tell by the officer's tone or body language if he was mad, glad or indifferent. She thanked him and asked if she could leave now, he nodded and she drove home.

As soon as Suzanne walked through the door, she called Betty Townson, "Betty, this is Suzanne, I'm in a little trouble and I need some help. You are the only person I can call."

"Suzanne, what's wrong?"

"Have you been alone all day?"

"Yes, why?"

"Have you talked to anyone on the phone since about ten thirty this morning?"

"No Suzanne, what's going on?" asked Betty.

"I have an uncle that Lloyd doesn't know about. I met my uncle at Latta Park this morning. When we were leaving, we witnessed what we thought was a man killing a deer right in the park, My uncle got mad and tried to take the gun from the hunter and was hit in the head."

"Was he shot?" interrupted Betty.

"No he was hit with the wood part of the gun. While I was helping my uncle, another man came up behind me. When I looked back, he hit me and gave me a shiner," said Suzanne.

"A what? A shiner? What's a shiner?" asked Betty.

"The son of a bitch gave me a black eye!"

"Oh my God! Are you all right? Do I need to come over there?"

"I'm okay, but I want the bastards punished for hitting my uncle and me. So I had my uncle call the police. I lied to them. I told them I was on my way to a friend's house, but had stopped at the park for a walk to clear my head. If I have to give them, or Lloyd, a name, can I give them yours?"

"Will I have to go to court?"

"No, the police, or Lloyd, may call you but all you have to tell them is that I called and said I was coming over. Then I called back and told you what had happened."

"Oh darn, sure I will, it's only half a lie. You did call and tell me what happened."

"One last thing Betty, don't tell anyone, even Hal, and please don't tell anyone about my uncle," pleaded Suzanne.

"Okay."

"Thanks Betty. I owe you. Bye."

Chapter 18

Mary Wilson had been awake for more then an hour. She glanced at the clock again; the red outline of a six, a one and an eight glowed back at her. There was no going back to sleep. Mary could see the sun through the crack in the drapes. She was more excited, than remorseful over the coming events of the day. Mary was more awed than intimidated by the number and variety of friends that had come to Al's wake last night. Jaw, as she was now beginning to think of him, must have known half the city.

She had peace about Jaw's death. Mary picked up bits and pieces of information during the brief encounters with his friends. The enormous pressures he must have had to endure began to surface after a little reflection. At his age, Jaw had been destined to burn out soon.

She showered and dressed in casual attire. It was important to her not to awaken James. She eased out the door and went down to the lobby. She looked around a moment for anyone who might be one of Jaw's people. The lobby was deserted. The limousine driver was sitting behind the steering wheel reading a newspaper. Mary exited by the other door and entered the cab parked at the curb. The driver put down a phone and asked, "Where to Ma'am?"

"Take me to the Beverly Hotel please," she said climbing into the back of the cab.

"Yes Ma'am," said the driver. "Do you live there?"

Mary crossed her fingers and replied, "Yes."

"Too bad about Jaw."

"Yes it is."

"I knew him pretty well. I used to be on nights. I couldn't venture a guess at the number of times he took a fourteen, fifteen, or sixteen year old hooker to the Bev. Usually it was around one or two in the morning.

Mary's face reddened.

"I guess it was about three months before I found out he wasn't a... a...well, you know."

Mary smiled to herself and said, "Yes, I know. "

"From what I heard, he got most of those girls to either go back home or get straight up jobs. Most of the time, he got the job for them. I sure wish I could have gotten in the program. I was trying when he died," said the cabbie.

The driver started again, "I went to his wake last night and met his wife." He glanced in the mirror for the first time. "Oh no! Mrs. Wilson! "Ma'am, I'm sorry. I really am sorry, Mrs. Wilson."

"Oh hush yourself," said Mary. "You didn't tell me anything I didn't already know. What isn't clear to me is how the candidates were selected."

"That isn't clear to anyone. When I heard about the program, all I heard was that there was a guy in town that would help the down and out, if they were ready to commit one hundred percent. All you had to do was let the street know on and on until one of them says the word is out on you. Then you just wait to be contacted," said the Cabbie.

"How long does it take before you know if you are selected?"

"Somewhere around a couple months or more. Somebody will come up and say, 'About the program, you're in or forget it,' and you go from there."

"I guess you haven't received your answer yet."

"No Ma'am, the word on the street is the program will go on but nobody believes it."

When the conversation finished, they sat in front of the Beverly Hotel for about a minute. Mary looked at the meter and began to pull money out of her purse.

"Don't bother Mrs. Wilson, you don't owe me a thing," said the Cabbie.

"You, my dear sir, have no choice in the matter, unless you want to get into an argument with Jaw's widow right here on the street. Think anybody who knew Jaw will hear about it?"

"Yes Ma'am, but Jaw and I had an arrangement on tips. There were no tips."

"I am not Jaw," said Mary taking her change and throwing a couple ones over the seat as she climbed out of the taxi.

"I can see that you were a match for Jaw Mrs. Wilson. My name is Terry Carnes and this is cab 321. Just call if you need to go anywhere safely."

As soon as Mary began to walk toward the hotel, Terry picked up his cell phone and said, "You were right. She snuck out and I dropped her at the Bev. Yes sir, I passed on all the info you instructed me to do. No sir, I don't think she did."

Mary walked into the lobby of the Beverly Hotel feeling both excited and sad. This is where her husband had spent all the years they had been apart. The lobby had a few chairs in it, occupied by men and women who were obviously down on their luck. Mary had no problem finding the Registration Desk. The Beverly did not have the opulence of her hotel. The desk clerk had his back to Mary, but he did look familiar. (She thought she heard a door open and close softly. Mary expected to see someone come around the corner. Then she definitely heard another door open and close. She thought little of it, assuming that the hotel must have a door or other things in the back.)

"Sir?"

Showing no sign of surprise either in voice or manner, Frances Zeigler turned and asked, "Yes Mrs. Wilson, what can I do for you?"

"I'd like to see Jaw's room."

Zeigler moved closer to the desk. As he did, he pressed a hidden button twice and said, "I'll have to call the police and see if they have any objections. They put a seal on the door just in case anything came up," said Ziegler as he dialed the phone.

"In case of what 'anything'?" asked Mary.

"It is standard police procedure in North Carolina. If someone dies without a doctor present, the coroner has to determine the cause of death. It will just take a second," said Zeigler.

110

Mary stood at the desk looking around. She wondered how old the hotel was. Mary could not remember being in a hotel that had rooms in sight of the lobby

Zeigler walked around the desk and motioned Mary to follow him. They walked to a corner room at the end of the hall. There was a yellow Police Seal on the door. Zeigler took the seal off the door and unlocked it. Mary grabbed his arm before he could open it. She moved directly in front of the door, took a deep breath and swung the door open, not knowing what to expect.

Mary took one step inside and stopped. The room had a television set, pictures, a couple chairs and a closed roll top desk. She could have guessed the roll top was in the room. Jaw loved roll top desks. Behind the door was a bed and nightstand. Mary looked at the wall pictures, there were none of her and James. She went to the desk and tried the roll top. To her surprise it opened. Laying dead center of the desk was an old worn Bible. She picked it up and thumbed through it. Immediately pages began to flop open to the weight of photographs. They were pictures of her and James, taken about a year ago. Tears rolled down her cheeks as she recalled her pose in one of the photos. She was at a wedding reception at the Polish Community Club in Binghamton. Mary was caught smiling up at a man who could have been asking her to dance. She laid the book down and closed the desk.

She walked around the room, touching everything with a light tap as though trying to get a feel of Jaw. When she came to the television, it felt hot. It caught her attention. Then she noticed a coke can sitting on the nightstand. It was sweating. She felt the can. It was cold. She looked at Zeigler in puzzlement.

"All right Zeigler, what the hell is going on here?" she asked demandingly.

Zeigler fidgeted a moment and said, "I don't know."

"You don't know or you won't tell me?"

"Honest Mrs. Wilson, I don't know," said a very uncomfortable Frances Zeigler.

"Look fella, the bed is made. The TV is warm. The coke is so cold the can is sweating. You tell me the police have a seal on the door and no one can get in. I heard doors opening and closing. I ask you again, what the hell is going on here?"

"Mrs. Wilson, I don't know what's going on and I wish I knew. Jaw left instructions. I was not to allow anybody in his room without permission of a certain Police Officer."

"Why?"

"Ma'am, the first thing anyone learns around here is not to question your husband. When he told you to do something, you did it. I was given instructions and I followed them."

"Where does that door at the end of this hall go?"

"To the supply room."

"Let me guess. It has a door to the back alley."

"Yes Ma'am."

"You can bet your ass I'm going to get to the bottom of this Ziegler," said Mary, as she stormed out of the room.

Chapter 19

Carl Gage could hardly stand himself. If he could tear his insides out and throw them away he would. What should he throw away was the question? His heart, his intestinal track, his stomach, all of them bothered him. Maybe he could do something like the Incas did and just reach in and pull the pumping heart right out of his body. He formed his hand into a spearhead and jammed his fingertips into his chest and began to laugh at himself for the foolishness of his thoughts.

In reality, he was surprised at himself. He did not understand the emotions that were released in him by the damn wake last night. It probably had something to do with his father. He hadn't thought of him in months. Gage had to shed the emotions so that he could write objectively, and not emotionally, in the exposè of Jaw. He knew Jaw ran some kind of rehabilitation center. He also knew that the Beverly Hotel Trust was as tight as legally possible. The fact that it was so tight intrigued him. Why should a rinky-dink hotel like the Beverly have such a sophisticated trust setup? Why have a trust at all?

Ted Holbrook was no easy matter either. He flat told Gage to lay off the Wilson story. "Jarvis Wilson is mine," Holbrook stated. "I've been working on him for years and if anybody is going to write his swan song, it will be me."

Holbrook gave Gage some hints about the material he had on Jaw. He must have just about penetrated the whole organization. All that information should have made Gage's mouth water, but it didn't. That bothered him too.

Without knowing it, he had met Jaw. He remembered the incidents as soon as he viewed the body. The first time had been at a city council meeting last spring. Gage had been covering the meeting that was supposed to vote on a zoning change that involved a company in which one of the council members was a silent partner. The council member, who had been silent all evening abstained, and the surprised Mayor had to cast the deciding vote. He had been angry because the council member had made no comments Gage could have used in his story about exposing the partnership. The man sitting next to him that evening had been Jarvis Wilson.

Wilson had leaned over to him and said; "Don't be so disappointed because we have an honest politician in town Mr. Gage. If you look around, you could probably find a lot of other good things about this city and its power people."

"He must have told the other members in private," Gage responded and remembered the man's look of contempt.

"That, my dear sir, is bull stuff and you know it. He has spoken against issues each one of the members had been strongly in favor of on multiple occasions. You wouldn't get a second grader to believe that story, let alone your editors."

Gage remembered having gotten up and leaving. The old man had the brass to follow him out and had stayed on his back saying, "Why don't you start writing your stories as they happen, instead of trying to slant them toward scandal? You are a damn good writer you know," the old man had persisted. Gage remembered his classic response. "Old man, if it wasn't for me writing my trash, the paper wouldn't be worth reading."

Gage never found out if it had been arranged or an accident, but a TV crew in the hall was "checking out its equipment" and happened to get the scene on tape. The station had run the segment that night on the evening news. It started three months of near war between the paper and the TV station. Gage had come very close to being fired.

The second time had been in the bar at the Holiday Inn. The conversation had started out placid enough, but soon turned to Gage's writing style. The old man had beaten him so badly in the 'Social Debate' as he called it, that Gage had walked out in frustration. The old guy kept hitting on one point, there must be something in this town that Gage could write a story on that would leave the reader with a good feeling. Thinking back to his response, Gage had loudly repeated, "If there is anything like that, I'll never find it and if I do find it, I won't admit it."

Gage drove aimlessly, immersed in his thoughts. He had no idea how he got there, but at the intersection of Fourth Street and Independence Boulevard, he decided to stop for a cup of coffee. He sat in a window seat, watching traffic while his mind wandered to last night's wake. Gage recalled his brief chat with the Wilson Family. He was taken aback by their admission that they had not seen Wilson in almost twenty years. They had not known where he was until Lloyd Miller had called and told them that Wilson was dead. When Gage had asked them if they were angered by his absence, they had almost answered in unison, "He's my husband/father!" Gage could not deal with the answer. He knew the void he carried in his life due, to a missing father. That was when he first got the notion that the Wilson's were imposters.

Gage was looking out the window, without seeing anything when he was jarred back to reality at the sight of a familiar automobile making a turn. Gage slammed a couple of bills down on his check. As he ran out the door and on to his car, he yelled to the waitress, " Keep the change!"

He was a block behind the car. He saw it pull into the hospital's Emergency Entrance. Gage turned in also, flashed his Press Pass at the security guard and parked. Inside the Emergency Room, Gage found who he was looking for at the admissions desk. Holbrook's face was covered with blood from a gash over his left eye. His face was swollen and becoming discolored.

"What the hell happened to you?" asked Gage.

"None of your business," responded Holbrook hiding his surprise.

"The hell you say! Who did that, Miller?" demanded Gage.

"Boy, if you don't get out of here and leave me alone, you and I are going to be a matching set," replied Holbrook.

"Yeah, right Gramps," Gage sarcastically responded.

Holbrook spun toward him growling. Gage's chin moved to the opposite side of his face from the impact of Holbrook's fist and looked as if it were headed for his ear. He was knocked backwards to the floor and lay spread eagle.

"That's how I got it boy, you want me to show you again?" Holbrook asked with contempt.

A nurse came running to him, "Sir, Sir are you all right? What happened? Did you faint?"

"To hell with him lady, I was here first. He tried to jump line," said Holbrook leaning on the admitting desk.

Some time later, after everything was straightened out, Holbrook and Gage left the hospital together. Holbrook had a slight concussion and Gage had one hell of a sore jaw. Both men were swollen about the same but Holbrook was already black and blue.

"All right you old bastard, how long have you been saving up for that punch?"

"You know Carl, I really should apologize for hitting you that way, but I'd be lying if I told you it didn't feel good. Another thing, keep making reference to my age, and I'm going to do it again. The next time, I'll finish it."

"Yeah right, how long have you been holding that pent up frustration Ted?"

"Boy, I don't know what put you on this ego trip. If you are referring to me having pent up frustrations over you, you better remember to hold your breath the next time you go bobbing for brown bananas in the commode."

"Damn it Holbrook, tell the truth."

"As far as you're concerned I just did. I got involved in a situation this morning. I wanted to hit the guy so bad I could taste it. But, as you can see, he hit me first and here I am."

"What did he hit you with a baseball bat?"

"Close but no cigar."

"So you're not going to tell me," said Gage, coming to the realization.

"Right."

116

"Why did you follow me to the Copal this morning?" asked Gage trying a new tactic.

"I didn't."

"Christ Ted, you looked at me. I saw you there when you were trying to get out of the parking lot before I could reach you."

"That doesn't mean I followed you."

"Then who were you following?"

"The person that was following you and Ms. Tarka."

"Why would anyone follow us?"

"I told you, Tarka works for Miller. I'm sure Miller is a member of the program. She didn't go straight to the office this morning. She went with you, and you two were followed."

"By who?"

"A bag lady in an XKE," answered Holbrook, knowing how ridiculous it sounded.

"Tell you what Ted, you better go back in there and tell them you're hallucinating. Bag women drive shopping carts not XKEs and I'm writing the Wilson story."

"Only if I let you boy," said Holbrook as he drove off in his car, leaving Gage with both ego and jaw damaged.

Chapter 20

Mary Wilson arrived back at her hotel as James stepped out of the elevator, "Where've you been Mom?"

"I went to the Beverly Hotel to see Dad's room. It was strange. Somebody was in there."

"You walked in on someone?" asked James as he led his mother to the dinning room.

"No." Mary went on to tell every detail of what had occurred at the Beverly Hotel.

"You're turning into quite a detective Mom. A cold coke, warm TV, did you find any fingerprints? Come on Mom, it was probably Miller."

"No, I don't believe it was Miller. I don't see him as a coke for breakfast kind of person. Your father would drink a coke once in a while for breakfast, as did some of his Marine buddies. Whoever it was, it was probably an ex-Marine."

They arrived at their table and without further conversation, ordered their meal. While they were sipping an after meal coffee, a man came to their table and asked, "Mrs. Wilson?"

"Yes."

"I'm Charles Mott, your late husband's attorney. I'll be waiting in the lobby. Please do not hurry at all. I have plenty of time."

"No, Charlie, I assume that is what Jaw called you, right?"

"That's correct Mrs. Wilson," replied Mott, smiling.

"Call me Mary, and this is Jimmy our son. Please sit down and have a cup. This is really excellent coffee. Besides, Jaw is paying for it."

Mott gave her a quick look as he pulled out a chair and sat down. They discussed the wake, Charlotte, the ACC football and basketball teams, along with a multitude of other things. Finally Mary invited Mott to her room.

In the suite, Mary sat quietly while Mott arranged papers on the counter. Satisfied, he cleared his throat and said, "Mary, for some reason Jarvis elected to draw up a new will two weeks ago. He also elected to have it done by another attorney. For whatever reasons he had for doing that, it has put me in the position of reading a will and acting as the estate attorney, without prior knowledge of what I am supposed to do. Jaw gave me verbal instruction to give this envelope to you and to follow your instruction without question." Mott handed Mary the envelope.

Without comment, Mary opened the envelope and pulled another envelope out with a note attached to it. She paused to read it. She checked the envelope and handed it to James, asking, "Do you agree that this envelope is sealed?"

"Yes," replied James, handing the envelope back to her.

She then handed the outer envelope to Mott as she read from the note, "Do you swear by the Beverly Code of Honor that this is the envelope Jaw gave you and you did not open it?"

Mott, slightly taken back answered, "Yes."

Mary opened the inner envelope and pulled out Jaw's will. It had a note attached to it also. Mary read the note, pulled it off and handed the will to Mott.

Mott finished reading the will and looked up at Mary, his face ashen. "Mrs. a-a- Ma-Ma –Mary, I don't know what to say."

"What's wrong Charlie?"

"I da-da-don't know what happened. According to this will, you inherit Jaw's half of your home. Then you and Ja-Ja-James get half of all his other assets wa-wa-which are all in this envelope attached to the back of the will."

"Okay, what is in the envelope?" asked Mary.

Mott became paler as he opened the envelope and looked in. He looked at Mary and said, "ta-ta-twenty thousand dollars."

Stunned, Mary looked at Mott and asked, "What about the hotel?"

"According to this will, he left it to the Da-Da-Downs Corporation, whatever that is."

Mary got up, walked to the window and looked out. She didn't move for several minutes. Then she turned to Mott. Holding up her hand she said, "Please Charlie, you look as though you're about to say something, don't. If this is what he wanted, then this is the way it is."

"Mom, I don't think."

"Please Jimmy," Mary interrupted, "it's what your father wanted and that's the way it will be. If you do anything to contest this will, never speak to me again."

Then looking at Mott she said, "Charlie, I've kept up our insurance policies at home. If you would please provide me with three or four copies of the death certificate sometime today. James and I will be on our way home on the morning flight."

"I can Mary," stated Mott.

"Charlie don't be an ass. I told you I will not contest the will, nor will I allow you to look into his personal finances. Neither you nor anyone else has made any indication that Jaw was not in his right mind. To me, that means he had or has a plan. It's over Charlie. Now, if you don't mind, I'd like to be alone."

Mott packed his brief case and let himself out as Jimmy walked over to his Mother and said, "Mom, I think you're making a mistake."

"Please Jimmy, I need you with me on this. The note on your father's will was personal. Part of it said to trust him for a while, that it would all work out," said Mary in resignation.

Mary walked into her bedroom. She sat in a chair thinking about the will as her eyes wandered around the room and finally to her bed. On the pillow lay an envelope with her name on it.

The note inside read:

Dear Mary,

Please keep the faith. I know this is very hard on you but hopefully it will soften soon. I am confident everything is going as planned. It will not be much longer before you have a pleasant surprise.

A Friend

Chapter 21

Much later, in Slick's office, the phone rang again. It was Pigeon, "Slick, this has to be one of the craziest mornings I ever spent. I was supposed to be watching this guy named Carl Gage. He came out earlier then usual but I'm in position to see him anyhow. He picks up Typer and I follow them out Wilkinson Boulevard, but I think I got a guy following me. I'm in the middle, so I slip out and U turn. Now I'm behind the guy I thought was following me, but he's following Gage too.

"So I follow the both of them to the Copal Restaurant. The guy following Gage turns out to be Ted Holbrook. So I high side them, walk back, warn Typer, and scoot. Somehow, Holbrook realized what I was doing and the chase was on. I run him into that area off Berryhill Road and lose him. I figured Gage was long gone, so I two-block follow Holbrook. He was one of my assignments some time back, so I knew who he was. All he does is drive around for a while and end up at the Register."

Slick assured Pigeon, "As Jaw would say, 'well done Pigeon'. I'll let you know if anything comes of this. Keep up the good work."

Miller pondered Pigeon's report then began running the entire matter of Jaw's death over in his mind for the fifth time. It still didn't come out right. There were too many things that hit him either wrong or out of place. Jaw's obituary first; why guard Malone's till midnight; who was going to appoint a new permanent head of the organization; who assigned Tarka to him, not to mention all Jaw had done in the past few weeks to enable the program to function at his death. The biggest things were Mary Wilson's knowledge in order to be able to ask the questions she had and the change in Jimmy Wilson. He slammed his fist on the desk. As if on cue, the intercom buzzed. It was Tarka telling him Beagle was on the line.

"Beagle, how did it go with Mary Wilson?"

"Ba-Ba–Bad, Slick."

"Calm down Charlie, take a deep breath. What happened?"

Beagle paused a few moments and said, "A couple of weeks ago, Ja-Ja-Jaw walked into my office and told me he had a new will drawn up. He gave it to me in a se-se-sealed envelope and said I was not to open it. I asked who could open it. He said it would be ob-ob-obvious when the time came. When Mary Wilson showed up, it became obvious. She opened the damn thing this morning. Jaw left Mary and James all his assets, which turned out to be a total of twenty thousand dah-dah-dollars."

"Are you kidding me?"

"I'm dead serious Slick. He left the hotel to the Da-Da-Downs Corporation, whatever the hell that is. I wanted Mary to contest the will but she cut me off at the knees."

"What the hell is the Downs Corporation?" asked Slick.

"Like I said, I have absolutely no idea who or what it is. I'll spend every favor that's owed me if I have to. I'm going to trace down the Downs Corporation."

Miller paused a few moments before he replied, "Beagle, something is wrong. There's too much strangeness going on, too many surprises since Jaw died. Call me with anything you get, piece by piece if you can."

"You got it Slick. Later."

Miller sat back in his chair trying to make sense of a gut feeling he could not identify. Tarka came in and asked if she could go to lunch.

"You are planning on going to the funeral, aren't you?" asked Miller.

"Yes, do you want me to change during lunch?"

"You can do it any way you want to but end up with casual clothes for this evening. We will be working late, " said Miller.

"Should I reserve some computer time and have a chalk board delivered?" she asked.

"Good idea. Keep me straight Nancy," said Miller smiling.

Tarka left the office and Miller called The Beverly to speak with Zipper. "How's it going?" asked Miller

Zipper sounded frustrated. "Crap Slick. It's going like crap. I don't know what the hell is going on. Everything is turning into a mystery."

"Now what happened?" asked Slick with resignation in his voice.

Zipper relayed the morning's events with Mary Wilson, including the cold coke and warm TV. He also explained the instructions Jaw had left with him about buzzing twice and calling the cop.

"What is really odd to me is that she didn't take any mementos or ask that anything be shipped to her. She just upped and walked out," said Zipper.

"Maybe she was waiting for the will to be read and then figure out what to do with the hotel. Her problem now is that Jaw didn't leave her the hotel. I'll get to that in a moment. When did Jaw give you those instructions?" asked Slick.

"They were in the envelope in the safe. He told me about them a couple three weeks ago," answered Zipper.

"Why?"

"Why did he tell me about the safe and stuff?" asked Zipper

"Yes."

"Hell I don't know. We were talking about the program and stuff. He was a little more serious then usual. It was just a feeling I had, but there again, he seemed very tired. What have you been into?" asked Zipper.

"Mary Wilson was there before Beagle read the will. All Jaw left her was twenty grand to split even with Jimmy. Then I find out that Typer is a plant," said Slick.

"Whose?"

"I thought yours, but she swore up and down she wasn't. Then I did the coin thing. She understood, her boss is two colors!"

Zipper was shocked and whispered, "Can't be. She's lying."

"I thought that too, but if she's lying, who showed her the signs? If you don't have an answer to that one, try this one. Jaw left the hotel to the Down Corporation, whatever that is."

There was a long silence on the line. Zipper came back with, "Later Slick," and hung up.

Miller was caught off guard by the sudden termination. What the hell is going on? His mind was a blank. The starting point of all this eluded him. It couldn't be Jaw's death, because it had been natural and there had been arrangements made in anticipation of his death. He began to make notes on his desk pad.

Miller had been mulling over his notes for almost an hour. One of the keys, he felt, was the change in Jimmy Wilson. Who or what caused the change in Jimmy was probably how Mary found out about the program and trust. An idea began to germinate, but the phone to his private line rang. He answered, "Miller here, speak."

A muffled voice said, "You need to be at the liquor store at Pecan and Central Avenue at one thirty this afternoon." The line went dead before Miller could respond.

Miller immediately glanced at his watch. He had twenty minutes. Was it a hoax, was it a set up, or was it real information? The voice, though familiar, was muffled enough to be unrecognizable. Miller figured he couldn't take a chance but he needed an edge. He called the Beverly Hotel and told Rock to meet him out front, across the street, in five minutes.

After telling Rock about the call they rode in silence. Rock was familiar with the area from his street days and had Slick drop him at the railroad track, down the street from the liquor store. Rock would come in from behind.

Slick proceeded up Central Avenue to the parking lot. Among other businesses, it contained the liquor store. It was one twenty five.

Slick slid down in his seat and waited In about ten minutes he spotted Rat walking across the parking lot from Pecan Street. He walked across the front of the liquor store, and looked down the side of the building. Then he looked around, as if trying to find someone.

At that time a car pulled in beside the store, leaving enough room on either side for a car to pass by. Rat walked over and climbed in. Slick studied a moment, and then drove around the building, coming up on the other vehicle's driver side and stopped abreast of the other driver. Looking across at Gage and Rat, Miller could see Gage give Rat money. Miller also could read Rat's lips as he yelled Miller's name. Gage spun to look and Rat bolted from the car and ran toward the railroad tracks at the back of the parking lot.

Gage did a double take from Miller to Rat and back to Miller. He tried to get out of his car, but the vehicles were too close. Gage rolled down his window to speak into Miller's open window.

"So, we meet again Lloyd, " said Gage smiling.

"Mr. Miller, to the likes of you, garbage writer," responded Miller coldly. "What happened to your face?"

"None of your business. Garbage writer huh? Well, let me tell you something, Mister Miller. That may have been trash that jumped out of my car, but that trash, and this garbage writer, are going to send you, Wilson, the program, and the trust into the sewer," grinned Gage.

"Too late Garbage, the trash just left town, permanently," Miller grinned as he drove off.

Gage watched as Miller drove to the near end of the shopping center building, stop, pick up the burly guard and slowly drive to the exit.

"Like you told him, Rat decided to leave town on the next freight. If Rat slows down, the train should catch him in the next county," said Rock.

Miller could not help laughing at not only Rock's statement, but also the mental picture of Rat racing down the tracks. Funniest of all was Rock's dry nasal baritone voice.

126

Chapter 22

Miller dropped Rock off at the Beverly and took a roundabout way back to the office. Driving relaxed him and he had a chance to think. He returned to his office. Tarka looked startled when he opened the door. She put her hand up to signal him to stop and spoke into the phone at the same time.

"Yes Mary, I'll tell him to call you as soon as he comes in. . . . I have no idea . . . .Is there anything I can help you with? . . . . Yes ma'am, I'll tell him."

Tarka hung up saying, "Carl is waiting in your office. He just stormed past me. I was going to get security up here when Speed called for you. I told him what was going on. He told me to let him stay. Was that okay?"

"It kind of narrows down where he is," replied Miller. "How long has he been in there?"

"About ten minutes or so. What happened?"

"I told him he was a garbage writer and I had run one of his sources out of town. Nothing to get mad over," said Miller innocently.

Before Tarka could respond, Gage came charging out of Miller's office and froze at the sight of Miller.

"I'm going to beat your arrogant ass," Gage said, as he threw a punch at Miller.

Miller avoided the blow. He pushed Gage's arm, forcing him to turn his back to Miller. Miller gave him several sharp kidney punches. Gage dropped to his knees, howling in pain.

"Garbage Man, you should work for Western Union. Anybody who can telegraph that good should have a future there," said Miller slightly out of breath. "Is it finished, or do you want to go to the athletic club and finish there?"

Carl nodded his head up and down, waving his hand. It was over.

127

"When you get up, come back in my office," said Miller, as he waved Tarka back down.

Miller was sipping bourbon on the rocks when Gage walked in. He motioned to a drink sitting on the corner of his desk. Gage sat down heavily and took a hefty pull on the drink, coughed and said, "I'm a beer drinker."

"You're an asshole," said Miller flatly.

Gage grabbed the arms of his chair to get up, but before he could, Miller said, "Sit asshole, or I swear to God, you won't be worth spare parts when I get through with you."

Carl had never feared a verbal threat, until now. Miller's icy stare assured Gage that he wasn't just blowing smoke.

"Mr. Gage, at this point in time I have too many important things going on to have to waste my time on an asshole like you. I'm..."

"First it's Garbage Man, now it's asshole, I'm..."

"You've been downgraded asshole, shut up."

"Don't call me an asshole. My father called me that, I hate it!"

"I can understand why."

"Why what?"

"Shut up and listen, yo..."

"Don't tell me to shut up. I'll..."

"Interrupt me again and we go round two here and now. You want to do a story on some program and trust you think Jaw was involved in. I'm going to give you the chance to do that story but, you're going to write it without your usual trashy slant," said Miller.

"You're the asshole. Nobody tells me what to write," said Gage getting up and heading for the door.

Miller rushed around his desk, grabbed Gage by the arm and spun him around. He blocked Gage's swing and gave him two hard punches to the stomach, the last of which raised Gage from the floor. Gage folded and slowly rolled to the floor gasping for air.

128

Tarka came into the office, stopping as soon as she saw Gage on the floor. Miller held up his hand saying, "Don't worry about it Ms. Tarka. It is just a severe case of writer's cramp."

Gage wanted to beg for help, terrified of what would happen next, but no sound came out. He watched in horror as Tarka slowly backed out of the room and quietly closed the door.

"Now Mr. Gage, this is how it is going to be. You're going to interview four people at the Beverly Hotel. You will not be able to see their faces. Your back will be to them at all times. They are going to tell you about Jaw. They will not lie. You'll write a story about Jaw based on their stories. I will approve or disapprove the story. I'll disapprove any story you write that is not based solely on what you are told at your interviews. It will all be recorded in case you protest any of my decisions. If it turns out that four are not enough and you can justify more interviews, I'll get them for you. There will be certain questions you cannot ask. They will all pertain to identity. There are a few other restricted questions but, should it become necessary, some information can be arranged.

"If you discuss this or any other interview with anyone at all, you will be, by both reputation and physical ability, unable to write in this city again. In the case of the latter, anticipate a lot of mental and physical pain until you leave Charlotte."

By this time, Gage was sitting on the floor with his back against his chair. Miller handed him his drink. Gage had sipped and listened as Miller spoke. Then he said, "Miller are you crazy? You are threatening me with physical harm if I write my article my way. I saw you run Rat out of town. That alone is a story. You and that gorilla could go to jail for that."

"I doubt it, but if you print the story, and if both Rock and I go to jail, you will spend many more months in physical therapy trying to regain use of your fingers and legs than we will spend in jail."

"Being a bit melodramatic, aren't you Miller?" asked Gage.

With his eyes like ice and a voice to match, Miller said, "No Carl, I'm being honest."

"You can have me writing for years before you approve the article," said Gage.

"Carl, if you are as good as Jaw thought you were, and you probably are, it won't take but about two or three re-writes," said Miller.

"He really thought that?"

"He thought you were the best this city ever had. How he could see that with the trash you write, I'll never know," said Miller knowing that now he owned Gage.

"I'll try it, but you best understand right now, I'm looking for a way out of this and I'll find it," said Gage.

"You're on," said Miller extending his hand to both shake hands and then to help Gage up. Gage shook the hand extended and was helped up.

Immediately after Gage left, Tarka walked into Miller's office hesitantly holding her steno pad in front of her with both hands and asked, "Is it safe to come in?"

"Yeah, I only beat women after six. By the way, what time is it?"

"One hour before I have to be out of here. Did you really have to beat him like that?"

"Nancy, when men build walls with stone or wood, you can see them and always knock them down with something. The walls men build with their minds are a different matter. They are built of perceptions. Men see things and perceive what they see. When it's remotely related to personal issues, the perception either adds to, or takes from, a mental wall. Some walls are thick and high, and some walls are low and of no consequence. The easiest way to break down the thick high walls in a man's mind is to crack it. That's what beating Carl accomplished. In Carl's case, once I had his attention, and he could see around the wall, the true Carl Gage came through. He knocked it down himself."

"How did you know it would work on Carl?" asked Tarka.

"He told me it would last night," said Miller. "When will the chalkboard be here?"

130

"It came while Carl was here. I'll get it," said Tarka.

Once the chalkboard was set up, Miller began making lists of what he did know and what bothered him. The thing that seemed to keep popping up to the forefront of his mind, besides the change in Jimmy Wilson, was the size of the crowd at the wake.

"Oh damn!" blurted Tarka, "Mary Wilson called and wanted you to call her back as soon as you came in. She was upset over some note."

Miller sighed, laid down the chalk and placed the call. "Mary what is this about some note?"

"How did you know about it?" asked Mary with a strange edge to her voice.

"You told Nancy about it. Explain it to me. Where did you find it?" asked Miller.

"I found a note on my pillow after Charlie Mott left this morning. Are you playing mind games with me?" asked Mary suspiciously.

"I don't know what you're talking about Mary. What kind of mind games?"

"This morning I went to Jaw's room at the hotel. Someone had been in his room. What the hell is going on?" asked Mary, anger building in her voice.

"Mary, I honestly have no idea. May I come over now and we'll talk about it? I'll be bringing Nancy with me, if you don't mind."

"Oh why not? Come on over, I'm better at looking at faces then I am at telephones," responded Mary.

Fifteen minutes later, Miller and Tarka were sitting in Mary's suite. Mary showed them the note as soon as they sat down. Miller read the note several times, as did Tarka.

"Mary, I'll be flat out honest with you. I did not have a thing to do with this note or what happened at the hotel. There is so much shi. . .,uh... stuff going on that...."

"Shit Lloyd. Shit. There's so much shit going on," Mary interjected.

"So much shit going on that I have no idea what the hell to make of it. I have been part of Jaw's operation for nine years. I've helped with scores of candidates and I've never seen half of the people that were at the wake last night. I talked to Charlie Mott today after he got the news of the Downs Corporation that neither he nor I had ever heard of. Mary, I don't have the vaguest idea of what's going on," said Miller earnestly.

"No, I guess you don't," said Mary who had been watching him very carefully. "How are we going to solve this puzzle?"

"Lets start with why you want the funeral to be at six in the evening?"asked Lloyd.

"I can't tell you that until after the funeral," said Mary.

"What?" exploded Miller. "Who told you not to tell me?"

"I can't tell you that either," said Mary quietly.

"You just asked me how we were going to figure out what's going on. The very first question I ask, you can't answer because somebody told you not to. Then why isn't that someone playing mind games with you?" asked Miller

"I'm sure he isn't."

"He, a man, told you not to tell me anything?"

"He didn't tell me not to tell you. He told me not to tell anyone."

"Then answer me this. Is he the reason for the big change in Jimmy's attitude?"

"That I will tell you and, the answer is yes," said Mary.

"Then this guy told you about the program, the hotel and the trust, correct?" asked Lloyd.

Mary nodded in agreement. Miller began to mull over what was said and then asked, "By the way, where is Jimmy?"

"He's on an errand."

"Mary, I'm better one on one than on the phone also. Where is he?"

"I don't know. The same man showed up just after lunch and asked if James would go with him. James and I agreed it would be okay," said Mary sheepishly.

"When will he be back?" asked Tarka breaking her silence.

"In a few minutes, we are supposed to leave here at five thirty for the funeral parlor."

At that moment, James returned to the suite with a man behind him. The man saw Tarka before she could turn. He dashed out the door. Miller saw only a shoulder disappear and sprinted after him. The elevator doors were about half closed when Miller grabbed one. Both doors hesitated a second and slid back open.

Miller walked through the door and said, "Good day Mr. Parkinson, nice day for intrigue."

The doors closed behind Miller as Parkinson spoke, "Slick get off at the next floor and go back up to Mrs. Wilson. She and James will need you more this evening than you need me to answer a few insignificant questions." Parkinson pushed the button for the next floor.

"Insignificant questions?" asked Miller incredulously.

The elevator stopped. The door opened and Parkinson said, "Beverly Code, Briefcase now go!"

A shocked Lloyd Miller stepped into the hall and the elevator doors closed.

Chapter 23

Miller waited for the up elevator to carry him back. Finally back on Wilson's floor, the elevator door opened and Tarka stood there waiting for a down elevator.

"Did you catch him?" asked Tarka.

"Yes," said Miller disgustedly.

"Well, who was he?" asked Tarka after a few seconds waiting.

A light clicked in Lloyd's head. "Your boss, Briefcase," said Miller.

"Who's that?"

"Parkinson, isn't he your boss?"

Tarka shook her head negatively. "I didn't know Parkinson had anything to do with anything," she said as they walked toward the Wilson's suite.

In the suite, Mary and James were both ready to go to the funeral. James walked over to Miller and said, "Mr. Miller, I apologize for my insult when we met at the airport. I had no idea of your importance to my father's organization or that he had an organization. I was bitter that he chose to abandon my mother and me."

"Just what do you know about the organization?" asked Miller.

"I've learned just about all there is to know about how it functions, about the hotel and the seven levels," answered James.

"Don't you mean five levels?" asked Miller.

"That will be discussed after the funeral. Hadn't we better get going? I wouldn't want to hold anything up," said James, as he helped his Mother put on her cloak.

Lloyd Miller was awestruck as he mumbled, "Well I'll be damned."

Riding to the funeral parlor, Miller was lost in thought. He vividly recalled the conversations and events that followed blow-by-blow, just as if it had happened yesterday. He remembered how Jaw had suckered him into becoming a real man again. the first time it had been on the front desk. Jaw would jump him unmercifully if he had been anything but totally respectful to anyone who had wanted a room for the night. That had lasted about three weeks before Jaw had sent him to work for a "friend" of his at a little credit company for a couple weeks until vacations were over. Miller had taken the job, but when payday had come, the "friend" had said he would send Miller's paycheck over to the Beverly in about an hour. Right on time, someone had dropped the check off at the front desk to Jaw. Jaw had called Miller as soon as it had arrived. He said he would cash it. The check had been for three hundred twenty dollars and Jaw had passed a twenty-dollar bill across the desk to Miller saying, "There's your end. You still owe me $2,123.78 so you go back next week."

"What the hell are you talking about? I don't owe you any two grand!"

"The hell you don't, plus one hundred twenty-three dollars and 78 cents."

"How the hell do you figure that?"

"You signed the registration card saying you were responsible for all charges and fees. You've been living here for over a month. I've been feeding you, and then there is the matter of fees, job placement and check cashing."

Miller had reached over the desk and grabbed Jaw by the shirt and tie and said, "Give me my money you damn crook!"

Jaw had grabbed the extended hand and held it in place. He rapidly stepped back, pulling Miller about half way across the registration desk. Miller's chin was now over the counter top. Jaw balled his fist and had slammed the top of Miller's head, driving his chin into the desktop. The result had been a visit to never, never land.

Miller had awakened in a chair in the lobby. Jaw had been writing something in a book on the registration desk. Miller had gotten up and walked over to Jaw and said, "Jaw, I want my money."

"Slick, if I have to knock you around again, I'll add sparing fees to your bill. Now you have twenty bucks to blow. I provide you with everything from room and board to toothpaste. Hell, you should give me ten back to put on your bill."

"Hell, this won't even keep me in cigarettes!"

"You should quit smoking anyhow, it's bad for you."

"I don't wanna quit smoking. I like smoking and wanna smoke. I choose to be stupid and smoke! That's my right!"

"Yep, it sure is your right, just as I have a right to be paid for services rendered, you have the right to smoke on twenty bucks a week."

The next payday, Miller had waited for his paycheck even though he had been told it would be delivered to the Beverly. He had gotten feisty with the "friend" and over his protests, had snatched the envelope with his name on it, and had gone back to the hotel. Jaw had been writing in some book as Miller had entered the lobby of the Beverly.

"I've got my pay check here Jaw and I'm going to get it cashed and then I'm out of here," said Miller with a wide grin on his face, cock sure of himself.

"You ain't going anywhere. Nobody will cash your check."

"What makes you think nobody will cash it? You going to call every business in town and tell them not to?"

"Don't have to, everybody will know it is no good."

"How's that?" Miller had asked. His smile had not been so confident.

Jaw had laid his pen down, looked up and had said, "Slick, sometimes you are dumber than dirt. You snatched up your check before Stan could run it through the signature machine. It ain't signed." Jaw picked up his pen and had begun writing again, grinning from ear to ear.

Miller had looked at the check closely for the first time. Sure enough, it hadn't been signed. Until that moment, he had seen himself puffed up like a Tom Turkey strutting in the yard. Now all he could picture was a turkey hanging in a butcher's window.

"Hate to bust your bubble Slick, but you ain't even gonna have smoke money till payday," laughed Jaw still looking down and writing.

Enraged, Miller had sprinted at Jaw and thrown a punch straight to the middle of Jaw's face. It had been at that moment that Miller learned that Jaw had a three-inch reach advantage. It was sometime later that Miller woke up in the chair again.

On the third payday, Miller hadn't even asked. He had just appeared at the registration desk for his twenty dollars. It had gone on that way for several weeks until one of Jaw's cronies on duty told Miller to go to Jaw's room.

Jaw had motioned him to a chair and offered him a beer, which he had taken. It had been the first he'd had in almost a month. He savored the cool liquid sliding down his throat.

Jaw had begun, "I been sort of teaching you for the past few months because I knew you needed it. We've had some good talks. I know enough about you to confirm my first impression of you. You are a good, decent, smart man, but you got no balls."

Miller had tried to speak but Jaw had held his hand up and continued, "Stan is really impressed with your work and so am I. I gather from our conversations that you have never been in a position where you could count on a strong income. That's the whole basis for you not allowing any relationship with a woman to get any further than laid now and then. Well, tomorrow I'm going to change that for you. I took the liberty of having your suit cleaned. At 9:00AM, we have an appointment with Newt Cramer. He's a friend of mine at First Nation Bank. You're going to interview for a job as a Commercial Loan Specialist. It pays thirty-five a year. In six months, if you do as good as I think you will, you'll probably go to forty or forty- five a year."

"What the hell is your finders fee for that?"

"It is going to cost you dearly Slick, and that is the only weak link in this whole program, as far as you are concerned. You are going to have to trust me completely. At a certain point in time, probably at the end of five or so months, you'll know you made the right decision, if you agree tonight."

"All I want to do is to get the hell out of Charlotte. Now, what does it take for me to get out of town?"

"Well," Jaw thought for a few minutes. "I'd probably have to knee cap you, then do something to your hands so they won't be able to pull some of your flashy stuff. It will mean about two or three weeks hospital time and three to six months physical therapy."

"Damn it Jaw, I'm serious."

Jaw looked coldly at Slick and had said, "Slick, am I laughing? I'm dead serious. I'll have you done tonight, right now in fact."

"Bull crap!" Slick said, as he walked to the door and opened it. Standing in front of him was a man dressed in near rags with what looked like a new axe handle in his hand. The look on the man's face told Slick he wasn't there for a convention. Slick had stepped back, closing the door."

"I can run while I'm at work," said Slick softly.

"Never get past my friends," said Jaw just as softly.

"I feel defeated."

"Not defeated Slick, scared. You don't want to risk failure. Failure is a part of life. Overcoming failure is one of the things that makes life worthwhile."

"Okay, I'm in." That had been nine years ago. Jaw had stayed on Slick's ass for the first six months while his bill kept growing. Then one Friday evening, Jaw had called Slick to his room.

"Slick, your graduation day has arrived, here's your accounting."

The ledger had shown every cent that Slick had earned and spent. It included the hotel room, meals, the six suits Jaw had made him buy, along with other clothes. It all came to just over eight thousand dollars. Attached to the bill had been a certified check for seven thousand, seven hundred forty-four dollars and sixteen cents. Under the check had been a thousand dollars, in cash.

"Don't worry about this stuff, it's yours. Worry about the contract you have to sign. It says that you agree to pay the program three times your debt. I usually round it off. It says that you agree to pay four hundred dollars a month until you pay off the twenty-four thousand to the trust. I assure you, you will not lose that money either, but you will not get it until you need it, or it goes to your heirs."

Slick had signed the contract and rented an apartment the next day. Slick was just starting to think about the apartment when Tarka said, "Here we are, Mr. Miller. Where have you been?"

Chapter 24

The limousine stopped in front of Malone's Funeral. Tarka and Miller walked through the crowd into the funeral home. Inside, Miller rushed to Zeigler who was standing at a window looking out.

"Who the hell are these people?" asked Miller, looking out over Zeigler's shoulder.

"I don't know Slick, but you and I have been summoned by the committee immediately after the graveside service."

"What committee?" asked Miller.

"I don't know," replied Zeigler. "I knew of a council, but I didn't know of a committee."

"Well clue me in," demanded Miller. "In nine years I never heard of either of them."

"Slick, I'll tell you what I know but one thing at a time. Let's get through the funeral first. We'll talk on the way to the tower," said Zeigler as they walked toward the parlor.

Miller looked around for Suzanne but could not find her. Finally, just before he was about to sit, he spotted her. He motioned for her to come sit with him but she shook her head no. Miller was not familiar with funeral etiquette, but he was surprised to see her wearing a veil. It seemed to him that only the wife and daughters of the deceased wore a veil.

Miller, Tarka and Zeigler sat behind Mary and James during the service. A preacher, who looked familiar to Miller, did the service, which took about twenty minutes. To Miller's surprise no one did a eulogy. No eulogy bothered Miller. It became yet another of the conundrums since Jaw's death.

The Wilsons, accompanied by Miller and Tarka, went immediately to their limousine. Miller was stunned to see that the two buses turned into five. There were now four more limousines behind the Wilson's. It took nearly thirty minutes to get organized and moving. Once moving, the trip to the cemetery was surprisingly fast but it took another twenty minutes to unload all the passengers and give them time to walk to the gravesite.

Miller tried to see who got out of the four other limousines but couldn't because of the moving crowd. He could not imagine where everyone had come from, or their relationship with Jaw.

Part of the delay was because of Mary's insistence that the flowers be brought to the graveside service. Once everyone was in place the service, which turned out to be only a single prayer. Mary murmured something to the preacher; who shook his head negatively and said something to Mary.

"I don't preacher. I said I want the casket lowered and it better be lowered now, or I'll do it myself," came Mary's voice above the din of whispers.

Malone himself stepped forward and began to lower the coffin, with the help of one of his men. Mary motioned to Miller, Tarka and Zeigler as soon as Malone started.

"Follow our lead. Grab a flower and throw it on the casket and head for the car. Jimmy and I will follow after everyone has thrown a flower on the casket. Pass the word to everyone what to do. The flower symbolizes the scent of love to follow Al eternally," said Mary.

The three turned and whispered the instructions to the crowd behind them. Once the coffin was all the way in the ground, Mary threw a Rose onto the casket, followed by Jimmy, Miller, Tarka and Zeigler. The crowd began to file past, plucking a flower and dropping it onto the casket. Tarka stayed with the Wilsons. Miller and Zeigler started toward the limousine.

On their way, two men dressed in dark suits, one a head taller than the other met them. They asked Slick and Zipper to follow them. The four walked silently through the cemetery to a leisure van sitting on a dirt maintenance road. The shorter man turned and said, "Sorry, we ran out of limousines."

"Where are we going?" asked Zipper.

"To the front of the tower?" replied the short man.

"What happens there?" asked Slick.

"We leave you there," answered the tall man.

Miller and Zeigler were directed to go to the bench seat at the back of the van. Short man drove while tall man rode shotgun. Slick noticed the tell tale bulge in tall man's jacket while he was calling someone on his cell phone. Slick thought he heard the man say, "Yes sir, we'll do it as soon as they... " The whisper grew softer.

"Frances," Slick whispered, "This isn't right. Did you hear what he said?"

"No."

"Zipper," he whispered again, the street name catching the man's total attention, "when we get out of this thing, you go first, stumble or something, but head toward the back of the van. When I slam the door, run like hell behind the van and disappear. Try to keep to the driver's side. I'll meet you at the Bev bottom. I think I know what is going on. These guys want to do us.

Slick felt Zipper stiffen, but he didn't look up or change his expression. They felt the van slow as their bodies were forced slightly forward by deceleration. Tall man got out and opened the sliding door. He stood with his back to the rear of the van. Zipper stepped out, faking a stumble and corrected himself as he passed tall man. Zipper headed to the rear of the van. Tall man looked back at Zipper. As soon as he did, Slick punched the man in the throat. A gun dropped from his hand. Slick pushed the man half way into the van, grabbed the gun and ran in the same direction as Zipper. They heard the screeching of tires as the van sped down the street. Then there was the deeper sound of tires wailing as the van spun around and came back.

Zipper ran into a parking deck and disappeared. Slick ran for the entrance of a familiar hotel and ran down the corridor leading to the restrooms. He leveled himself against the Men's room door looking back and waited. In about ten minutes he saw the two men from the van casually walking around the lobby. They split up and the tall man came toward him. Slick glanced to his left. The Ladies Room was ten feet away. No one had entered while he was waiting. He went in and into a stall. He sat and put his feet against the door.

During the little over twenty minutes he spent there in hiding, Slick was privy to several conversations, none of which were flattering to the ladies' male companions.

On his first attempt to get out, a lady entered just as he was about to lower his feet. He made it to the door on his second attempt but met a lady coming in who yelped in surprise. Slick's face reddened as he said, "God! I wasn't paying attention. I'm lucky no one was in there." He then rushed into the men's room. Slick waited another ten minutes before he walked carefully back to the lobby. As luck would have it, the lady he had encountered in the rest room was walking toward the exit and ended up beside him along with her escort.

"I bet you will read the door signs from now on," she said giggling. Slick reddened again.

It took Slick almost an hour to make the five block walk to the Beverly Hotel. As dusk was blending into darkness, he had to be even more careful of every nook and cranny as he worked his way toward the hotel. Finally he had one more street to cross. He was about to make the dash for the hotel when he noticed a shadow shift from side to side. The back entrance was being watched. He wondered where Zipper was. Had he gotten away? He must have. Both men who were after him were in the hotel. As Slick was backing away, he wondered if that meant they had been after him all along? What the hell have I done? He kept backing carefully away from the corner when suddenly an arm went around him and he was lifted into the air in a spiral. Another hand clamped over his mouth. With his arms pinned and his mouth clamped shut, all he could do was wiggle in terror.

"Calm down Slick, its Rock," came the deadpan whisper. "I'm gonna put ya down now. Don't make any noise, please sir."

Rock put Slick down on his feet, but Slick just sank toward the ground. Rock held Slick up by the back of his suit coat with one out stretched arm and looked at him. Slick just hung there, holding his chest and trembling. His legs wobbled like a balloon head, paper-legged doll at a fair.

"Rock, if my heart doesn't explode, if I catch my breath, and I ever stop shaking, I'm going to kick your ass from here to Gaston County."

"Please don't try that sir. Jaw said I don't have to take any abuse. He said I should be careful and not kill anybody," stated Rock.

"Did he tell you that when you scare the shit out of somebody, they have the right to beat your ass?" asked Slick breathlessly.

There was a pause, "No sir, he didn't say anything about that."

"Well damn it, it's true," whispered Slick.

"You want I should let you go?" asked Rock innocently.

Enraged, Slick swung his head up to look at Rock. The innocence of the giant's face washed out the rage immediately. Slick sighed, "No pal, I'm still a little shaky, give me a moment yet." Slick hung there until he felt his heart rate slowing to normal.

Rock slowly let Slick's feet take on the load of his body. When Slick was back to breathing normally, Rock totally let him go.

"Have you seen Zipper?" asked Slick

"No, I was told to come out here, find you and keep you safe from the guys watching the Bev," said Rock.

"Who told you that?"

"I don't know, a message was passed to me at the cemetery."

"How do you know it was a real message?"

"She gave it to me as Bev Code Flash."

"She? It was a woman? What exactly did she say?"

Rock looked at Slick helplessly, "You know I ain't that smart."

"Okay, tell me in your terms, but tell it all."

"She said something like Bev Code Flash, Slick and Zipper are in danger. Go to the First Nation Bank Tower. Yous were in a van. If I couldn't find ya there, I was supposed to hunt yous guys down before yous got to the Bev," said Rock proudly.

"What are you supposed to do with us?"

A big smile came across Rock's face as he said, "I don't know. She passed me a cell phone and told me to tell you to hit redial. She said I could keep it after I found you two guys."

Slick took the phone from Rock. He pressed redial, then send, it was answered immediately with, "Talk"

"Slick here."

"Go to a land line and call here." The voice hung up.

"Rock, we need a pay phone," Slick said urgently.

Rock started off walking down the alley. Slick soon realized where Rock was taking him and asked if there were any pay phones nearer the Beverly. When Rock answered no, Slick told him to find a different phone, knowing that this one would be watched. They tramped through alleys and across side streets for fifteen minutes. Rock finally took Slick up a flight of stairs. He knocked on a door, identified himself, and the two men were let into a well worn, but neat apartment.

"Sandy, this is my friend Slick. We got some trouble. We need your phone," said Rock.

To Slick's surprise, Sandy was bigger then Rock. Although the two men stood six foot eight inches, Rock was mostly muscle. It was hard to tell how much of Sandy was muscle. Also, Rock had two arms.

"Yeah, sure, it's in the kitchen, over there," said Sandy. His voice struck Slick as sweet.

Slick called the number back. Again, it was answered on the first ring with "Talk."

"Slick here."

"Are you calling from a parking lot?"

"No, some friend of Rock's. A one-armed guy."

"Slick, you are in danger. This thing of Jaw's has backfired. We have a weasel in the organization," said the voice.

"No shit! They tried to kill Zipper and me earlier. Who are you?" asked Slick.

"For your safety, the organization's and mine, I can't tell you that."

"What the hell are you talking about? What backfired? Damn it to hell, I've got to have something. If I hadn't realized the lie about the limousine and overheard a part of the phone conversation, Zipper and I would be dead!"

"It is just because of those attributes that Jaw wanted you to become chairman of the council. Your good instincts are going to have to take you further then we anticipated.

"What the hell are you talking about? What council? Where's Zipper?" asked Slick.

"Zipper has been taken by the Misotas. He is being held in a house on Matheson. There are two ways to get him out. We can call the police and the organization will become public or you can go get him. Which do you prefer?"

"Who's holding him? For christ sakes, what the hell is going on?"

"I can tell you this much, our organization had been infiltrated by criminals. They want to use our network for drug deliveries, prostitution, racketeering and fencing. They know about the Downs Corporation and want to take control of it. You still do not know what the corporation is about. At this point, that is not relevant. What is relevant is that Zipper will be forced to tell all he knows. When he does that, all will be lost. The council wants you to free him. You may take Rock and Sandy with you."

"What the hell! You want me to go up against real crooks, unarmed, with two unarmed gorillas, one of which has only one arm? How the hell do you know I was calling from Sandy's any way?" Slick asked, not mentioning the gun.

"I know Rock's patterns. You are at his brother's apartment. Not even Zipper knows of Rock's brother. Jaw told him to keep that secret."

Slick thought a moment, "Okay, but I'm not taking Sandy. Where on Matheson?"

"Cab 321 will pick you up in ten minutes. Now put Rock on the line," said the voice.

In twelve minutes cab 321 pulled along side the three waiting men. The result of Rock's final conversation was that either all three go or Slick goes alone. Rock walked around to get in behind the driver. Sandy got in the front and immediately rolled down the window. Slick sat in the back next to Rock. Without a word, the cab started off. The driver reached for his radio. Sandy beat him to it, tore it off the dashboard and handed it to Rock. The driver began to protest until Rock wrapped one of his paws completely around the driver's neck.

"I ain't supposed to kill nobody tonight but if I find out that Terry is dead, I'm gonna hunt you down and stomp you like a slug," said Rock.

Slick, who sat watching the events play out said, "I take it you know Terry?"

"Yeah," said Rock side ways. He turned back to the driver and asked, "Where's Terry?"

The driver just gurgled, Rock lightened his grip saying, "Try it again, where's Terry?"

"I don't know," said the man in a harsh breathless voice.

"Then you better learn to breath through your ass hole," said Rock and he squeezed again. The driver waved his arms and jumped around while Sandy steered. The driver had his foot off the gas pedal and the cab slowed. He finally nodded his head up and down. Rock loosened his grip. The driver sucked air into his lungs with loud gasping breaths. Rock let him have a few breaths and slightly tightened again.

"Talk to me. Where's Terry?" asked Rock firmly.

"In the trunk," gasped the driver of the now motionless cab.

Sandy took the keys from the ignition and handed them to Slick, who rushed out and unlocked the trunk. Terry was hog tied and gagged in the trunk, but alive. Slick freed him and helped Terry out of the trunk. Rock passed the driver to Sandy saying, "Here hold this." Sandy gripped the driver's neck.

Terry explained to Slick and Rock that he had a separate little portable radio for Jaw. A note had been dropped in his cab to have it on after Jaw's funeral. He had a fare about thirty minutes after Jaw's funeral from near the Beverly to the Hilton. Evidently the two guys had left something in his cab in order to listen in on what he said. As soon as he had gotten the call on what to do, the same guys had forced him to the curb. They tied him and threw him into the trunk.

Slick called, "Show him to us Sandy"

Sandy jammed the man's face into the window while Slick asked, "Is this one of them?"

"Hell, I can't tell," said Terry looking at the face flattened against the window.

"Sandy, let the dumb shit roll the window down. We can't tell what he looks like all mashed up like that," said Rock.

The window came down and Terry got a good look at the driver. "No he ain't one of them," said Terry.

Slick bent and looked the sweating driver in the face. He moved a bit to look at Sandy and told him to get a better grip on the man's throat. Sandy did as instructed.

The driver shuddered. Slick looked him in the face again and said, "Don't be stupid. If you want to die, lie. If you want to live, give. What exactly were you supposed to do?"

"I'm supposed to take you to the house where they have the other guy, drop you off and leave. That's all. I swear it!" said the driver desperately.

"Yeah right! Do him slow Sandy. I want to watch him turn black," said Slick, leering at the driver.

"No! No! Honest, I told you everything," gasped the driver.

Slick slapped the man's face hard enough to get his attention. Through gritted teeth Slick said, "Do not insult my intelligence. I'll have your arms and legs broken and leave you where hungry rats will find you before anyone else. I want to know what house on Matheson and what was going to happen to Terry."

The driver was now trembling uncontrollably. "I don't know the address. It's the second house from the corner, off Tryon. Then I was supposed to go back to the Beverly Hotel and send the cab through the front door with him in the trunk,"said the now crying driver.

"Where are the other two guys?" asked Rock.

"They are waiting at the house. I got nothing to do with them. They are mad as hell. I heard somebody on their cell phone chewing their ass off about being out smarted by an old wino and a pussy loan shark."

Slick almost slapped the man again, while Rock made some kind of disgruntled noise that Slick took for suppressed laughter. Instead, Slick told Sandy to put the man in the trunk. He walked around the cab to let Sandy out. Sandy dragged the driver like a rag doll. One handed, he threw the man into the trunk and slammed the lid.

Chapter 25

3rd Day 11:50 PM

The cab rolled down the dark street stopping in front of a nondescript house at the end of the block. Slick and Sandy silently stepped out of the cab. They walked into the yard while the cab continued on, turned around and drove out. Silently, they began working their way back up the street, using the houses for concealment. Their objective was four houses back. They moved quietly, as if in slow motion.

Sandy, following, reached up and pointed to a clump of bushes at the corner of a protruding porch. He signaled Slick to stop and pulled Slick back behind him. Sandy felt around on the ground. He found a flower garden rimmed with bricks in front of the house. Sandy quietly pulled a brick out.

As he turned back to Slick, a soft female voice said, "Boy, you best have a good reason for taking my brick."

Sandy froze and turned to see a large black woman standing on the porch above him. He was speechless.

"You boys here to help that little ol' man they took in that house?" she asked, nodding toward the house with the bush.

"Yes Ma'am," whispered Sandy and Slick in unison.

"You, with the brick, you best bring my brick back when you're finished or I'm gonna get me a brick and we goin' to lump city," said the woman.

"Yes Ma'am, I promise," said Sandy. He turned in relief and eased up to the corner of the lady's house. Sandy waited for a car to pass. As it did, he threw the brick into the bush.

"Ow! Damn ratty ass neighborhood. Jerry, come here! Some bastard threw a brick from that car that just passed. The son of a bitch hit me on the side of the head. I think I'm bleeding," said the bush, in a loud whisper.

"Damn it Pete, shut the hell up. Those guys are overdue. They could be standing right next to you," Jerry whispered loudly.

150

"Damn it, they ain't. I'm the one who got hit. Come here, I'm hurt," said Pete the bush.

After a few moments, Pete the bush repeated his demand. "Damn it Jerry, come here!" After a short lapse of time, Pete the bush anxiously whispered, "Jerry, Jerry? You okay? Jerry!"

Slick and Sandy heard a thud and something fall in the bush. The form of Rock came out from behind the bush, dragging what Slick assumed was Pete, now not a Bush. Rock dragged Pete to where Slick and Sandy were standing and dropped him.

"What's wrong with this picture?" asked Slick.

Sandy, who didn't see anything wrong asked, "What do you mean?"

"They may think I'm a pussy loan shark, but I'm not stupid. The jerk off driving the cab said there were two of them. Why are they both outside? Did they want us to go in?" asked Slick.

Rock had wandered off and came back with two semi-automatic pistols and four magazines. Handing them to Slick he said, "You take these. Guns scare me. I'll go get the rest of the garbage."

"I'm going to find the brick. She might be able to take me," said Sandy facetiously.

"You damn right I can boy, now git ma brick!" came the voice from the brick's home.

Sandy headed for the bush, as Rock came back dragging Jerry. Rock held Jerry up while Slick searched him. Slick had no idea what he was looking for but he knew when he had found it. Jerry had an electronic detonator on him. Slick immediately took it apart, putting the battery in one pocket and the device in the other. In Jerry's other pocket, Slick found a small flashlight. Rock dropped Jerry to the ground and yanked Pete up. Slick found nothing else of interest. Pete was dropped.

Slick went up on the porch and flashed the light into the house. He could see Zipper gagged and tied to a chair. Slick turned the light into his own face. He could see Zipper shudder. Slick realized the mistake and moved the light up to shine directly into his face. Zipper recognized him. Slick pointed to the front door. Zipper shook his head no. He pointed to the window he was standing at, and Zipper shook his head in agreement.

Slick tried the window. It was locked. He kicked the window in and climbed through. Slick flashed his light at the front door, seeing a five-gallon gas can, a whitish wad of dough with a short black tube sticking out. Wires ran from the tube to the front door. There was some sort of box attached to the door to receive the wires.

As soon as Slick remove the gag, Zipper started, "I know more about what is going on. It's a takeover; somebody high in the organization has turned. It has to be a council member."

"That much I know, but what's the council?" asked Slick, frustrated at the mention of it.

"I'll tell you that on the way. Let's get the hell out of here before they start to check on their guys," said Zipper.

"Okay but do you know how to defuse that door?"

"Yeah, there's a small black box in the dough over there. By the way, that dough is C4. Pull one wire out of the box, then remove the box and take the second wire out," said Zipper.

As Zipper and Slick climbed out the window, they could hear Sandy yelp, "Gotcha!" Zipper jumped, but Slick calmed him immediately, explaining that Sandy was Rock's brother and that he was hunting a brick.

"There is so much shit going on, I'm not even going to ask," said Zipper as they walked toward Rock, who was guarding the two men.

As Sandy came back from replacing the brick, Slick told Rock to take the two thugs down the back yards and tie them to a pole or something. Adding that he didn't want them to get loose until someone untied them.

Cab 321 came back down the street and stopped in front of Slick and Zipper. The two men climbed into the back seat and waited.

"Terry," Slick said, "Beverly Code?"

152

"Tipster," responded Terry.

"How many coins do you have?" asked Slick.

"Three silver and a penny," said Tipster.

"How is it I never heard of you?"

"Do I really have to answer that?"

"No, not really," responded Slick, as he shook his head in resignation. Slick sat and contemplated his situation. Suddenly a notion struck him. In all the years he had known Zipper, he had never asked. "Zipper, how many coins do you have?"

Zipper answered, I have four silver plus two copper."

"For christ sakes, am I the lowest man on the pole? If I'm three coins silver, and all you guys outrank me, why the hell am I in charge? There has to be many others in the Beverly more senior than me; you two for instance. Why am I the only one in the dark?"

"We are going to take care of that next," said Zipper.

There was a noise on the hood of the cab that sounded and looked like a bundle of rags. Rock stuck his head through the window, grinning from ear to ear and said, "They pissed Sandy off. He beat the shit out of them, then tore their clothes off of them and said they made a lousy team. One guy grumbled that this was the first time they had worked together. So Sandy tied one of the naked asses over a low bar on a gym set with the other guy on top of the first guy. He then stood in front of them and informed them that he used to be a bouncer in gay bars and that he was sure he'd seen at least one of them in there. The guy on the bottom started screamin' that he'd never been in a gay bar before and the guy on top didn't say nothin'." Rock repeatedly stopped to laugh while telling the story.

"I don't care about having fun, but are you sure they won't get away?" Slick laughed.

"Naw, the guy on the bottom is spread eagle and the guy on the top is grinning. They won't be along for a while," laughed Rock.

"Get in, we best get out of here before someone comes checking," said Zipper.

"Where? How?" asked Rock.

It was finally figured out that Sandy would ride up front, while the other three were crammed into the back seat.

"Sandy," asked Slick as they rode out of the area, "how many coins do you have?"

"About seventy five cents, if you mean in coin, a couple hundred if you mean cash."

Terry, Zipper and Rock burst out laughing while Slick said, "Thank you, at least there is more then one person a lower grade than me."

"You calling me low life?" grunted Sandy, as he spun reaching for Slick's neck.

With great effort, Rock stopped the hand saying, "No insults here Sandy. I'll explain it to you later, trust me."

Slick told Terry to go someplace where they could talk without being disturbed by cops or night watchmen. It took ten minutes for Terry to find the place he had in mind and to park.

"Sandy, I can't tell you enough how much I appreciate your help tonight. If there is any way I can return the favor, let Rock know and we will do our best," said Slick.

"I need a job," said Sandy. "Hell, I'll tear off arms, break legs whatever you want if you'll just help me get a job."

"We'll work on it Sandy," said Slick. Then turning to Terry and Rock he said, "You two take Sandy home. Zipper and I need to talk privately. Come back here when you're finished."

As the cab drove off, Slick said, "We have three guns with full clips and four full clips in reserve. Now, before I work up the brass to point one of these things at you, tell me about the council or committee or whatever the hell they call themselves."

"Slick, I'm sorry man, but I still have to be candid with what I can tell you. There is a Charter Committee; with about six or eight members. I just found out about it myself. These are, or were, very heavy hitters in the community. They guide the investments of the Downs Corporation and oversee the council. The council is like a gathering of middle management. Each council member is responsible for keeping track of around fifty

Bev members. They keep up with their charges through the guys they have working for them; it kind of flows down hill. Each foreman has about twelve guys who can call him for help and it is passed up the line.

"The council makes decisions on who can join the program. If a man is nominated, the council member can only speak against the nominee. If no one speaks against the candidate, he is in. If someone speaks against one, the investigative arm of the committee verifies the accusations. There is no such thing as a black ball because you don't like someone. I'll tell you one thing I'm not supposed to. You think I am Jaw's right hand man. Actually there are seven of us," said Zipper.

"What seven lieutenants! Why the hell didn't I know about this shit?"

'That I can't tell you. Jaw had a special plan for you, which only he and the Charter Committee are privy to. That's all I can tell, pal. Please don't press for more," said Zipper.

"You realize you created more questions than you answered."

"Yeah, sorry, but that's how it is," said Zipper.

"I'll think about that later. Right now we have to figure out what the next play is. If they have trouble getting to me, who else can they go after?"

"They could go after the Wilsons. They may think the Wilsons still have a stake in the Beverly," suggested Zipper.

"They could go after my wife just as well," said Slick wishing Rock was back with the cell phone. "If it is a council member that is feeding them information, he or she would know who the other lieutenants are, and snatch one of them."

"No, I got caught because I made a warning call. The lieutenants and your family are safe," said Zipper.

"That leaves Mary and James," said Slick as headlights came around the building. They were about to jump behind a nearby dumpster when Zipper saw the cab roof light through the glare. Slick and Zipper ran toward the cab.

"We needed to be at the Wilson's hotel twenty minutes ago!" said Slick as he and Zipper dove into the back of the cab.

Chapter 26

Terry guided the cab through the early morning traffic, stopping with a screech of tires at the front door of the Wilson's hotel. Slick, Rock and Zipper rushed into the building.

Zipper hurried to the Registration Desk asking, "Ben, anyone go up in the last hour?" he asked.

"Two or three guys went up about a half hour ago."

"Give me the pass card Ben, do it now!" demanded Zipper sternly.

All three ran toward the elevator bank. On the Wilson's floor, they let Rock out first because he was possibly an unknown but there was no guard. They rushed to Mary's room. Zipper put his ear to the door. He could make out voices but could not distinguish the words. He thought he sensed fear, alarm, or panic in a muffled female voice. They eased away from the door and back down the hall a short distance.

Whispering, Slick explained his plan. He described the layout of the rooms and cautioned them not to kill anyone. He remembered when James came back, the door made no sound opening. Zipper was to stay behind with a gun to cover him and Rock. They were to go in fast and hard.

They quietly walked back to the door. Zipper's job was to unlock the door, push it open and step back. Rock insisted on going in first. His job was to start throwing bodies as fast as he could. Slick was supposed to follow with gun drawn. Zipper was not to enter until everyone was subdued or else rescue them if anything went wrong.

Zipper unlocked the door and gave it a push. It swung silently till it hit the wall with a soft thud. Rock was on his way before the door reached the wall. There were two men talking to Mary as she sat crying on the couch. James was tied to a chair. A man wearing kid gloves was standing in front of him. James

157

was bleeding from the mouth and his left eye was almost completely swollen shut.

Rock had two men in his arms before they had a chance to react. The men crashed to the floor. Rock was punching the men as he landed on top of them, first in the back of the neck, then he rolled them over and sent several punches to their faces.

Slick pointed his gun at the man standing in front of James and yelled, "Freeze!" The man instinctively reached inside his jacket

"You die if you try," said Slick. "You'll have two in the chest before your hand clears your jacket."

Rock picked each man up by the jacket and punched him again. He left them lying in crumpled heaps on the floor. When Rock was finished, Slick told him to search the men. Rock removed a pistol and wallet from each of them. He threw the items on the couch next to Mary. Then he walked over to the third man standing in front of James. He was still frozen in position. Rock reached inside the jacket and the man began to grimace. Rock pulled the hand out squeezing it to the grip of a 45 automatic. Rock yanked the gun from the man's hand and squeezed even harder. The man twisted in pain.

"You want to talk to this son of a bitch or can I crush his hand?" Rock asked Slick.

Just then, Mary Wilson screamed, "You son of a bitch! You coward! You, you scum! You tied my son to a chair and beat him!"

The thug tried to back away but Rock was still crushing his hand. As soon as Rock saw the gun in Mary's hand, he swung the thug clear of himself and moved him in front of Mary.

"I'm not sure what knee capping is," said Mary, I think it's when you shoot kneecaps. If I'm wrong, tough shit," said Mary.

"Mary! Mary! Wait don't do that! We need to know who they work for. If you shoot him, he will only scream and holler. We need information!" pleaded Slick.

"We can get that from the other two. This son of a bitch beats people tied and defenseless. He's a fighting legend in his own mind," said Mary as she walked toward the thug with a gun from the sofa and evil in her eyes.

"Mary, please let us handle it. Shooting him will bring the police. That will ruin all of Jaw's work. Please let us handle this," said Slick as he slowly approached Mary.

Slick reached over and took the gun from Mary's hand. She swung to Slick enraged. For a few seconds they stared at each other but finally Mary relented. Then with another sudden whirl, Mary turned back to the man and kicked him with all her strength on the left kneecap. The thug howled in pain as he fell on the floor. Rock, who was still holding the thug, let him drop. Then he picked the man up by the belt and carried him to the other two men and dropped him so that he landed on both of the other intruders.

"Lloyd, you should have let me shoot that son of a bitch," said Mary as she untied James.

Mary helped her son to the bathroom and began to put cold water on his face. Slick and Rock used the intruder's belts to tie their hands behind them. They were engrossed in their task as Zipper sprinted through the room and into a bedroom. They had just finished binding the groggy men when a voice behind them spoke.

"God damn, where am I supposed to get any reliable help?

Rock and Slick turned to see two men standing behind them, one with his gun drawn. The man speaking was Emile Misota. Slick knew him from newspaper photographs. Misota had recently been acquitted of racketeering charges.

"Ya know it ain't funny when you think about it. If ya want something done right ya gotta do it yourself," said Misota.

"Never send boys to do a man's job," said Miller.

"Thank you Miller, I'll take that as a compliment," said Misota.

"Don't, boys grow up to be men. I doubt you will ever make it that far," said Slick.

"I heard you were a smart ass Miller. After I get through here, I'm going to give you a smart ass lesson you won't forget," said Misota, anger building in him.

"You get out of my apartment," yelled Mary from the bedroom door. Jimmy remained hidden.

"Shut up bitch," said Emile, "move over here where I can see you."

Mary moved next to the bar. There were several uncapped liquor bottles sitting below the counter within easy reach. She casually hung her hand over the edge of the bar and clasped a bottle just below the neck. As Misota turned his head toward Slick and Rock, she flung the bottle at him. It traveled the twenty or so feet to Misota in a fraction of a second. The side of the bottle hit him in the chest. The contents splashed up to his face and in his eyes. The impact of the bottle staggered Misota back a few steps. His arm hit his companion's forearm, knocking the gun from his hand.

Slick sprang toward Misota but tripped over the coffee table. Rock dashed at the same moment for the second man. Rock raised the man from the floor and jammed him into the edge of the open door. Turning to Misota, Rock picked up the screaming man by his necktie and belt Jimmy Wilson sprang through the bedroom door. Rock ran Misota's head into the edge of the door. Using the ropes that tied Jimmy, Misota and his aid were quickly tied.

Jimmy had taken an awful beating. His left eye was swollen shut; his lip split and his front teeth were loose. Mary ranted and raved about what she would like to do to all five men. Rock stood over the pile of men hoping one would try something.

"How did they get in here?" Slick asked James as they paced around the apartment trying to calm down from the adrenaline high.

"I couldn't do a thing. Mom opened the door and they grabbed her. I was in the bedroom. I heard her yell. When I came out, they had a gun to her head. All I could do was submit. Now I want to know who sent them here," said James.

160

Jimmy walked over to Misota and yanked him up to a standing position, about five feet in front of Rock saying; "You catch him if he makes me get rough."

"Wait a minute Jimmy." began Slick.

"Shut up, Miller. It was my mother that got the shit scared out of her and I almost got the shit beat out of me. You just shut it."

Jimmy moved to Misota till his nose was about six inches away and asked, "Who do you work for? I'm only going to ask once.

"Up yours," said Misota.

Jimmy's eyes were locked with Misota's. He reached into his back pocket and pulled out his handkerchief and draped it over his own face, covering his eyes and mouth.

"You going to play boogie man with me, you stupid ass? YAAAAHA!" screamed Misota.

Without warning, Jimmy's forehead smashed into Misota's nose, flattening it as blood gushed onto the handkerchief. Misota staggered back to Rock who caught him and immediately pushed Misota back toward Jimmy.

"God damn! You broke my nose!" screamed the bleeding man struggling to free his arms.

Jimmy and Misota were about four feet apart when Jimmy coldly told him, "I'm going to tear your left ear off if you don't answer my question."

"You're pretty brave when a man has his hands tied behind him," said Misota.

Jimmy moved his shoulders slightly and from the standing position, he leaped into the air, spun completely around and kicked Misota in the left ear, tearing it with the heel of his shoe. It took every bit of Rock's strength to catch the flying man and not fall backward himself.

Misota screamed in agony as Jimmy said, "I'm a fast learner. Your scum taught me to fight guys who are tied up. I think I'm doing pretty good for the first time, don't you?"

161

Misota was now staggering back toward Jimmy, begging for mercy. "You want mercy? I'll give you mercy!" Jimmy hit Emile straight in the mouth. Emile's feet almost walked out from under him as he dropped to the floor unconscious.

Jimmy turned to the men laying on the floor saying, "Okay, let's try the guy who taught me to win the easy way."

"No!" yelled the man in terror, "I'll talk. We work for his daddy. Mr. Misota sent us over here to find out about some kind of trust fund. Once we got someone to talk, we were supposed to call Emile but he got impatient and came up before we called."

"Get that one too Rock," said Jimmy pointing to the guy that came in with Misota.

"Hey! I ain't done nothin'!" the man yelled in terror.

"You're here because Misota wants to know about the trust. You're Emile's right hand man so you know more then the hired help." said Jimmy. He watched Rock stand the two men up beside each other. "One of you is going to tell me who the informant is."

"What informant?" asked the aide.

"The one who told Misota there was a trust fund," said Slick as he moved to Jimmy's side.

"You don't know how Carlos Misota operates. He keeps everything in the family, blood family. If you ain't blood, you ain't in on the plan. Guys like me get assignments. They have a special room where they hold their conferences. In three years, I've only seen three guys go in there that wasn't blood. One of them was about four or five days ago," said the aide.

"Who?" asked Slick.

"Who was the last guy?"

"Yes, stupid. Who was he?" asked Jimmy.

"How the hell do I know, they don't introduce their business partners to us."

"How do you know he was a business partner?" asked Slick.

"Nobody in their right mind would sell insurance to the Misotas. I figure he was a business partner and a nervous one too," said the aide.

162

Slick was about to ask another question when he noticed Zipper standing at the edge of the bedroom door. Zipper waved Slick to him.

Slick said, "Jim, you and Rock watch these guys. Your mom and I have to have a private conversation." As soon as Slick and Mary entered the bedroom, Slick asked, "How the hell did you get in here?"

"I did it while you and Rock were playing Rodeo, tying up the bulls. I heard the elevator door open and stepped into the room. When they started toward us, I closed the door and ran for the bedroom," said Zipper.

"Why the hell didn't you shoot somebody?" asked Mary.

"For the same reason I wouldn't let you shoot," said Slick, then jerking his thumb over his shoulder he said; "I think they are telling the truth about not knowing anything else. Now what the hell do we do with them?"

"I think they are talking about Dot-Com," said Zipper.

"Yes, that sort of confirms his story, but what about these guys?" asked Slick.

"Let me make a call," said Zipper.

Zipper went to the phone. The few minutes he mumbled into the phone seemed like forever to Slick. Zipper hung up and said, "The police will be here in five minutes. Get everybody turned to the wall so I can get out unseen. They don't know I'm here and I don't want them to see me now. Give me your guns. The cops will let you and Rock go and take statements from Mary and James. You and Rock will have to make statements in the morning. We meet in the ally out back as soon as the cops release you."

"I think we should have let Jimmy smack them all around before you called the cops, "Mary stated. "First you didn't want any cops, now you called them."

"I called our cop, Mary. Things will go our way now," said Zipper.

Slick went out and whispered to Jimmy what they had to do. "No, I can't let that happen like that. That piece of shit tied me to a chair and beat my ass," said Jimmy walking toward the thug. In one motion, Jimmy leaped up, spun around and kicked the thug's jaw sending him into the aide and both fell on top of the other men.

"Now you do whatever, but he wasn't going to leave without a mark," said James.

They followed the plan and held the men captive with their own guns. The police arrived, took Slick and Rock's names and addresses and as stated, let them leave.

Chapter 27

"What the hell do we do now?" asked Slick standing in the dark alley.

"You're the boss, you tell us," said Zipper.

"No he isn't. We still have to go to the committee," said Terry.

"Nothing's going to happen until I call Suzanne. Rock can I borrow that phone you are so proud of?" asked Slick.

Rock grudgingly handed Slick his prized possession.

"Suzanne are you okay baby?" asked Slick.

"Yes, where are you. Everyone is looking for you. Are you all right?" asked Suzanne breathlessly, her voice obviously on the verge of tears.

"Don't worry about me. I've got a couple of friends with me. I have to go to a meeting. Is there anyone with you?" asked Slick.

"Yes the Townsons stopped by after the funeral. When no one could find you, they stayed for support. Nancy called; she's still at your office. Lloyd are you sure you're safe?"

"Yes sweetheart, I'm okay. I should be home in a couple hours. Later," said Slick.

"Later." he repeated.

"Oh, honey..." but it was too late. The phone clicked dead and clicked again. Slick thought about it for a moment and filed it away.

Slick immediately called his office hoping Typer would still be there. He was rewarded with, "Mr. Miller's office, may I help you?"

"Typer, do you have anything for me?" asked Slick.

"No sir, are you okay? Everybody is worried about you. We heard that guys with guns chased you and Zipper down Tryon Street. Then we heard that Zipper was captured and taken

165

somewhere. Is Zipper okay?" asked Typer.

"How did you learn all that?"

"You know the street has no secrets Slick. There were a few people who couldn't get to the funeral. Somebody had to watch the store."

As Slick listened, he slowly worked himself away from the crowd. When a safe distance away he spoke again. "Zipper and I are both okay. I'll tell you about it in the morning. Have you been studying the black board?"

"Yes sir, it's strange. Nobody really said what Jaw died from. It almost seems as though he knew he was going to die. From what you told me and what I found out myself, I made a chronological listing of the sequence of events. Did he have cancer or something like that?"

"There was no mention of anything, not even natural causes. I have to meet with some people now. It's too late to do much tonight. Come in around ten in the morning and we will try to figure this thing out together," said Slick.

"I won't argue with that. Goodnight sir, and Slick, please be careful," said Typer,

Walking back to his companions, Slick said, "Okay, if I have to see this damned committee, lets get going."

The cab headed to I-77 North to exit 28. Along the way, Slick queried Zipper about the council but was told to be patient. They made a series of lefts and rights to a dirt road. The road kept narrowing until it was all but a game trail. Just as it seemed the trail was ending, the cab entered a clearing in which sat an elegant two story brick house. The cab crossed about fifty feet of lawn to a black grit track that circled the house.

"Now your questions will be answered. I hope you're ready," said Zipper.

They exited the vehicle. Rock walked into the yard, taking up a guard position. Slick followed Zipper to the front door. As they crossed the porch, the front door opened. Stanley Parkinson stood directly in the center of the doorway while Ted Holbrook held it open.

Stunned as he was, Slick still noticed Holbrook's face and asked, "What happened to you Ted? That isn't what Gage did is it?"

Holbrook grunted, "No it's a long story. I'll tell you about it later."

"Welcome Slick, glad to see you made it," said Parkinson. "Zipper, are you alright?"

Slick was silent, but Zipper acknowledged that he was okay. The four men walked down a hall and turned into a large room with a conference table that looked to be around forty feet long. There were about thirty places set up counting both sides of the table.

At the far end sat four men. It was arranged so that three men already sat to the left side. One man sat in the second chair on the right. The chair at the head of the table was empty.

As they walked toward the head of the table, Parkinson said, "If the table looks familiar, it should. I borrowed it from the bank for this meeting. This is my lake house. I had it built in my wife's maiden name so it would be a true getaway."

As they approached the table, Zipper sat on the left side, Holbrook walked around and took the third seat on the right. Parkinson stopped short and took the first chair on the right. Slick stopped and started back to sit next to Zipper.

"No Slick, your seat is there," said Parkinson, motioning to the head of the table.

Slick walked back and sat down in the chair as if it were electrified. Parkinson began, "Mr. Miller you have been chosen on the recommendation of Jarvis Wilson and with the approval of this Charter Committee to become the Chief Executive Officer of the Downs Corporation. You will also be the Chairman of the Board of Directors of that corporation.

"The Downs Corporation is a corporate entity whose purpose is to invest the repayment extracted from those the Beverly Hotel returns to society. The purpose of the investments is to gain a return so as to provide income to take care of the administrative costs of the organization overall and provide the

Beverly Hotel clientele with a retirement fund of which they have no knowledge and therefore cannot fall back on during hard times or periods of financial stress. We will not allow them to become homeless or die for lack of funds for medical procedures. However, many times a retirement fund is used as the easy way out at a time when hard work and determination could have obtained the same end. What I have told you is only a generalization. You will be thoroughly briefed by each of us but as of this moment you lead this organization and are in charge. The one damper on this occasion is that I fired you." Parkinson was now smiling.

"What the hell do you mean, I'm in charge? In charge of what?" Slick demanded.

"I may be able to help you there, sir. I am Beverly Code Notes."

The man speaking was seated directly to Slick's left. He strongly reminded Slick of Mr. Peepers from the old TV show except Notes was fat. Slick had the impression that they had spoken before.

Notes continued, "At present you have a staff of four. Myself, as secretary to the corporation, Mr. Ziegler as head of the Beverly Program, Mr. Holbrook as head of Security, and we have taken the liberty of engaging Typer as your personal secretary.

"At the present time there are 1468 members of the Beverly Fraternity, of which, 708 have repaid debts and are making only light contributions. Another 653 are paying their debts, as either hotel debts, or business loan repayments. There are yet another 107 in the program being trained.

"The corporation is currently owed, in round numbers, fifteen million dollars. It has assets, cash, stocks, bonds, etc of twelve million dollars, again in round figures. I do of course have the actual numbers, which are available to you on command."

Some of the double talk and comments Slick had heard during the past few days began to make sense. His mind raced through the period since Jaw died. There were still some answers he needed but now the questions became clearer.

"As my first act, I am tendering my resignation," said Slick.

Parkinson laughed, "That damn Jaw. He told us that is exactly what you would do. I am glad to say that you cannot. When you spoke to Notes by phone this evening, he told you the truth. We have been infiltrated. We are sure the traitor is not someone in this room, the Charter Committee. The traitor is in the council. That is why this table is so large. We could have met at my dining room table if we were the only parties involved. The council will be here in about thirty minutes.

"We did not realize we were infiltrated until two months ago. We were forced to look for an alternate plan before the thieves went too far. You were the best we could come up with and I am glad to say there were no dissenting votes. You are well respected in this circle.

"You and Jarvis are the only two who we feel can get to the bottom of this. That is why if he died, you were to take over."

Slick glanced around the table once or twice while Parkinson spoke. More and more the others were beginning to frown in either confusion or ignorance of the plan.

"Now we can watch from the sidelines while the infiltrators try to take over. Do not forget, there is over twenty-seven million dollars here that can be converted to cash. They were going to kill you and Zipper tonight. The criminal elements in this city want this organization very badly. A few dead players along the way means nothing to them."

"You make it sound like Jaw's death was mandated. If that's the case, Jaw was either murdered or his death was faked. Either way, I should have been consulted. I had no idea the program was so large. Notes said there were over a hundred in the program. I know of only a dozen or so. You are talking fifteen million in debits, I know of only a couple hundred thousand at most. How the hell do you expect me to run this organization?" asked Slick.

169

"You run this organization like I taught you in a microcosm," said a voice behind Slick.

Slick heard gasps from around the table, Slick stood, and without turning said, "Gentlemen, may I present the winner of this year's Mr. Bull Shit Contest, Jarvis Alvin Wilson."

Chapter 28

4th day 2:35 AM

"Who was it, Samuel Clements who said, "Reports of my death have been greatly exaggerated?"" asked Jarvis Wilson.

"Just what the fuck is going on here?" asked Slick exasperated.

"Watch your mouth boy, you're a CEO now. They don't talk like that," said Jaw.

"They do when they have been made a fool of," said Slick, still not turning around and seeing nods of agreement from most of the committee members.

Jaw walked up and stood between Parkinson and Slick. He said, "It was not my intention to make a fool of anyone, but that must be the view from the eye of the beholder. At first, all I wanted to do was get out of the Beverly thing, the program and the trust. I wanted to go back to my wife. I wanted to make sure that you were ready to take over. This thing is doing well, far beyond what we thought it would do in the beginning.

"We all have been planning your takeover for about six months. We were about to start you "hands on" when we found out about the mole, spy, traitor, or whatever you want to call him. Once we figured out it was the Misota bunch that were trying to break in, we reversed the process and broke into them. That is how we found out you and I were about to become dead meat. We discovered that about three weeks ago.

"The reason we feel the traitor is not in this room is because we made the decision six months ago and told the council a little over a month ago. Then, a week or two after we told the council, you and I were on a hit list and we didn't sing. This plan is the fastest Briefcase and I could come up with. We thought they would try to take you in, but we were wrong. It makes no real sense to kill you before they know you can't be bought. Killing you would just raise a lot of stink. Maybe that is why they decided to include Zipper, to make it look different.

171

"Slick, you've a sixth sense about things that I don't even begin to understand. I sincerely hope I don't get you killed before this is figured out.

"As far as Mary goes, we've been planting doubts in her head from day one. Parkinson went over to their hotel the first thing and told Mary all I've been into and lied a little about how much I talked about them in private. He told them I wanted to come back but, I had to turn the organization over to you first."

"Do you know that Jimmy got beat up by the Misota's tonight?" asked Slick.

"No! How bad is he?"

"He's okay. Did you know he is some kind of Martial Arts expert?" asked Slick

"I started him when he was a 'pup'. I didn't know he still practiced."

"Let me tell you about the "pup"," said Slick. He went on to tell the entire story of the evening in the Wilson's hotel room. Jaw smiled when Slick told about Mary wanting to "knee cap" the thug and throwing the liquor bottle. His expression turned to complete surprise when it came to Jimmy's part of the evening.

Jaw looked at his watch, "The council is coming. I have to disappear. I'll be in touch."

The rest of the committee sat awestruck, looking at Jaw. Parkinson realized as he led Slick from the room, he would have a lot of ruffled feathers to smooth.

Jaw walked to a door at the far end of the room while Parkinson led Slick to a side door saying, "The council members don't know about the committee but all committee members are council members. We have to sort of blend in separately as committee members arrive."

"Do you have a yard big enough to hold all those cars?" asked Slick.

Parkinson laughed, "No, Driver and his fleet are bringing them out. Of course, they are going to use the front entrance."

They could hear the din of voices in the next room as the Council Members mingled awaiting everyone's arrival. Parkinson opened the door a crack and said, "It looks like they are all in there, and I see Driver. I'll go introduce you. Watch for my hand signal."

Parkinson went in and immediately called the meeting to order. "Ladies and gentlemen, I have sad news. Jarvis Alvin Wilson, known to us as Jaw, is dead. This is our first official meeting since his death. This announcement is for the record. In our meeting some months back, we agreed to choose a successor to Jaw in case of retirement or death. I am sorry to say we have to deal with the latter. Jaw is no longer with us. In his honor, not of his death, but of his achievements, take one minute to ask your God to give whatever assistance Jaw may now need. Please bow your heads."

While every person in the room had their head bowed in prayer or meditation, Parkinson waved Slick into the room. When exactly one minute had lapsed, Parkinson shouted, "Now stand and greet your leader, Lloyd Miller, Beverly Code Slick!"

Everyone in the room stood and applauded Slick. He felt a small sense pride he had never felt before. He also felt inadequate to the tasks before him. After a bit, Slick held his hands up to quiet the council.

Slick began, "My Beverly Code name is Slick. I have that code name because I tried the twenty-dollar switch scam on Jaw my first night in Charlotte. It didn't work of course and I got smart-mouthed and was treated to a display of Jaw's mental and physical dexterity. A treat that many, if not all of us have been privileged to receive."

A light laughter rippled through the room. He went on, "I don't know of anyone who got the best of Jaw. I promise you if there is one, I'll find him. We have a traitor, in the ugly sense of the word among us, which leaves me in one hell of a predicament. I have to try to fill the shoes of a man who, in every sense of the word, was a better man than I, and I must find someone who got one over on him. I may be naïve, but

I think that there is someone among us who is being forced to compromise the program either by extortion or bribery. My phone number is 555-3323. If anyone here has that problem, please call me tomorrow morning, we can lay a trap that will solve your problem. In the meantime, I'm not Jaw. I can't operate the way he did. I beg each and every one of you, to help me keep the program going at least to the same end though maybe not the same path.

"We could all use some sleep. Thanks for your confidence in me. I'll do my best to live up to your faith in me; good night."

As everyone rose to leave, Slick turned to Notes and asked, "Does anyone have a roster of who was here tonight?"

"No," replied Notes, "but there was a videotape made that you could get."

"Good! You get it and then use it to make me a roster of who was and wasn't here tonight."

"By the way, " Slick continued, "do I have an office somewhere? I got fired today you know."

"Yes sir, the entire top floor of the Beverly. Everything from your office at First Nations is being moved as we speak," said Notes.

"Including your man Tarka?"

"Yes sir, including my person, now your person, Tarka."

"The whole top floor? What all is going to be up there?" asked Slick.

"Obviously your offices and mine. Now that Jaw is gone we'll need a small staff to keep up with everything. All the records will have to be transferred from the basement to a vault room. I've been putting everything on computer for the last year or so, but we still have a need for hard document storage," said Notes.

"You're boggling my mind Notes. I'm too tired to think straight. We all need some sleep. How do I get home tonight?" Slick asked.

174

"Your vehicle has been taken to your home. Driver will be back in a few minutes to take you home," said Notes. "Do you have any idea how you are going to find the leak?"

"I think I found one. If that's all there is we might be in good shape. I just have to figure out how to corral him," Slick said to an astonished Note.

Slick and Notes sat at the table talking while waiting for Driver to return. Slick was most interested in the computer filing system that Notes had mentioned, as well as in the depth the files went into concerning personal histories and cross-referencing abilities. Their conversation began to shift to other matters as Driver and Holbrook walked into the room.

"Slick, do you mind if I ride with you? asked Holbrook. "Driver can drop me off on his way back from your place."

"I don't have a problem if Driver doesn't," responded Slick.

As Holbrook and Slick rode through the dark night Slick said, "I thought I had been surprised when I learned Parkinson's name was Briefcase, but finding you in the organization has been a total shock. You're supposed to be the enemy," said Slick.

"I really did break the story, but when I saw the good that was coming from the Beverly, I couldn't turn it in. Then Jaw got hold of me and converted me. In fact, he surprised the hell out of me when he asked me to investigate the trust from the outside. I found a couple holes and they were quickly plugged. I don't think that even the FBI could break in now," said Holbrook.

"Well, I have to find a way to deal with Misota. I might have to arrange a crack in the wall under one plan, but I have several other thoughts on that," said Slick.

Holbrook started again, "There's something else I have to talk to you about, but I don't want you to get excited. Everything is okay," he reassured Slick. The worst part is that you can't fix what I think you'll see as something very distasteful.

"I met with my niece this morning at Latta Park. There was an incident there with some toughs who had shot a deer. That's

175

how I got this bruise, on the side of my jaw, where some guy hit me with the butt of his shotgun. The damn thing hurts like hell. They had been there to do more damage to me but they hadn't counted on my niece, who elbowed the guy in his nuts. His buddy punched her in the face and she's now sporting a beaut of a black eye."

"I'm sorry about you and your niece, Holbrook, but what's that got to do with anything here?"

"The reason they didn't do anything else is because Pigeon started yelling for the cops. The thugs grabbed their deer and ran. The result was, I wasn't snatched, nor was my niece, but she was in danger.

"My niece is married. On Jaw's insistence, her husband doesn't know that I'm her uncle. We did that. At the time I didn't understand why. About a year ago, Jaw filled me in. He hadn't wanted my judgment influenced by a personal relationship. He thought there would be time for that later."

There was absolute silence in the limousine. The two men could see each other by the dim strip of lighting that circled the cabin. Slick grimaced and said, "If you think for one second I'm going to call you Uncle Ted, you're out of your rabbit-ass mind."

"More importantly, what about Suzanne?" asked Slick. "Are you sure she's all right? I saw her at the funeral and tried to motion her to come over to me, but she shook me off. I guess I know why now."

"I called her just after the committee meeting. She's okay but still pissed off at the guy who hit her. The cops caught them and I have their names and addresses," said Holbrook.

It was three thirty in the morning when the limousine finally arrived at Slick's home. The front of the house was fully lit up. As they got out of the limo the front door sprung open and Suzanne came running out and lept into Slick's arms. Slick felt her trembling.

"Lloyd, Mary Wilson called for you. She told me what happened, are you okay? Where the hell have you been? My

God, I've been so worried!" rambled Suzanne as her pent up worry for her husband released like a floodgate.

"My wife comes running to me with a shiner she got during a rendezvous with a secret uncle that is my arch enemy, plays with some guy's nuts in the park and she's still worried about me?" asked Lloyd in mock surprise.

Suzanne jerked back, hunched her shoulders and held her arms out, palms up. She had been caught off guard by her husband's assessment and could only utter, "A-a-well!" From the corner of her eye she caught what she thought was movement by the limousine. Quickly turning her head she saw Uncle Ted, wearing a Cheshire grin, emerging from the limousine's cabin.

Both Slick and Holbrook examined Suzanne's shiner. Although it hurt Slick to see his wife's face marred like that, it didn't stop him from bragging about a shiner he had once had. Holbrook then elaborated on his own past shiner story. Not to be outdone, Slick came back with yet a better shiner story, which Holbrook promptly topped. Both knew the other had moved from truth to fabrication, but they kept it up.

In total frustration and aggravation Suzanne screamed, "What the hell is going on here? Have you forgotten that I'm the one with the headache from hell? It's my nerves that are shot because my husband was almost blown up, shot, and, and, and, almost beaten half to death, and you two ass-holes are out here lying to each other about shiners!"

Holbrook never liked domestic disputes, especially ones he had helped to fuel. Being the "gentleman" that he was he sprinted toward the limousine as he hurriedly shouted over his shoulder, "Gotta go." He was in such a cowardly hurry to make his exit that he literally dove through the limousine's open cabin door. Driver spun the limo's tires as he followed Holbrook's orders to, "Get the hell out of here, quick!"

Slick put his arms out protectively as he backed away from his oncoming wife saying, "Honey, I'm sorry. Don't look at me that way Hon. I really am sorry."

Suzanne cocked her arm, fist clinched, high in the air and rushed at Slick swinging at his head. Slick stepped just forward enough to slip his arms around her and hold her tightly to him. She responded in kind, whispering in his ear, "You really are a bastard you know."

"You sure you're okay? You haven't had double vision or been dizzy, have you?" asked Slick softly.

"No." she responded as her anger lessened with Slick's concern for her.

"I mean dizzier than normal," Slick whispered, with a smile on his face

"What?" she exclaimed, as her anger level escalated to its original fury.

"I'm only kidding," he said, holding her tighter. Planting a kiss on her forehead he said, "All teasing aside honey, are you ok, other than your headache?" Slick's concern was real.

Suzanne's fury fizzled like air rushing out of a balloon, as she replied, "No, just this headache, and of course this damned shiner." They hugged and then started back toward the house.

As they approached the house and started up the front steps Slick looked up to see Hal Townson standing in the doorway smiling. Townson's eyes suddenly went beyond Slick and widened. Townson yelled, "Get down, Slick! Suzanne, get down!"

Shots rang out in the night. Bullets struck the brick steps next to Slick as he shoved Susanne down. Instinctively and protectively he crawled over and covered Suzanne's body with his as he pulled out the gun he had taken from the thug at the house. He twisted and returned fire over his body in the direction of the flashes. A voice yelled and the firing stopped. A door slammed and a vehicle could be heard spinning tires as it drove off.

"Suzanne are you okay?" asked Slick desperately.

"Yes," she answered sobbing and trembling. "Why is someone trying to kill us? What is going on Lloyd?"

"Not kill us Honey, scare us. Those guys don't miss. Let's get inside." Slick helped her up and rushed them to the door.

Once safely inside Slick sent Suzanne to wash her face and compose herself. Betty Townson, who had been in the kitchen when the shooting occurred went with her. Hal was laying on the floor sweating and trembling like a leaf in a gale. He tried to talk, but the words were just a jumble of sounds. Lloyd brought him a shot of whisky. Townson slugged it down as if it were water.

"My God Lloyd! They were trying to kill you! They were shooting at you," Hal finally choked out.

"I know. I was there. Before the girls get back, tell me why you turned on the organization," Lloyd said.

"Why what?" asked Townson.

"You heard me Hal,"said Slick coldly.

"I haven't turned on the organization. How could you even think that?" Hal. asked incredulously.

"Why were you listening in on my conversation with Suzanne?" asked Slick.

"I- I didn't!" exclaimed Townson.

Slick pulled his gun out and rammed it under Townson's chin. "You son of a bitch, Susanne could have been killed twice today! Now you better start telling me the truth, or I swear to God, you're dead meat!"

"Okay, okay, I admit it. Please don't kill me. I didn't know they were going to do that," Hal pleaded.

Slick slipped the gun back into his pocket. Townson sighed in resignation and said, "When Jaw found me I was a drunk. I had to quit gambling because I couldn't afford to do both. Jaw never knew about the gambling. I'm into Misota for over half a million. He was going to do Betty in if I didn't help him."

"Why didn't you go to Jaw, or somebody for help?"

"There are over a thousand people who have gone through the program. I didn't want to be the first failure." Townson sounded pathetic.

179

"You self-righteous son of a bitch, how could you even remotely consider yourself more important than the thousand you just mentioned?" demanded Slick.

"I'm not a strong man. I never won a fight even as a kid. They intimidated me. What am I going to do Lloyd?" asked Townson.

"The first thing you're going to do is get your sorry ass the hell out of my house, before I start wondering if you had anything to do with the shooter having been here tonight. Tomorrow you go to your office and wait for my call," Slick said in disgust.

The Townsons left as soon as the ladies walked back into the room. How quickly they left and how cold Lloyd was to Hal, had startled Suzanne, but she said nothing.

As they prepared for bed, Lloyd told Suzanne what he could of the evening, but did not mention that Jaw was still alive. He explained some of the attempted take over. Then, in a moment of inspiration, he told her about Sandy, and his future role as her bodyguard for the next few weeks.

Chapter 29

Miller was surprised at how well he felt the next morning. He and Rock had been to the police station to give their statements.

The Misota gang were all being charged with terrorism, assault, assault with intent to do bodily harm, carrying concealed weapons and several other charges, all of which Mary and James Wilson had promised to come back and testify to. The two naked guys, found off Matheson, were a different story. One guy had been arrested for sodomy, caught in the act. The other was charged with assault on a police officer, which happened while the sodomizee was trying to kill the sodomizor. Misota had posted bond for all of his men, except for the sodomizor and the total had come to well over a million dollars in cash.

Slick met with Typer in his new office. He related the events of the evening to her from the ride to the tower, to the ride to the lake house. Slick didn't mention his appointment, or that Jaw was alive. He only told about a high level meeting.

"That answers most of the questions," said Typer "but it still doesn't satisfy my distrust for coincidence. I do not believe in coincidence. Jaw doing all he did in the last two or three weeks could not have been because he thought he was going to die. He was either murdered or is still alive. I just can't see how he could still be alive. Of course I don't see how he could've been murdered and it not be seen or found out. I forgot to tell you, Rock said that Sandy was on post."

Slick smiled at her. "Thank you. Lady you are amazing."

"What does that mean?"

"A little later," smiled Slick. He made a few phone calls, one of which was to Mary Wilson, convincing her to stay at least one more day. He decided to call Holbrook, who turned out not be at work yet. Slick then consulted his list and called Holbrook's house. The line was busy. Ten minutes later, the line was still busy. Slick called Suzanne. The phone rang. At least he knew that Holbrook was not talking to his niece. Suzanne finally answered on the third ring.

"Hey, Honey, how are you and Sandy getting along?"

"What a waste. A big beautiful man like that and he's gay," replied Suzanne.

"You'd never know it in a fight. You'll be safe with him around. Talk to you later. Love ya," He hadn't wanted to upset Suzanne by asking about her uncle.

Slick called Holbrook again. The line was still busy so he called Zipper and asked him to send someone to check on Holbrook.

Miller had just returned from lunch when he received a call from Beagle.

With near panic in his voice Beagle said, "S-S-S-S-S-Slick, s-s-s-something is ga-ga-ga-going on. B-b-b-but I don't know what. M-M-M-Mrs. Wilson asked me to p-p-p-pick up a few copies of the death certificate. They have n-n-n-no record of Jaw's death!"

Slick said, "Charlie, I need you to come over here. Stop asking questions about Jaw till you talk to me. Do you know where I am?"

"NE-NE-New office. See you in about t-t-t-t-twenty minutes."

Charles Mott was flustered, wringing his hands and sweating profusely as he sat tensely in front of Slick's desk.

"Damn Charlie, it's not that hot out," said Slick.

"Ja-Ja-Jesus Slick, there's no r-r-r-record of Jaw dying in the whole place. They duh-duh-don't even have a r-r-r-record of a call to pick up his body. It's like it never happened," said Mott.

"Easy Charlie, take a deep breath and calm down. Do you have any out of town clients?"

Charlie Mott paused a moment and took deep breaths trying to calm himself. He then asked, "What the hell does that have to do with Jaw?"

"Answer the damn question Charlie," said Slick coldly.

"Well yes, I have N-N-N-Nick Dresden in Hickory. Why?"

Slick pushed the intercom button and said, "Typer, you and Rock come in here."

The two appeared. Slick began, "Rock, you are to accompany Mr. Mott to the front desk and register him under the name, 'M. Smith.' Be sure he gets a room on the seventh floor and then take him to the Manager's Office. There Mr. Mott, you will call your wife and tell her you had an emergency call from Hickory, and for whatever reason you make up, you have to go there. Tell her not to be surprised if you stay the night. Give your wife any kind of code, that we find out about, and Charlie, you will be spoon-fed, lying on your back, the rest of your life. Tarka go with them and make sure Mott doesn't get cute on the phone. When that is done, Rock take him to the room and sit with him. Only Tarka or myself can come get him. Do you understand me?"

Typer and Rock nodded their complete understanding.

"What the hell is going on?" asked Mott, who received a cold stare from Slick.

Mott looked at Slick and in almost a whisper asked, "Ha-Ha-How did you know?"

"My first hint was the new will. The second was that you didn't know about the Downs Corporation. That meant Jaw knew and why you are now scared shitless over Jaw's death certificate. Only someone who is compromised would get as scared as you are," said Slick.

"I beg you S-S-S-Slick, duh-duh-don't do this. M-M-M-Misota said he would get me through my wife and son."

"I'll have them protected Charlie, but for now I need you here for advice."

As they started out the door, Slick instructed Tarka, "Send Notes in, now."

While waiting for Notes to come in Slick's phone rang. He answered it.

"Slick," said Zipper, "Holbrook was beaten bad and left for dead. His entire house was ransacked. The police are there,

183

investigating the scene as we speak. Holbrook was taken to the Medical Center."

Slick looked up as Notes entered his office. Not wanting to continue this phone call in Notes' presence Slick spoke officiously into the phone and said, "Ok, keep me posted on any other developments."

Hanging up the phone he motioned for Notes to sit down in the chair in front of his desk. "Notes, tell me about the Charter Committee members."

Notes started listing members and information about each. "Well, there's myself My code name is 'Notes,' and my given name is Marshall Watts. I'm a former CEO of a 500 company. There is 'Briefcase,' whose given name is Stanley Parkinson. Stanley is a current CEO, whom you know. 'Kid Gloves' given name is Thomas Manning and he is a now retired, self-made millionaire in the stock market. Then there is 'Archer,' whose given name is Norman Holloway. He has never worked, but is a millionaire, many times over. 'Stinger's,' given name is Martin Reams, and he is a retired Marine General. Finally, there is 'Writer,' whose given name is Ted Holbrook, whom you are also familiar with."

"How did they all check out?" asked Slick.

Notes sat there just looking at Slick.

"Notes, you forget, I'm one of Jaw's students. Now answer my damn question. How did they check out?" demanded Slick.

"Jaw told me not to tell anyone we even checked, but everyone came up clean. No money problems, no big bank transactions that weren't on the up and up. Not even any private stuff, except that Holbrook would get drunk once in a while and go to the same hooker each time."

"Was she checked out?"

"Why? She isn't part of the organization."

"Get her checked out fast. Somebody tried some shit with Holbrook yesterday and this morning somebody beat him half to death. I don't think it was a random happenstance."

Slick asked Typer to come into his office. "Typer, Notes has a computerized list of anyone who had ever received assistance from the Beverly, or any part of the organization. He's going to give it to you and I want you to initiate a general warning. If a message was left, insist on a return call to confirm that the message was received. When you leave, have Rock bring Mott into my office now.

When Mott came into the room Slick motioned him to a chair and asked, "Charlie, who else rolled over to Misota?"

Mott, who was now calm, and resigned to his fate answered, "I don't know, but a few of the questions they asked led me to believe there's someone else. They asked me about safety deposit boxes."

"What did you tell them?"

"Nothing, I don't know anything about safety deposit boxes."

"Charlie, Ted Holbrook was beaten up this morning. I want to know why. You better give me an answer or you best learn to fly because you're going through the window," said Slick grimly.

"I don't know Slick. I haven't had any contact with them since before the funeral."

Typer and Rock were still in the office. Slick wrote a note, handed it to Typer and said, "Take care of this." She read the note, motioned to Rock to follow, and they left the room.

Slick looked menacingly back at Mott. "Charlie, I never killed a man who didn't ask to die, but if I twist this around enough in my mind I can absolutely justify killing you. What I want to know, and to know now, is why Holbrook was worked over," shouted Slick.

Mott jerked in his seat, "I-I-I da-da-da-don't know! M-M-M-Maybe they thought he knew something because of his contacts with the paper and the few articles he had written, making insinuations that he knew more than what he had put in the articles."

"Charlie, did you tell them Holbrook was a council member?"

"I don't think so. I told them about the money in the trust and how it was all hidden."

Slick sat behind his desk, looking hard at Mott. As time passed Mott became more nervous. After a full two minutes, Slick stoically glared at him and said softly, "I see no way to keep you alive or your family in good health without your input." Having said that, Slick leaned back in his chair and unflinchingly watched Mott sweat and squirm in his seat for the next ten minutes.

Finally, the door opened. A nervous Hal Townson walked in, followed by Rock and Notes. Slick motioned for Townson to take a seat next to Mott. Rock stayed at the door and Notes took a seat near the door. Slick straightened himself at the center of his desk and leaned forward on his forearms.

"Hal, do you know what happened to Ted Holbrook," Slick asked quietly. Townson nodded his head affirmatively and began sweating even more.

Slick nodded his head a few times and asked, "Did you know that Mott had rolled over to Misota?"

"No."

"What did you tell Misota about the safety deposit box at 1st Securities?"

Townson began to tremble, "I-I just told them that there was one," mumbled Townson.

Loosing his patience, Slick pushed back in his chair and disgustedly said, "Rock, throw him out the window."

"What?" screamed Townson, jumping from his chair and right into Rock's grip.

Mott watched in horror as Rock carried and dragged a screaming Hal Townson toward the window. Rock looked at Slick. Slick made a gesture and Rock nodded.

About five feet from the window, Rock raised Townson off his feet and threw him at the window. Townson flew through the air screaming and his face and chest slammed against the window. He bounced back, as if off a trampoline, and lay on the floor sobbing. He was totally defeated, in body and mind.

"Jesus Christ!" exclaimed Mott in awe.

Townson's mouth and nose were bleeding. He looked up at Slick with pleading eyes and begged for mercy. "Slick, for God's sake, have mercy on me man. I don't know any more."

"Mercy my ass! You listened in on my call to Suzanne. You told Misota what time I'd be home and almost got Suzanne killed. You potentially ruined the lives of a thousand people because of personal pride. YOU want mercy? I'll show your ass mercy! Rock, try again!"

Before Townson could react, Rock snatched him from the floor and threw him at the window again. Screaming, Townson bounced off again.

"Damn it Rock!" shouted Slick "I said throw him out the window, not play hand ball with him."

"Want I should try again?" asked Rock, in his calm, deadpan voice.

"Want he should try again Hal? Anything you want to talk to us about?" asked Slick.

"Yes, yes, I mean no, don't try again. Yes, I'll tell you everything."

"What about you Charlie?" asked Slick.

"You have my attention," was his grim answer.

Mott and Townson told everything they had related to Misota. The information they shared included the names of almost all the council members, and unknowingly, some of the committee members. They also told what they knew of the bonds and available cash.

"Notes, we have the capability of electronic transfer of funds, right?" asked Slick.

Notes nodded affirmatively.

"Who sets up new accounts?" asked Slick

"I do, but to get any money into the account, I have to let Charlie know which account it's from and what account it's going to," said Notes.

"Charlie, have you given Misota any cash account numbers?" asked Slick.

"Yes, he asked for them last week. I gave them to him yesterday."

Slick looked to Notes, "Do we have a hacker?"

"Dot-Com, but he disappeared. We've been hunting him all morning. Word is that he left town," said Notes

"Well boys, then exactly how did Misota find out about Dot-Com?" asked Slick.

The two men looked at each other, hoping the other would answer. Townson finally admitted he had given Misota, Dot-Com's name.

"Rock, take these two ass holes to Mott's room. If they try anything smart, break some serious bones," Slick commanded.

Once they had left Slick asked Notes about the number of accounts that had cash in them, and how much was in each of them.

"We have nine including the Hotel's. The hotel keeps around five thousand, and the other accounts should total around a million and a half."

"How many banks?" asked Slick.

"Three."

"Can we get another hacker? We need someone that can tear those accounts a new ass."

"I don't know of anyone. Let me ask around. Do you need anything else?"

"Do we have anyone high enough in our banks to waiver policy?"

"I think I know where you are going with this Slick, but I believe that's built into the bank's program. I'll check for you though, to verify everything." Notes rose from his chair and headed for the door.

Miller heard a phone ringing in his desk. He opened the drawers on the left side and found a ringing wooden box in the second drawer. As he reached down to the box he caught sight of his wristwatch. It was 11:20 AM He opened the box and found a telephone receiver, raised it to his ear and said, "Hello."

"Slick, Jaw here. I understand you need a computer expert to deal with Misota. I finally met with Mary and Jimmy. Damned if Jimmy isn't a computer whiz."

"The way I see it," said Slick, "I need more then a computer whiz. I think one of the Charter Committee members is in with Misota. As I understand it, you and the Charter Committee have been together since the beginning. None of you ever thought this thing would blossom the way it has. Think back a bit. Have any of the committee members been suggesting changes over the past few years? If somebody gets hold of those bearer bonds, it would bankrupt the trust."

"We are essentially the same group of guys. Notes joined us about six years ago. By then the program was showing its potential and we really needed someone like him. I believe it was Briefcase who ran across his résumé when he applied at First Nations.

"The system we have now, started about five years ago. Kid Gloves said he and Notes were talking about bearer bonds and the thought occurred to him that we could do that. Briefcase was against it at first, as were Stinger and Archer. I think Stinger was the last hold -out against it," said Jaw

"What was Notes' input?"

"I don't recall him having much to say. It almost seems now, thinking back on it, all he ever had to say had been in the form of a 'what if' question which always seemed to lead to a resolution of a question the opposition had. Why?" asked Jaw.

"We are working with three banks," said Slick. Each bank has a safety deposit box containing the bonds. They have a key and we have a key. That's two. The committee has to approve any transfer of bonds. That's seven. Notes carried out the instructions. That's one. When you had the Charter Committee checked out, who checked out Notes?"

"That was a hell of a guess. Yes I had the guys checked out, but to my knowledge Notes hasn't been checked out," said Jaw.

"Then, I do believe I need to talk to Parkinson," said Slick.

189

"Don't bother. I'll take care of this. By the way, my source with the Misotas has an urgent message for me. I should have it within the hour," said Jaw

They both hung up. Slick studied the phone a moment and realized there was nothing to it but a cradle. As he sat there pondering it the phone rang again.

"You can't dial me," said Jaw. "Just call me aloud and I'll answer. Your office is bugged." Lloyd made a mental note to fix that.

Chapter 30

Mary and James Wilson ate breakfast in their room. The events of the previous night had drained them of all energies. In fact, James looked worse than he had the night before. His bruises varied in color from black to a sick green around the edges, however, his eye was open a little, even though the socket and all around it was black.

Mary awoke first and immediately ordered coffee and a newspaper. She scanned half the paper before realizing that everything from the previous night had been happening as the paper was being printed. The phone rang, and she answered it.

"Mary, are you alright?" asked Stanley Parkinson, who was on the other end of the line. "I was worried about you and Jim and about your safety. Would it be ok if I came over to see you right now?"

"Stanley, I'm tired, but otherwise fine. If you insist on coming over now, then at least give me an hour. I insist on that."

Exactly one hour later Parkinson arrived at Mary's.

Mary opened the door and took one look at him and said, "Stanley, I don't want to sound rude, but you look like hell. You must have something really terrible to tell us."

"Actually Mary, I have no idea how to describe to you what's going on. You and James have been threatened, Miller and Zeigler were almost killed, and Zeigler was kidnapped. Fortunately, Miller got Ziegler back. I think I'm getting a little old for this kind of life, but be that as it may, I need you and James to come with me now."

"I really wanted to see the noon news about what happened last night," said Mary.

"You'll get to see the noon news afterwards, if you are still interested," said Parkinson.

191

Mary motioned James to get their coats. They followed Parkinson to the limousine parked in the hotel's executive pickup area. It was a short ride to the Beverly Hotel. They walked inside to the elevator. Parkinson pushed a button and the doors opened almost immediately. They stepped into the elevator and he pressed a button that took them down. Parkinson turned to Mary saying, "I can't tell you the agony some of us have been through for the last two weeks. The last three days have been the worst. I beg you and James not react to anything until you have heard everything that's going to be told to you now."

The elevator stopped. The doors opened up to a drab, musty smelling basement. Parkinson led them out of the elevator and over to a door that opened into a medium-sized, sparsely furnished office, which contained a phone on a gray metal desk, a couch and two stuffed chairs. Three walls were bare, but it was the fourth wall that immediately caught Mary's attention. Photographs of her and James almost completely blanketed it. As Mary and James walked toward the wall, Parkinson slipped quietly from the room. Mary stood, transfixed, looking at the wall of photos.

James turned to ask Parkinson a question and exclaimed, "Jesus!" A different man was standing quietly behind them.

"Yeah," said Mary, not taking her eyes off the photographs.

"Mom, Mom," James excitedly and insistently repeated as he tapped his Mother's shoulder, and kept his eyes fixed on Parkinson's replacement.

"What is it?" snapped Mary, who was visibly aggravated as she looked at James and then at where he stared.

Mary Wilson gasped as she spun around and was knocked backward to the wall with astonishment. Her eyes flared open as she stared at the man standing there sheepishly looking back at her. It was none other than Jarvis Alvin Wilson, her not-so-dead husband.

"Mary. James. Please forgive me for what I've put you through these last few days. I'm so sorry. I didn't realize that everything I've worked for all these years was so close to being lost. A lot of good people could be hurt very seriously if this thing doesn't work. I just can't put you through any more," said a tearful Jarvis Wilson.

"You son of a bitch Al. You're alive!" yelled Mary as she ran to him and threw her arms around him. She held their embrace, as if in desperation letting go meant he would once again be gone from her. He in turn held her as if he would never let her go.

Suddenly, Mary's eyes snapped and slapped Jaw across the face as hard as she could saying, "You bastard, you put me through all this shit! Why the hell didn't you tell me this was all fake?"

"I couldn't Mary. If I had, you would have spilled your guts last night. I hadn't anticipated what happened, but if you had known, you would have said anything to stop them from beating James. As it stands now, I think we both have a greater respect for our son."

"You might have, you bastard," screamed Mary as she forcibly shoved Jaw away with from her with both hands, " but I've been living with him all this time. I know what he can do!" She turned her back to him and started to walk away. Instead of walking out she turned and ended up walking in a complete circle.

"O-O-O-O-o-o-o-o-o-o-o-o-o," she uttered as she ran back to Jaw and clung to him, as if he would disappear forever if she let him go. Tears flowed down her cheeks like tiny glistening rivers. With her mouth slightly open and her face contorted, she wept for joy.

Tears also began to stream down Jaw's face. He knew after all these years he would now have his Mary back. He silently promised never to leave her again. James, with moist eyes, walked over and put his hand on his father's shoulder.

"Dad," said James softly, "Mr. Parkinson told me about you the first night. You've done wonderful work here in Charlotte, but I have to admit, it still doesn't take away all of my resentment for having to grow up without a father. We'll have problems with it. I think we can work it out."

"I hope so James," replied Jaw, fighting back tears. "I know I'll give it my best shot."

"Do you know the woman lied to you?" asked Mary.

"I found that out two years ago when I bumped into a high school friend of mine in a hotel lobby. We got to talking and somehow he knew I was involved in that scandal. I swore him to silence about having seen me. I offered to pay him for taking pictures of you but he had gotten mad because I had offered him money. Richie would be glad to do it but had insisted he wouldn't intrude on your privacy."

"Why didn't you contact us then?" asked James.

"I almost did, but Stan Parkinson reminded me of my schedule. I'm on the go as much as eighteen hours a day. That's when I started grooming Lloyd Miller to take over the organization. I worked him in a microcosm of the whole organization. We were just about to take him to the next level when we figured out we were being infiltrated by crooks. They turned out to be the Misotas. At first we thought they just wanted our street network, until we figured out they had wanted it all. Carlos Misota is the boss of organized crime in Charlotte and most of North Carolina. His biggest moneymaker is drugs. Anyone who brings drugs into North Carolina has to pay a fee to Misota or else end up in jail, or worse, dead. He also brings in his own drugs and that's what he wanted our network for. I figured out that Charlie Mott had rolled over to Misota, but I had missed Hal Townson. I had Lloyd Miller's office bugged. Somehow he figured out Townson had rolled over also.

"I don't know if anyone told you, but before Miller came to your hotel room he had helped Zeigler escape from some thugs that were going to kill the both of them. Miller had figured out what the jerks were going to do and set up the escape. Miller made it, but Ziegler got caught. The thugs set Zeigler up in a house and then booby-trapped it. Miller got him out of that too. You know what happened in your room. He left there and was appointed CEO of the entire organization. The man has been busy the last eighteen hours.

"I overheard some of the conversations in his office. I think I know what he is going to try. We need a computer whiz. The only one I know, that's good enough, has rolled over to Misota."

"No Dad, only one of us has disappeared, I'm still here," said Jimmy.

"You're hot on computers?" asked Jaw.

"I'm the most dangerous kind of Hacker there is. I have a master's in computer science, and I have common sense. I work from home Dad, but I also work for the government," said James.

"Hot damn Jimmy, will you help us?" asked an elated Jaw.

"It will cost you Dad," said Jimmy.

"How much?"

"When this shit is over with, you have to come home with us."

"Deal."

Chapter 31

"Zipper! Zipper!" yelled Shoes as he ran into the lobby of the Beverly Hotel. "They just grabbed Typer out front!"

"Who did?" asked Zipper as he hurriedly back stepped toward his office.

"I think it was Misota's boys. At least I'm sure one of them was anyhow," said Shoes.

Zipper turned and ran the rest of the way to his office. He hurriedly picked up the phone and called Slick. "Slick, Typer was just grabbed! Shoes thinks that one of Misota's boys was in on her abduction."

"Can he describe the vehicle?" asked Slick.

In a few minutes Zipper came back on the line with the vehicle's description and tag number.

"Zipper, put this information on the street, and offer a big reward in anything: booze, clothes, food, cash, or whatever the informant wants... Then call our cop and let him know what we have. Let's see who finds her first."

"You got it, Slick!. I'm going to drop a few twenties on Shoes for some quick thinking. I'll have to do it over a few days though or he'll be walking around in a pair of new Air Jordan's."

Even with the stress of the moment, Slick smiled as he visualized Shoes, who was the scariest looking person he had ever seen. In fact, Slick thought that Shoes made a made-up Jack Elam look like a sex symbol. Shoes was a few inches short of seven feet tall, skinny and wore a size seventeen shoe, thus how he rightfully came by his name.

Slick called for Jaw and immediately the secret phone rang. He explained what had happened and gave Jaw a run down on what he thought Typer knew.

"She initially worked on your instructions for Notes. Depending on what was explained to her will be what Misota

196

learns from her. She doesn't know you are alive." Notes wanted Jaw to know he had figured out who had assigned Typer to him.

"You're right, Slick. I put them together. I told her an associate of mine was going to contact her and set her up to help a friend. Notes told her not to let the friend know he was being helped. She was to report everything that happened to him as soon as she got off work, regardless of the hour. The last time she had talked to Notes, she told him she wasn't going to report to him anymore and that she was one hundred percent yours. If he didn't like that, then he was to tell me."

Slick told Jaw about the restaurant meeting and the coin display.

"Notes told her more than he was supposed to," snapped Jaw.

"No shit, Buckwheat, do you think that's why she was snatched?"

"That's a hell of a leap. I just can't figure what could be gained by setting Typer up for a grab. I'll have to think that one through. What are you doing about her?"

"The street is looking for the van she was taken in. All we can do is wait. Like it or not, I have to leave this one with Zipper. I have too much going on right now," said Slick as he hung up the phone.

Mary looked quizzically at Jaw and asked, "What was that about Nancy?"

"She was abducted by Misota five minutes ago," Jaw grimly answered.

"My God Al! How many people will get hurt by this charade of yours?" asked Mary

"I don't know. I just hope Slick is smart enough to get my stupid ass out of this jam and get Tarka back safely," Jaw tearfully replied.

197

Chapter 32

Carlos Misota sat alone in his conference room. He was livid as he tried to access the damage caused by his son's stupidity. Not only was his son beaten half to death, but the embarrassment of having lost to a rank amateur was almost more than he could bear.

Finally Carlos called his men into his office. They stood in a line in front of his desk while Carlos paced back and forth in front of them. In a voice reminiscent of Anthony Quinn he said, "I don't know what to say. I send my best men out on a simple assignment and what happens? All of you get your ass kicked. You embarrass me! Not only do you get your ass kicked, but one of you actually accomplishes getting your ass pumped!" He was now yelling at the top of his lungs.

"You fucking idiots work for Carlos Misota! I am a Don, not a circus owner! I have soldiers working for me, not clowns! I don't accept failure! When you fail me, you attack me! You attack me, you better kill me because if you don't, I will kill you!" He screamed into the face of the man at the end of the line. Then he walked down the line and into each man's face he repeatedly shouted "and you," even into his son's face.

"The only reason I don't kill you now is that my heir, my own idiot son, failed me too!"

"Papa please, not in front of the men," Emile softly pleaded.

"Why not? They already know you're an idiot. You don't follow instructions. You were supposed to wait for a phone call. Did you wait? No, you go charging in like the Lone Ranger. You insulted me and you insulted your men! When you walked through the door you told your men, "I don't trust you. You are not good men!" Carlos yelled.

"Donnie, did I say that when I walked in?" asked Emile.

Carlos continued pacing back and forth. Emile spoke up and Carlos all but sprinted back to his son and slapped him mightily on his bandaged ear. Emile howled in pain, stumbled to the side and nearly fell to the floor.

"You shut your stupid mouth," said Carlos through gritted teeth.

Just at that moment the phone rang. Carlos looked at Emile and motioned with his head for him to answer it. After listening to the person on the other end of the phone Emile laid the phone down and whispered into his Father's ear.

As Carlos walked to the phone he said, "All of you, out of here!"

Carlos picked up the phone and looked up to see Emile, "I said ALL of you!" A red-faced Emile left the room.

Speaking into the phone Carols said, "Good morning sir," as he kept nervousness from his voice.

"Carlos, you have a problem. Have you heard the news casts this morning?"

"Yes Sir."

"You've brought attention to us in the most stupid way. You know Emile is impulsive, yet you send him out on a man's job. Why Carlos?"

"He got a little anxious."

"I ask you again Carlos, why do you send an impulsive boy on a man's job?"

"He is my son. I must send him occasionally. This is the first time he screwed anything up. He conducted himself properly during the trial."

"Carlos, we are not here to run a kindergarten. There are millions at stake here. If you have a problem with your kid, solve it on your own time. He isn't the only screw-up you have working for you. Luckily Holbrook is still alive. I told you to rough him up a little, not beat him half to death. Your men have no class. I am now beginning to wonder about you.

"However, right now we have new business. We've made arrangements for another purchase. You have been given a credit line of sixty million in your real estate purchase account. When the delivery is made, release forty million to Hays, Hays and Seigniot Attorneys, account number 0441-579-6637-DRZ-114. Did you copy that?" asked the voice.

Carlos read the account number back along with the instructions.

"That's correct. Earmark the transaction for the purchase of K.R.T. Refining Company, Inc. Two days later the lawyers will contact you and tell you that for another twenty million, you can purchase the company's drilling rights in several areas proven to have oil and gas. Accept and send them the balance. In the meantime, get the information we need to drain the Beverly Trust. Your ass is on the line. That Beverly network will be invaluable to us." The line went dead.

Carlos sat at his desk fuming. Emile had screwed up seriously, but so had the other men. The rules were the leader or the man who didn't follow orders was responsible for failures. In this, Emile was both. He was the leader who didn't follow orders. Carlos had ordered the death of many men for doing what Emile had done. But he could not bring himself to order the death of this only son. As far as the rest of the men with Emile were concerned, that pussy loan shark and his gorilla had captured them. Carlos wished he owned the gorilla. Like that union guy, Carlos could have the others put in a 55-gallon drum and dropped at sea, but the word was already out on Emile. Carlos was forced to give Emile, and the others, a second chance. If it didn't work, this time he would have no choice in the matter. It was at that moment that he decided to add Rock and Jimmy Wilson to the hit list. Carlos called everyone back into his office. They were all nervous, including Emile, who seemed even more nervous than the rest.

"Emile." said Carlos. Emile stiffened visibly. Carlos continued, "You take two men and take out the gorilla named Rock. He was last seen at the Beverly Hotel. Don't try to take him up close. Use a rifle. I've seen guys like him before. You can shoot him dead five or six times, and he'll still come at you."

"Yes sir," answered Emile. He immediately chose two of the men that had been with him the previous night and they left the room.

Carlos continued, "Pete I want you to glue yourself to Hal Townson. Here's his picture. He left his office this morning and took a cab somewhere and hasn't been back to his office. He works at 1st Security's Tryon Street building. Hang around there and do a little talking to the cabbies." Carlos handed Pete the photograph and Pete acknowledged the instructions with a nod in return.

"Oh Pete," said Carlos, "keep a patch on your ass and watch out for falling bricks."

The embarrassed man nodded again and rushed from the room.

"Hank, you know what Lloyd Miller looks like?" asked Carlos.

"Yes sir."

"Well, find a few more boys and keep an eye on the Beverly. Let me know as soon as you spot him. We know he's in there. Surround the place. I personally want that son of a bitch," said Carlos with hatred in his eyes.

"Yes sir."

"Oh Hank," Hank prepared himself for the insult, "don't let any broads near your balls."

Carlos turned to his aide, Tony Deluca. "Get Charlie Mott on the phone." In a few minutes Tony returned to say that Mott was in Hickory and may not be back until the next morning.

Carlos wondered what the hell Charlie was doing in Hickory. How the hell am I supposed to keep up with what's going on? Things at the Beverly should start jumping now. Wait a minute. If Mott is the one who transfers the money to new accounts, then they won't be able to transfer anything if he isn't here. I guess I do know what is happening - absolutely nothing.

Deluca came back in the room and asked, "Sir, did you know Miller has a personal secretary named Nancy Tarka? She went with him to the airport and funeral home. I think there might be a connection there."

"No I didn't. Indeed there just might be a little something to that. Do we have a picture?"

"No sir, but there is no mistaking Nancy Tarka. She's one of the most beautiful women in Charlotte. If you want her, I'll have her snatched," said Deluca.

"Make it history," said Misota.

Then Jimmy Wilson came to his mind. He immediately planned that he and Emile will do him together...

Misota's apartments were above his office. He spent most of the day in his apartment mulling things over. At sixty-two, Misota was at the pinnacle of his success. He had risen through the ranks of the crime syndicate, taking on any and all assignments successfully.

He was on his third cigar, puffing like a steam locomotive. A cloud of blue white smoke hung throughout the room. He paused to look into a mirror. Again, for the ten thousandth time, he reflected on dyeing his hair back to black. He grunted and resumed his pacing.

His thoughts centered on Emile. The boy was trying hard. However, Carlos had seen instances where the gentleness of Emile's Mother stuck its crippling head out. In this business, compassion and kindness have no place. Either one could get you killed by your competition and you rarely knew who the competition was. A rival organization could be less of a threat than someone in your own family.

While Emile had a real mean streak in him, it took something personal to set it off. You had to slap him or hurt him, anything that put the insult on a one-on-one basis. Emile lacked solid reasoning in terms of organizational planning. . He couldn't understand how the street people of the Beverly could be coerced into being drug runners and bagmen.

The kid had wanted to go to college. Maybe he should have. Carlos remembered that as a kid Emile had wanted to build bridges and roads. The kid definitely had the brains for it, but being his only son, and child, it was understood that Emile would take over the business. Until Emile's mother died in an auto accident, which was caused by a drunk driver, there had been many heated debates over that issue. Carlos had loved her very much and had taken great delight in watching her killer die a very painful and slow death. It didn't relieve his grief and loneliness.

This assignment would settle it. Carlos sent his aide out to check on what was going on. Emile had the rifle. He was going to be the shooter. If he could shoot Rock, there would be a chance for him. To order a man killed, you yourself had to have killed. You had to know the gut wrenching feeling when you pulled the trigger for the first time. Then you would have a better idea if the man you ordered to make the hit would do it, especially if it was his first hit.

A knock on the door brought Tony Deluca into the living room, "Boss, we have Nancy Tarka at the warehouse."

"Good, let's go talk to her," said Misota.

After the conversation with Nancy Tarka, Misota was beginning to think his organization was coming apart. Two of his best men had been too stupid to tie and blindfold the woman. How could he do anything with an empty talent pool? Not even his kid was anything to brag about.

A few hours later Tony Deluca again knocked on the door, "Boss, it's nine thirty now. We haven't found Townson and the guys at the Beverly seem holed up for the duration. What do you think we should do, wait it out or come in?"

"Call them all in and leave a fresh man at the Beverly. Tell him to call us if there is any activity. Be sure the new guy knows what Miller and Rock look like."

"What about the Wilson Kid? Anything you want done there?" asked Tony.

"He's being taken care of as we speak."

"Yes sir," replied Tony, and he left the room.

Chapter 33

Slick was sitting in his office trying to figure out the best way to do in Misota and hoping Zipper could get Typer back before she had been hurt. Damn! There were so many things to think about.

In detailed conversation with Notes, Slick learned that each loan to a Beverly graduate had been from a bank, not from the Beverly Trust. The Trust put up money to cover the loan in an account. Once the loan went through, a bearer bond was substituted for the cash, and the cash had been withdrawn. The cash was then returned to the Trust's account, normally in the same bank, less the cost of the bond, which was added to the graduate's bill. The trust in turn purchased bearer bonds from the open market. The Beverly had a secret agreement with each of the three banks. If a loan defaulted, the bank received the full payment amount of the bearer bond, and in ninety days, the bank refunded any excess over the defaulted loan. The bank had the free use of the excess over repayment for ninety days. It was equally as sweet for the bonding company because the Beverly guaranteed half the loss for the first five years. Thus far, the Beverly had not paid out a single extra cent.

All negotiable bonds were held in safety deposit boxes in the three banks the Trust dealt with. It took Charter Committee approval to remove any bond from any of the three boxes. Due to each committee member's financial position, all three banks had agreed to their control.

The control of the Charter Committee is what had Slick worried the most. At this moment the Trust had guarantees on fifty-eight loans totaling just over three and a half million dollars. The loss of the three and a half million would have a serious impact, although not a crippling one. The loss of all the other stocks and bonds would be crippling to the Trust, almost to the point of bankruptcy. The problem with that thinking was that a member of the Charter Committee would have to have been in with Misota for him to have had that knowledge.

A knock came on the door and Notes walked into the room wearing a big smile. "I have to admit Slick, you are good. I just received the information on Vera. She is one of Misota's top hookers. I don't doubt that she passed on everything Holbrook said to Misota."

"Hell, Notes" Slick spit out. "That was a couple of years ago! Could they have been planning this takeover that long?" asked Slick.

"I hadn't thought of that. I guess they could have been or they might have just started asking around, and found out that Vera had conversations with Holbrook when he was investigating the trust. We don't know when they compromised Speed and Beagle."

There was silence in the room while both men contemplated what had been said. The ringing of the phone shattered the muted moment.

"Slick, we got company," said Zipper.

"Who?"

"The guys that had Jimmy last night, plus a couple others," answered Zipper.

"If there are spies out there, the young Misota will be among them too... Send a couple guys around the area. I'm sure you will find Misota within a block or two. Tell them to be sure and check the side streets and alleys. Let me know when you find him. What about Typer? Anything?" asked Slick.

"Nothing to get excited about yet. The guys are still out there looking," replied Zipper before he hung up...

Notes left the room as soon as he had heard the news on Tarka. As soon as Notes closed the door, Slick's desk drawer phone rang. "Slick." spoke Jaw. "Misota has upped the hit list. Rock is now on the list, but he wants to do you and Jimmy personally. He's looking for Mott and Townson. I know

Misota, and from what I know, he is old school. I think he wants Jimmy because of the beating he gave his kid."

"That's a pretty good assumption. We'd best keep Jimmy and Mary here for the time being. In the meantime, I'm going to get Mott and Townson up here to solidify their alibis."

Slick called Rock and had him bring Mott and Townson up to his office. While he waited, Slick called Suzanne at the hospital. He had notified her earlier. She and Sandy were in the room with Holbrook. Sandy answered the phone and passed it to Suzanne.

"He's conscious now and out of danger. He's mad as hell," said Suzanne.

"Have they said how long they are going to keep him?" asked Slick.

"The Doctor said at least two days. He has a broken jaw, two cracked ribs and several bruised ribs. The worst part is his broken fingers, because they broke fingers on each hand," said Suzanne as she began to weep.

"Did he say how they broke his fingers?"

"He told the police they held him in a chair and hit his fingers with the handle of a butter knife," said Suzanne, who was now openly sobbing.

"Did he say who the guys were?"

"He told the police he didn't, but he talked to Sandy before they wired his jaw. Sandy has something to tell you. If it's what I think it is, I want them in the hospital for months."

Sandy got on the phone. "Sandy here, Mr. Miller. Mr. Holbrook said that it took four guys to do this to him. Two of the guys were at the park. He said to tell you first chance I got, and this is my first chance."

Slick thanked Sandy and pressed the button for an internal line. As soon as Zipper picked up he said, "Zipper, Misota has put Rock on the hit list. Have you found Emile yet?"

"No, we checked every street, alley and car for two blocks."

"Well if there is a hit on us, try looking above ground level. Try parking decks and rooftops. If they find him, don't let him know. Let me know where he is."

"Next thing is," said Slick wryly, "two of the guys that beat up Holbrook are the same two who had the shotguns yesterday. Check with our cop friend and find out who they are and see if you can snatch them. If you can, take them to the warehouse. No need to be gentle," said Slick wryly.

"You got it."

In a few minutes, Rock came in with Townson and Mott. Both had regained most of their composure. They sat in front of Slick's desk, like two school kids in front of their principal.

"Charlie, you need to call your client in Hickory. Get him to cover for you in case Misota starts checking on you. You can use my phone," said Slick, as he pushed the instrument toward the edge of the desk. Slick got up and motioned Townson to follow him. They walked to the back corner of the room.

"Talk softly," said Slick with a cold stare. "How long has Misota had his hooks in you?"

"It started a couple of years ago. When I first started gambling again, it was through a bookie. I did horses, football, basketball, all the standard stuff. I didn't know Misota owned the bookie. One day I walked in on another guy placing a bet and later saw him at Frenchie's Bar. We got to talking and seemed to hit it off pretty well. After a while he started giving me a tip now and then. I began winning more than I lost. It all happened within four or five months. Then he invited me to a floating poker game. I lost my ass the first three quarters of the night, but then I began to come back. I ended up down only a couple hundred. We played several times after that and I'd win a few hundred, and lose a few hundred. One night I was really hot and walked away with twenty-five hundred. That was the last time I was a big winner. I'd win a few hands, but when the big pots came up, I always lost. They kept taking my markers. I paid them, for the most part, but I couldn't catch up. So, I kept playing to get even and to get out. That took about three months. About a year ago Emile Misota visited me in my office one afternoon, and that's when I turned.

"Sounds like a set-up to me," said Slick.

"Looking back now, I'm sure it was. Do you remember when I slipped and hit the edge of my desk and got this scar?" asked Townson, pointing at a scar above his eye.

"Yeah, Misota?"

Townson nodded and asked, "Can I call Betty now and tell her I'll be late?"

"No, call her and tell her you're in an all-nighter and won't be home tonight."

Mott finished his call, so Townson made his. During Townson's call, Slick questioned Mott and found the time frame to be about the same. When the final call was finished Slick sent them both back to their room.

Alone, Slick reflected on what he had learned. The Misota's had been planning this for at least two years. That would obviously make it a long-range plan with nothing tied in so there wouldn't be a critical closure date, unless it was a takeover. If his takeover dictated the closure date, would that account for the hit or would the hit be revenge for what happened to Emile? The first attempt was before the incident with Emile that put it before the takeover plan.

That gave Slick two tracks to think down. What difference would it make if he had the reins or not? The difference would be a new system if he chose to incorporate one. He probably would eventually. If there were a Misota man inside who would be concerned about less power or access to the money, he would have to be high up. There weren't many "high ups".

The ringing of the secret phone startled Slick out of his thoughts. Immediately a tense Jaw said, "Slick, they are on the move. Misota sent somebody, probably a team, to get Jimmy, maybe Mary too."

"I'm on my way. Let Zipper know that I have Rock and have him call a warning to Jimmy and Mary."

Slick burst into Mott's room. Instantly he was grabbed and thrown over a chair onto a couch. It was reflex action. Too late, Rock recognized Slick and thought is was over for him.

Slick immediately rose to his feet as indifferent as Peter Sellers would have been in "The Pink Panther." He looked at Mott and Townson saying, "If you two guys leave this room before I get back, you're dead meat." Then turning to Rock he said, "Let's go!"

As they rode the elevator down, Slick told a very relieved Rock about the hits ordered by Misota and that Misota was on the move.

Chapter 34

4ᵗʰ day 2:30 PM

The last thing Tarka remembered was standing on the sidewalk in front of the Beverly Hotel. A man asked if she was Nancy Tarka. She had answered yes, saw a flash of white cloth and all had gone black.

Tarka awoke lying in the fetal position on a filthy couch that stank of oil and grease. She fought off panic as consciousness slowly allowed her to become aware of her surroundings and situation. Not opening her eyes she remained motionless and listened for any sound in the room. There was none, but she was sure there was someone there... She slowly opened her lower eye. She could see a pair of men's shoes, with trousers hanging over them. They were in front of a set of chair legs. She assumed the man was sitting. She closed her eye and waited. Shortly she heard the squeak of a door. She opened the same eye. A man chuckled and a pair of feet walked across her field of vision and disappeared.

"Fred, you really are a pervert. You should cover the woman's ass. Go over there and pull her skirt down. What the hell are you doing, daydreaming about her ass?"

"Up yours Ted. When she wakes up she can cover it herself if she wants to," said Fred.

"What the hell do you think she's going to do, wake up and see that tiny pickle sticking out of your pants and throw her clothes off?" teased Ted.

"You're as funny as a baby on a meat hook," spat Fred.

"The boss said no touching. If you do, you'll be dead in a New York minute," said Ted.

Tarka realized her butt must be showing. She began to moan and rolled over. She could see down her body that her skirt was indeed above her panties. She overcame the knee jerk response to immediately cover herself, thinking they had already seen all they were gong to see. She rolled over onto her back, keeping her legs together, and looked around. Then she lazily looked down and nonchalantly pulled down her skirt.

"Well there goes that idea Fred," laughed Ted.

"Where am I?" asked Tarka fearfully.

"You don't worry about that," said the man, whom she now recognized as the voice of Fred.

"Don't let Fred scare you Miss. If you answer the questions truthfully, I won't let that pervert get you," said Ted nodding at Fred.

"In your dreams," said Fred.

Tarka figured the questions would be about the Beverly. She pondered her problem and realized she had not been tied up. Sarcastically she said, "I don't see any way I'm going to get out of here without getting hurt or raped or both. I have an idea what you want to ask me. I don't know anything. I hope one of you is man enough to handle a real woman."

Fred spat, "You watch it bitch, or I'll show you what kind of men are here now!"

"You already have... Do I turn you on, or do you have a Bic in your pocket?" asked Tarka.

Laughing, Ted said, "Easy Fred, the boss is on his way here now. You know how he is about slapping women around."

"She better watch her nasty-ass mouth."

Tarka looked around the room for something she could use for a weapon. There was nothing in the room but two chairs, an empty wooden coat rack near the door, a pedestal ashtray between the chairs, and a large wooden desk with a high back wooden chair behind it. The walls were bare without even a fire extinguisher hanging on them.

Tarka heard voices approaching. "Be sure that the hacker doesn't leave the office for any reason. Whatever he wants, you get it for him. He's our ace in the hole to snatch the money from the trust accounts."

The door swung open. A huge man, in a black suit, walked in and quickly scanned the room. Then a distinguished looking man in a gray suit followed him into the room. Another stocky man dressed in black followed. Obviously the black suits were bodyguards with the bulk of NFL linemen.

"Hi boss," said Fred. "We have her safe and sound."

The distinguished looking man immediately started yelling, "What's the matter with you two idiots? She isn't blindfolded! She isn't even tied up! She's seen all our faces!"

Fred and Ted jumped up looking stupidly at each other. Fred finally mumbled, "No one told me to tie her up or to blindfold her."

"Do I have to tell you to clean your ass when you shit? Get the hell out of here! I'll deal with your stupid asses later."

One of the bodyguards walked over and yanked Tarka from the couch and sat her in Fred's chair. She was terrified.

"Nancy Tarka, you are indeed a very beautiful woman," began the Boss. "However, if you want to live, forget you ever saw our faces, or your mother dies first, and then you."

"Yes sir," whispered Tarka.

"Tell me everything you know about the Beverly Hotel Trust," he demanded.

"I figured that was what this was all about and that puts me in big trouble because I was assigned to Mr. Miller's office only two weeks ago. Until some guy named Jarvis Wilson died, I didn't even know there was any kind of program, let alone a trust fund," answered Tarka.

"Punch her in the stomach," ordered the Boss.

The blow came immediately and it sank deep into her stomach. All the air was expelled from her lungs before she could scream from the pain. The only sound she made was a strong grunt as she folded and began to fall off the chair. The guard caught her before she fell, and pushed her back into the chair.

"Nancy, it's going to get worse. We're going to punch your tits, your crotch, and belt your naked ass until you tell us what we need to know. Provided you're still alive, just imagine the pictures they'll take of you to be shown in the courtroom, if...."

If you're stupid enough to press charges against us think of your shame in court while you morn your mother's death.

"I'm not really interested in having you beaten. First I want your information, and second your silence. Just to refresh your memory..." A nod of his head brought a second penetrating punch to her stomach that felt worse than the first. "This is just the beginning until you tell us what we want to know about the trust. I'm going to give you some time to think about it before we get serious," said the Boss.

He rose and walked out of the office, followed by the two guards. The sound of the office door slamming jarred Tarka's nerves. Realization of her dire circumstances hit her hard. Rescue was out of the question. No one knew where she was. She wasn't sure anyone even knew she had been abducted!

Chapter 35

Zipper immediately put word out on the street about Tarka's disappearance, including the van's description and tag number. He also notified the cabbies he knew to keep their eyes open for any leads. He soon learned that the tag had been stolen, ending that lead.

Almost immediately, word got back that Fred Purser and Ted Comer, two Misota men, had been seen hanging around the Beverly hotel about the time Tarka had been abducted. Zipper put this information out on the streets too.

Within forty-five minutes of the latest tidbit getting on the streets, a medium built man, with broad shoulders, a surprisingly small waist and long dirty shoulder-length blond hair, wearing an army fatigue jacket, observed Carlos Misota being driven from his office. The man watching was Weeds, a street name he had acquired because of his unkempt hair and his favorite smoke. Weeds hailed a cab and with the help of other cabbies, followed Misota to a warehouse in North Charlotte.

Twenty-five minutes later Weeds called the Beverly and spoke to Zipper. "I just came back from a warehouse in North Charlotte, where I followed Carlos Misota and his men. I snooped around outside. I'm sure Typer was inside."

"How do you know that?"

"I overheard Carlos yelling at his men that they were stupid and useless for not blindfolding and tying up some woman they had inside. His last instruction to them before leaving was, 'Go back and tie the bitch in a chair, if you know how!' I quickly ran and hid in the dumpster next to Misota's car. As his men got into his car I overheard someone say, "We may have to grab a few more hostages to get the information we need."

214

"You've done a great job, Weeds!" exclaimed Zipper appreciatively. "Thanks."

In twenty minutes, Zipper had three cabs loaded with men at the warehouse. Armed with lengths of pipe, axe handles and bricks. Weeds immediately began to organize them.

"Jaw may have been a Marine, but I was Special Forces. You guys do what I tell you and we'll get that chick out in a heartbeat," instructed Weeds.

As Weed's people were getting in place, Fred and Ted walked into the office. Fred held a rope in his hand and leered at Nancy...

"I'm gonna tie you up sweet cheeks. When I get done with you, you won't have any secret places I ain't seen," said Fred.

"No, please. I won't move. Please don't tie me," cried Tarka as she leaned away from him.

Fred hesitated, "What do you have to trade for my not tying you up right now?"

"My purse is over there. I have money in it. I'll pay you," pleaded Tarka.

"I already own your money. How about a little pussy?" asked Fred grabbing his fly.

"No! No! Please no!" begged Tarka as she leaned further in the chair, and almost fell.

The two men approached her walking menacingly side by side. Tarka jumped toward them and sprayed perfume into their eyes. The men grabbed their faces, howling. Quickly Tarka grabbed the pedestal ashtray, held it by the bottom, and swung it like a baseball bat, connecting with the side of Fred's head. Fred was knocked sideways into Ted and then fell to the floor. Tarka pushed Ted. He rolled over the desk, onto the chair and finally fell to the floor. Tarka grabbed her purse, and still carrying the ashtray, dashed for the door.

In seconds, Ted came charging out of the office after Tarka. Just as he cleared the doorway, a fist connected with his chin and nearly tore his head off. Tarka, still running in panic, came upon the Beverly men that had been sent to rescue her. She raised the ashtray to attack and stopped when she recognized each of the men. She let the ashtray fall behind her and collapsed, weeping, into the nearest man's arms.

Thirty minutes later, Tarka was at the Beverly. Fifteen minutes after that, her mother was sitting in her own room on the Beverly's third floor.

Tarka and Weeds immediately reported to Slick. Each told what they had experienced and what they had overheard. Slick thanked Weeds for the excellent work in rescuing Tarka and promised him a sizable reward.

"I don't have to take this shit!" spat Weeds. "She's one of us. Why the hell are you cheapening helping our own?"

Stunned, Slick said, "I apologize Weeds." Smiling his understanding and appreciation, Slick said, "Then may I shake your hand for a job well done?"

Weeds looked at him for a moment before sticking out his hand. The two men shook hands. Weeds walked out, wearing a satisfied grin and with a swagger to his step.

Chapter 36

As Slick and Rock entered the lobby, Zipper walked up and said, "We checked again. Now we have a new guy out there. We never did find Emile but the other two are gone. Maybe they changed guards. We may have another problem. Tinker just came in and said he saw one of Misota's guys watching the front of 1st Securities this afternoon. Think they were looking for Townson?"

"Probably. I thought about them earlier and had both Mott and Townson cover their asses," Slick said to Zipper. Then he turned to Rock and said, "Let's use the basement."

The two men hurried down the stairs to the basement, along a corridor and out the back door. The reflection of the lights from the trucking terminal behind the hotel made it seem like twilight. They were forced to take advantage of whatever shadow they came upon, which for the most part kept them close to the building. Then they ran for the rusted cyclone fence separating the terminal from the hotel, and hid themselves in the overhanging vines. They worked their way along the fence until they came to an opening.

Rock and Slick were now behind the distribution warehouse. Long trailers backed up to the building and road tractors moving about to hook up. It was busy enough there for the two men who didn't want to be noticed passing through, to easily make it.

Slick led the way to the back of the Wilson's hotel, entered and took the service elevator to the Wilson's floor. The elevator opened to a small recess at the end of a hall. Slick stealthily eyed around the corner and saw a man standing in front of the Wilson's door and looking straight ahead. He knew the man would pick up any movement in his peripheral vision.

"Have any suggestions Rock?"

"We could shoot him."

217

"What if he's a cop?"

Rock shrugged, "Tell them a Misota guy did it."

"No, Rock," said Slick. "Cops are on our side."

"Jaw had Pigeon teach me to read better. I been practicing reading the newspapers. I ain't so sure the cops are on our side."

Slick smiled shaking his head, "Here's what we'll do. You know what being gay is, right?"

"Yeah," answered Rock cautiously. "I ain't into that stuff Slick, so don't ask."

"We're going to fake it."

"No sir, WE ain't gonna fake nutten. You gonna fake it. I ain't gettin' down on my knees in front of nobody's fly," said Rock stubbornly.

"Not like that. You just keep saying 'Come on sweetie. You grabbed it, now get on it,' and I'll keep trying to get you to my room. We'll talk in normal voices. The guy will come to see what's going on. When I say 'now' you turn and punch his head," explained Slick.

"I ain't gotta pull my wang out do I?"

"No, now let's get started before something happens to the Wilsons."

Rock played his part to perfection. Both men got louder and louder. In a few seconds the man came to see what was going on.

"Now!" said Slick. Rock spun and punched the guard in the face, sending the man crashing against the wall. He fell unconscious into a crumpled heap.

Rock quickly removed the man's gun and threw it to Slick. They silently ran down the hall to the Wilson's door. Very lightly Slick tried the doorknob. It noiselessly turned all the way. Slick squatted, flung the door open and yelled, "Freeze!"

Everyone in the room jumped. Parkinson, who had been talking to Mary, jerked toward Slick, before immediately recognizing him yelling, "What the hell's the matter with you?" You just scared the shit out of us!"

Mary, who was standing in front of Parkinson, screamed in fright. Jimmy vaulted over the couch and landed in front of his mother in a fighting stance. Rock sprinted past Slick, almost knocking him down.

Slick regained his balance a few feet into the room and sheepishly tried to explain that he thought Carlos Misota was on his way to get revenge for what Jimmy had done. Suddenly there was a strange look on their faces; Slick's head exploded in a flash of pain. Everything went black.

The first time Slick awoke he was face down on the couch. Mary Wilson was putting cold compresses on his neck. He raised his head enough to see broken furniture all over the room before he went out again. The second time he awoke it was to the stimuli of smelling salts being held to his nose by a medic. He tried to jerk his head back but the pain was too intense.

The room was a shambles. He looked to find Mary and Jimmy. Mary was crying and seated on a chair across from him. Jimmy was lying on the floor, being attended by a medic.

"You're a lucky fellow, Mr. Wilson," the medic was saying to Jimmy. "You'll only need tape, no stitches. The gash may be long but it isn't deep. You may have a slight concussion, but the doctor will have to determine that.

"What the hell happened?" asked Slick as his head began to clear.

Parkinson walked over and said, "While you were 'napping,' Jimmy Wilson and Rock fought World War III here."

"Rock? Where's Rock?" asked Slick.

"He's on his way to the hospital with a knife in his chest. The guy who put it there is outside lying on the roof of a cab. I've never seen anything like it in my life," said Parkinson.

"Where did they come from?" asked Slick.

"While you were standing with the door open, looking foolish, three barefoot guys in black pajamas came in behind you. One knocked you out and then they started on Jimmy. He fought them off pretty good for a while. Then Rock came rumbling in and grabbed one of the guys from behind and threw him against the wall. That guy stayed there till the police took him away. Then it was one on one. The little bastard that fought with Rock beat the stuffing out of him 'till Rock finally got hold of one of his legs. Rock threw him at the wall, but it happened that either his arm or leg hit Jimmy and knocked him sideways. The guy fighting Jimmy pulled out a knife and slashed Jimmy across the chest. Luckily, Jimmy warded off most of the blow. Rock charged the guy and the little shit stuck Rock in the chest with the knife. Rock jerked the guy over his head and threw him out the window and then collapsed," said Parkinson.

"Is Rock going to live?" asked Slick.

"I don't know. They rushed him out of here fast."

Mary came over and sat next to Slick. Wringing her hands, she looked at him and whispered, "I can't take any more of this shit Lloyd. Tell Al to get hold of me. I have to get Jimmy out of Charlotte. Those men were here to kill Jimmy. They were probably hired by that young snot that Jimmy slapped around last night."

"I'll let him know as soon as I get back to the Beverly," reassured Slick.

A police officer took Slick's statement, which was rather brief and only half true. Later, he asked Slick if he knew anything about the guy they had found down the hall. They knew he was one of Misota's men but they couldn't figure out what he had been doing at the end of the hall.

In the lobby, Slick called the Beverly. Zipper answered. He asked for Jaw.

"Something going on?" asked Zipper.

"Yeah, " said Slick. "Misota just made another attempt at Jimmy. Rock is in the hospital with a knife in his chest. Find out which hospital and get someone there to assure payment and the best care. I'll fill you in later. Right now I need Jaw."

Zipper quickly put Jaw on the line.

"Yes?" came the familiar voice.

"Jaw, Misota made another attempt at Jimmy. Rock's in the hospital with a knife in his chest, Jimmy has enough cut for fifty or sixty stitches, I need a head transplant and Mary wants to go home. We have to move on Misota now.

Chapter 37

Jarvis Wilson sat in his basement office trying to plan a coup on Misota. He had called Mary and had been very unsettled from the conversation. He thought he had maybe made a big mistake by fighting for the program in this manner. He could have approached it several other ways, but as Mary said, he always went for the flamboyant. Now he would have to just do it and get it over with.

After a brief rap on the door, Slick walked into Jaw's office. In total silence the two men sat contemplating each other. Slick finally said, "Well, 'Mr. What's-His-Name.' A fine mess you've gotten us into this time or whatever the hell that saying was in the old movies."

"No shit," retorted Jaw in total frustration. "I never in my wildest dream thought it would turn out like this. I'm surprised the Committee let me get away with this. Of course I know why. They didn't know for the most part. News flash. Parkinson just let me know a few minutes ago that Notes is Misota's man."

"Damn, that means Misota knows you're still alive."

"I don't think Notes told him yet. If he had, I doubt they would have taken the action they had tonight. Hell the only people that knew I was alive was Parkinson, Malone, Copper and Mouse at the Coroner's Office," said Jaw.

"You mean you pulled this whole thing off with only four people?" asked Slick in awe.

"Why the hell not? I died alone. Copper told his guys it was a hush-hush thing. Mouse covered the Corner's Office for any inquires. Malone did the mask, and sent the obituary. The newspapers take them as a matter of course from an undertaker. Parkinson did the legwork, but the hell with that stuff. What are we going to do to stop Misota?"

"You said he was into drugs. That takes cash. Do we know where he keeps it?"

"You've been watching too many movies. Misota washes some cash, it ends up in a business account and the payment is made by electronic transfer," said Jaw.

"Okay, what about the Beverly Trust's stocks and bonds?" asked Slick.

"They are in safe deposit boxes in the three banks we use. The only way to get them out is for Notes, or me, to call our man at each bank and make the arrangements. Notes gives the key to our messenger and the messenger gets what we authorize our man to give him," said Jaw.

"Where do the loyalties of the bank contacts lay?"

"I hope with you. I'm dead."

"Do you have the phone number of the contacts?"

Slick looked at the three names. One man was a council member. He was called first. Slick told him that as a council member, he had his complete trust. He explained there was the possibility of a shake-up and that he needed his cooperation. The man, impressed with his own new stature, readily agreed. Slick also asked him to inform the other two that they could call him to verify that Slick was now in charge. The man agreed without hesitation. He closed the conversation by telling the man he would be contacted the next morning. Slick then called the two other contact men, and repeated this same information to them. Telling them mostly the same things. They too were equally impressed. Slick felt they were his.

As Slick was explaining his plan to Jaw, the phone rang. Jaw listened a moment and then said, Send someone down. In a few minutes, Mary and Jimmy walked into the office.

Jaw paled at the sight of his son's dozen inches of transparent tape covering the wound.

"Dad, you know they don't stitch surface cuts anymore? Look here, they taped me up," said Jimmy as he opened his shirt and sat gingerly in a chair as his mother silently went to the couch and sat down.

Jaw's eyes moistened. "I really screwed this thing up," he said sadly. "I'm sorry son."

"You should be, you old bastard," spat Mary.

"Dad, you didn't cut me. You didn't force Misota to send someone after me. Misota made the decision and we have to make him pay," Jimmy adamantly responded.

"Jimmy, are you as good on a computer as your dad said you were?" Slick asked.

"Slick, if hackers had judo degrees, I'd be a twelfth degree Black Belt."

"Can you follow a system penetration back to its source?"

"Can an eagle soar?"

"Then by three tomorrow afternoon we'll own Misota," gloated Slick.

Chapter 38

Carlos Misota almost didn't want to get out of bed. The past two days had been full of frustrations. That silly ass accountant had gotten away, his kid had screwed up, and not only gotten his sorry ass beaten, but had been put in jail. The bitch got away, and he had found the ass holes that had been guarding her, hanging from a chain fall, covered with car grease. They were now in the hospital losing one, maybe two, layers of skin. The punk karate guys had gotten themselves either caught, or killed, and that yellow bunch of cowards wouldn't come out of the Beverly Hotel.

The frustration remained with him until late morning. His first ray of light came when Mott had told him to get ready for some big transfers because he was going to move the paper and money that afternoon. Then a half hour later, Townson called and told Misota that he was to make arrangements to be at First Nation Bank at three. Townson said he would be going to all three banks to pick up all the paper and transfer it to a vault in the Beverly. That confirmed what Mott had told him. Misota smiled to himself realizing those two jerks were working in tandem to bring the Beverly Trust down, and they didn't even know it!.

There was one issue still eating at Carlos. He knew that Miller and his people were probably meeting at the Beverly this morning, planning to bring him down. He thought it was incredulous that they would even think they could do him in. For God's sake, they had enough trouble just taking their pants down! The thought of that bunch of yokels even thinking they could take him, was an insult. They would never succeed. But, deep in the back of his mind was the realization that so far they had thwarted his every attempt.

The thought that they had the brass to think they could take Carlos Misota out would not leave him. The brazenness of the

225

punks began to consume him. Misota decided he would personally do the hit on the Wilsons and Miller. He knew where they were. Misota forced the thoughts of revenge out of his mind and turned to the business of killing them. Revenge would come later and be all the sweeter.

First, he had to deal with milking the Beverly Trust using the information the informants have given him. He would catch everybody in the Beverly Lobby and get it all in one sweep. Misota planned it so the runners would walk into an ambush. His boys would be spread around the lobby to snatch the paper, lock everyone in a room so they could be out in less then five minutes. Misota instructed his men not to shoot anyone unless a gun was pointed at them.

At 2:30 that afternoon Misota's computer hacker was busy emptying the bank accounts of the Beverly Hotel. He contacted the first account with little problem. The screen was titled **Withdraw-Deposit**. The next line read **Transaction Type**. One box read **Normal,** and the other read **Special**. Not wanting to take any chances, the operator hit the **Special** box. The next screen had two boxes, **All** and **Part**. The **All**, box was struck. As the transaction took place, the hacker noticed a momentary blink of the screen, but it fixed itself. He knew immediately what was happening. The hacker smiled to himself, kept quiet, and went on to the next two accounts. In less then two minutes he was finished.

"It's all yours Mr. Misota. I don't think I did half bad for being the first time on your program," said the hacker.

"Dot-Com, it's just amazing what you can do with a computer these days. In the old days, you'd have had to plan for three months and have ten guys to help you with a million dollar heist. Here you did it in less than a minute," marveled Misota.

"Electronics, Mr. Misota, it's really something," responded Dot-Com.

"How much did we get? I had sixty-mil. in there before. What's in there now?"

Dot-Com tapped rapidly over the keyboard and stopped. He started again, and stopped again. He started a third time, "Are you sure there was money in those accounts, sir? It shows a zero balance," said Dot-Com nervously.

"I'm gonna bust your ass if you don't tell me how much is in that account right now!"

"Sir, the account shows a zero balance..."

"Hacker, if you lost sixty million bucks, I'm going to kill you real slow. I'm not only going to kill you slow, I'm going to kill your mother, your father, sisters, brothers and maybe some cousins. I'm going to kill them slow and make you watch," said Misota softly, yet menacingly. From that point on, his volume increased evenly to a scream as he yelled, "You better start looking for my money or I'm going to start pulling teeth out of your head right now!"

At three fourteen, a white van stopped in front of the Beverly and discharged eight men, six of whom were carrying boxes. The men walked single file into the lobby. As soon as all eight were inside, armed men, yelling at them to drop the boxes surrounded them.

Everyone was herded to a small office and locked in along with Zipper and several men who happened to be sitting in the lobby when the Misotas took over. They huddled in the locked room for about thirty seconds before Zipper produced a key to unlock the door from the inside. The couriers ran from the room with guns drawn, taking positions around the lobby.

The Misota men grabbed boxes and ran out the front entrance. As they began to clear the door, police officers appeared from behind parked cars and adjacent building entrances. The front of the hotel was surrounded. They yelled for the robbers to drop the boxes and raise their hands. Some of the thieves tried to get back into the lobby. All the couriers were police officers. One of them yelled at the returning thugs, "Freeze Police!" The first man back through the door froze and threw his hands up in the air. The men outside were blocked

227

from going anywhere. They were surrounded by police officers and disarmed. Not a single shot had been fired.

An hour and a half passed as Carlos sat thinking about the implications of losing sixty million in mob money. He began sweating as he listened to the frantic clicking on the keys by Dot-Com. If the money wasn't found he was dead and so was Emile. He was jarred out of his thoughts by the ringing of the phone. He grabbed the receiver.

"Carlos," said the voice at the other end.

"Who's this that calls me by my first name?"

"This is Jarvis Wilson, better known as Jaw."

"Bull shit! Wilson is dead."

"I assure you Carlos, I am alive. I took your sixty million because you were trying to get my money."

Thoughts flashed through Misota's mind. This would have to be Wilson. Somehow he found out about the takeover. How the hell did he find out? Better yet, how did he get my money?

"If you are Wilson, why are you calling me?"

"No ifs about it. I am Jarvis Wilson. Carlos you're pretty sure of that yourself."

"Mr. Misota to you thief!"

"Yeah, right, Carlos. The men you sent to steal my paper are all in jail. They were involved in other crimes and their bonds have been revoked, including Emile's. However, I called to give you a chance to get your money back."

"Chance's ass. No deals Wilson. Give back the money and I'll let you out of town alive."

"Odd you should say that Carlos, because that is how you can get your money back. You and your whole organization leave North Carolina, and your money will be waiting for you when you open a new account in some other state."

The line was silent. Misota was so angry; he thought he could be having a heart attack. Then he screamed into the phone, "You fucking, stupid son-of-a-bitchen-bastard. Nobody tells Carlos Misota to get out of anywhere. I'll down every street creep in this town while you watch. I know you have a wife and kid. I'll chop them both into stew meat while they are alive. I'll..."

"Blow it out your ass Carlos. You aren't going to do a damn thing until you get your money back, and I told you how that was going to happen," Jaw interrupted, sarcastically. "That bunch of yahoos you have working for you don't have the mental capacity to threaten a cub-scout troop, and that includes your 'can't follow simple orders' kid!"

"You're dead meat!" yelled Misota.

"I'm tired of this shit. I'll call you back in an hour for your decision," Jaw said disgustedly. He slammed the phone down, laughed and turned off his voice recorder.

Chapter 39

That same morning, at nine thirty-five, two men had walked into the First Nations Bank and asked for Ralph Thompson. Mr. Thompson had greeted the men like old friends and had escorted them to the Safety Deposit Boxes. Mr. Thompson produced one key and one of the men produced another. They inserted their keys and opened Box 1220.

Mr. Thompson then produced two more keys and opened box 1235. One of the men pulled a list from his pocket. As the second man moved packets from one box to the other, they were checked off on the list. When the transfer had been completed, both boxes were closed. Mr. Thompson made of copy of the inventory, and gave the men a copy of the new key before the men had left the bank. The entire transfer had taken approximately eight minutes. Simultaneously, the same transaction had taken place at 1st Securities Bank and Charlotte's Farmer's Bank. The six men had returned to the Beverly and given the keys to Zipper.

At nine AM, Slick, Parkinson and Notes began a strategy meeting to evade Misota's attempt at taking over. It was quickly agreed that a secret transfer of stocks and bonds to the Beverly Hotel Vault would be the easiest. The transfer was set up for three that afternoon in order to have time to set up a gauntlet of Beverly people along the routes. The biggest problem facing them was hiding the cash. It was decided that the cash should be withdrawn from the banks, leaving a thousand dollars in each account. Following Note's suggestion, the transaction would be made after the transfer. It made sense to handle one thing at a time and the setting up the paper transfer would take several hours, just due to finding enough people to set up the gauntlet.

Slick then turned the meeting to an in depth analysis of the stocks held, the earnings projected, the bonds and their yield, and finally the status of the notes owed the trust. The longer the meeting went the more uncomfortable Notes seemed to become. The meeting ended at ten forty-five. Slick then called down to Weeds, who was sitting with Mott and Townson. He told him Typer would be down to release the two and give them instructions.

When Zipper realized the meeting was over, he called Slick and informed him that the paper transfer had gone smoothly and everything had been arranged for that afternoon, as they had planned earlier. Slick went immediately to Notes' office. Notes was gone, and so were the keys to the old safety deposit boxes. Slick took a list of accounts Notes had made for him to Jaw's office, where Jimmy was waiting with his lap top computer plugged into one of the phone lines.

Jimmy began. The clicking of computer keys was all that could be heard for the better part of the next hour. Finally, Jimmy said, "Done."

"What's done?" asked Slick, sitting on the couch equally anxious and bored.

"We're in all three main frames and sitting on our accounts. As soon as someone tries to electronically hit any one of the three accounts we will know. The transaction will be reversed. We'll grab their money and throw it into the account Dad set up at the other bank."

"You can't do that!" said Parkinson, who had come while Jimmy had been clicking away.

"Sir, you can't do that. I can. I do work for a living. It's hardly noticeable, but I do work. The folks north of us, and south of Binghamton, pay me to do just this sort of thing. They pay me exceptionally well, and for the most part legally," responded Jimmy to an awed Parkinson.

"What happens now?" asked Slick.

"Just like fishing, we wait for a bite," Jimmy replied assuredly.

The phone rang. It was Notes, looking for Slick, who had left a message in Notes' office to call him as soon as he had returned.

231

"Notes," said Slick. "I've got a couple appointments this afternoon. How about cutting the checks and I'll take them with me? I'll meet the runners at the banks and make sure everything goes as scheduled. You, or Parkinson, can check on the stocks and bonds to ensure they all make it here."

"I'll take care of it sir. It might be a bit inappropriate for Stanley to invade his competitors," answered the secretly elated Notes.

At one forty-five, one man walked into each of the three banks with a check, slipped from the back of the checkbook. A contact was waiting for each man, because due to the size of the check, pre-approval was required. The contact escorted the men to the teller. A certified check had been issued and each man had been out of the banks by one fifty-nine.

The men had been picked up by Slick and taken to the Mecklenburg Bank and Trust Office where the certified checks had been deposited in the account Jaw had opened earlier.

At 2:30, Jimmy Wilson jumped to attention in his chair. One of the accounts was being hit on again. Jimmy had watched the hits when the accounts were emptied. This hit was external. It was what he had been waiting for. Jimmy's nimble fingers flew over the keyboard.

In a few seconds he said, "I'm in." A few seconds later he gloatingly shouted, "I've got it!" as his fingers began to fly even faster. As suddenly as it had begun, it was over. In less time then it takes to get comfortable with the evening paper, Carlos Misota's account had been emptied.

"How much did he have in there?" asked Jaw.

"Let's see," responded Jimmy, his fingers flying over the keyboard. My God!" said Jimmy incredulously, "We plucked sixty million from him!"

The room was ghostly silent.

Chapter 40

Carlos Misota stared blankly into the phone. He knew he had been had. He could not even consider pulling out of North Carolina. He would be considered a failure by the mob. He couldn't call the Boss and tell him he had lost sixty million to a bunch of amateurs, in fact, he couldn't tell the boss anything about this because he had attempted to co-mingle company money with stolen money. That in itself would be enough to get him killed, especially after all the trouble and expense that had been gone through to wash the money. Now he had lost them both. On top of that, the cops were probably waiting for him to make a move at the Beverly and take what was left of his men. What the hell were his alternatives now?

First things first, he had to clear his head. so he headed for his exercise room. He threw his suit jacket and necktie on the floor as he walked. He unbuttoned his shirt a few buttons. Carlos went directly to the wall weights, grabbed the handles and began to exercise. He pulled the handles hard and fast to raise the weight, then slowly lowered them to an inch or two from the floor. He began in earnest to repeatedly pull fast, and lower slowly. Finally, he lowered the weights for the last time and dropped the handles. He was breathing hard and sweating profusely as he leaned over and braced himself on his thighs for a few minutes. He began walking around the room, shedding the rest of his clothes until he was down to his socks and shorts. Carlos kept walking, until his breathing had returned to normal before walking into the shower room. Naked, he entered the shower and turned the water on full. He directed the blast of tepid water to his neck and shoulders allowing the massaging water to work out the last of his anxiety. Slowly he cooled the spray. He stayed under the cooling water until he stopped sweating.

Forty-five minutes after having left his office he had returned to it. Now, dressed casually and refreshed, his mind cleared, he was ready to plan his vengeance. His first call was to a police friend inquiring if there were any special assignments tonight that would require a lot of officers. He was told that there were none. He sat at his desk pondering his problem when the phone startled him.

"Jaw here Carlos, you ready to start packing?"

"I'm packing, Wilson, and you can bet your sorry ass I'm going to use it on you! Nobody gives Carlos Misota orders! Who the hell do you think you are?

"Who do I think I am? I think I'm the guy who has your sixty million," said Jaw.

"I told you, it's Mr. Misota to scum like you Wilson."

"I'm sorry you are so uncooperative Carlos. I should have known anyone with the balls of a piss ant and the brains of a slug would be impossible to deal with. You know where to find me. It will be a new experience for me to take trash like you off the streets." The line went dead.

It took thirty minutes of pacing and two cigars for Misota to calm down. He called his driver and had him take him near the Beverly Hotel. He then directed him to go into all the parking decks, alleys, and basement garages; anywhere a contingent of police could hide in ambush. There had been no sign of anything unusual. He was driven back to his office. Later, Carlos contacted his outlying areas to call in more men. Forty-five minutes later he went on the same drive again. Still nothing.

Later that evening around eleven o'clock he was driven around the Beverly Hotel again. All was peaceful, as it had been during his earlier trips. Suddenly, he realized there was one area he hadn't checked. He had the driver circle around his own area and found one policeman parked in the lot of a closed service station   His dome light was on and, through field glasses, Misota could see he was writing a report. The officer didn't look up as they drove past and returned to his office.

234

Misota had twelve men in the room, giving them instructions on what was to take place at the Beverly Hotel. He showed the men photographs of the people who were not to be killed, unless their own life was in danger, and they had better have a witness. The pictures included Jaw, Mary, Jimmy, Lloyd, Townson, Mott and Notes. Anyone else who gave them a problem was fair game. Everybody was to be knocked out, or worse. All twelve began to understand the importance of this mission when Misota announced he would lead them in. They climbed into a delivery truck and were driven to the Beverly Hotel Delivery Entrance.

The men easily broke down the door and charged into the dimly lit hotel basement. They were at the beginning of a long corridor. Misota was third through the door. Within a few seconds the lights brightened. They saw Jaw and Lloyd standing at the end of the passageway. They all stopped. Both men were holding guns.

"Shoot the bastards!" yelled Misota. "Try to wing them. I want to kill them myself!" He stepped forward and began firing his Uzi Pistol.

Lloyd and Jaw immediately fell apart to the sound of falling glass. Slick had set up a large mirror at the end of the darkened hallway and had it angled so it reflected his and Jaw's images down the hall while they stood out of the way of danger.

A thought flashed through Misota's mind, that something was wrong, but his rage at the ploy drove him into override caution. Misota urged his men down the passage to the now closed door while he stood stationary. The door was steel and locked.

One of Misota's men said, "Boss these walls are fake. They're made out of cardboard or something."

Misota pushed against the wall. It rocked and gave a little. "Push!" yelled Misota. The wall slid a few inches and began to fall away. Spotlights immediately flooded their eyes. Instantly, twenty men holding automatic rifles materialized. Misota's men shaded their eyes in stunned confusion.

"FBI, drop your weapons!" yelled a voice.

"Bull shit! It's another scam. Those are probably street creeps. Beat their asses!" yelled Misota as he charged out the back door.

"Gentlemen, I assure you, this is FBI Agent Allen Packer. Some of you have talked with me before. Do any of you recognize my distinctive voice?" asked Agent Packer, in his throaty Texas brogue.

"I recognize it," one man said.

"Then ya best put your pieces on the floor and back off. You boys are lined up like ducks in a shooting gallery. If ya don't do it now, ya'll gonna die," Packer stated flatly.

The men started putting their weapons on the floor. Then a Misota man yelled, "These are only pussy Feds you guys. They can't shoot unarmed men. Make a run for the door!"

Both groups charged for the exit and collided near the doorway. Fists began to fly. There weren't enough Misotas for one-on-one fighting. As Misota men began to hit the floor, agents who were not fighting handcuffed them. When an agent went down, he was replaced. The fight lasted several minutes. Final score: FBI- twelve, Misota's - zero, and one had gotten away.

As the fighting had come to the pre-determined end, Agent Packer and another agent had run from the basement in pursuit of Carlos Misota. They didn't have far to go. On the ramp to the basement, Carlos, Jaw, Jimmy and Carlos's driver/bodyguard were locked in battle.

Carlos and Jaw were fighting with fists. Jimmy and the Misota soldier were fighting with fists, feet, elbows and knees. At one point, Carlos knocked Jaw to the ground, just about the same time that Jimmy had knocked the soldier down. As Carlos was about to stomp on Jaw's face, Jimmy leaped and kicked Carlos in the chest. Jimmy fell to the ground from the impact, hitting his head. He lay dazed on the ground. Jaw and the soldier got up at the same time. The soldier kicked Jimmy in the stomach, as Jaw planted a fist on the soldier's chin. The soldier was sent spinning.

The agent with Packer was about to interfere when Packer stopped him saying, "I know the background here. Let 'em finish."

Jimmy got to his feet, as did the two assailants. Jaw went for Carlos, and Jimmy went for the soldier. As blows were traded, father and son were forced back to back. Jaw glanced over his shoulder and said, "I'm getting tired. Lets finish it."

"Yes sir."

Both father and son became more aggressive. The tide of the battle turned immediately. Jimmy put his man down as Jaw's final three punches to Carlos's face downed him.

Carlos held up his hand and said, "Enough."

Jaw turned to Packer and said, "He's yours."

The other agents were marching the handcuffed Misota soldiers out of the basement during the closing minutes of the fight and watched the ending. Carlos slowly got to his feet and leaned against a dumpster. His mouth and face were bloodied, his hair askew and this clothes filthy. He looked like a candidate for Jaw's program. Misota bent and pulled a small caliber automatic from an ankle holster and stood back from the dumpster.

"Gun!" somebody yelled.

"Don't Carlos," pleaded Packer, as he walked forward. "You don't have a chance."

"Stay back. No matter what, I can at least get you," gasped Misota. Packer stopped.

"You know I can't let you take me," Carlos said softly.

Agent Packer, suddenly realizing Carlos's intention, said, "No, Mr. Misota, not here, not next to garbage. You're a man of honor. You deserve better than that. Let us take you. You can post bail and then do it out in the clear, maybe under an Elm or a Maple tree with lots of grass around it, but not here in a driveway for garbage trucks."

237

"Thank you Allen. You've pissed me off many times, but I've always respected you as an honorable man. Don't you see I have already lost my honor," said Misota, his eyes full of tears. He slowly raised the pistol to his head. There was a loud report from a fired weapon and everyone jumped in alarm. Misota stood ashen faced, holding his wrist.

"Good shooting Hank," said Packer. "If you had hit the weapon an inch or two higher, the impact wouldn't have broken the man's wrist."

Chapter 41

As Notes walked out of jail on bond he was met and "escorted" to the Beverly Hotel where he was taken to Slick's office. Slick and Jaw were waiting there for him.

"Notes," said Slick. "Jaw and I flipped a coin to see who throws you out the window. Jaw won. He gets the first try. Then we alternate." said Slick.

Sweating profusely Notes said, "I'll tell you anything you want to know."

"Who owns the sixty million?" asked Jaw.

"The family I work for in New Jersey."

"How do you contact them?" asked Slick.

"Usually by computer."

"How much money can you scrape up?" asked Slick.

Notes paused a moment and said, "about a million and a half."

Jaw sighed aloud. Shaking his head in disgust, he walked over and jerked Notes out of his chair. Notes began screaming. Jaw dragged him toward the open space in front of the window despite Notes' best efforts to fight him. Jaw easily spun Notes around. He led Notes by his shirt collar and belt, took two fast steps and threw the screaming man at the window. There was a cracking sound. The base of the window moved slightly.

Notes lay on the floor sobbing. Almost incoherently he said, "I can come up with five million eight hundred thousand."

"How fast?" asked Slick.

"By the end of the day!"

"Damn Notes, that's more then we need," laughed Slick.

They took Notes to the computer room and put him to work contacting his boss. Once contact had been made, Slick instructed Notes to ask if they could call in some manner that would be secure for both parties. It was settled to call at a designated Charlotte pay phone that Notes knew of in one hour.

The site turned out to be a pay phone outside a library within easy distance of the Beverly Hotel. They could make it there with plenty of time to spare. Luckily they arrived twenty minutes early. They found the phone in use with two more people waiting in line. About ten minutes to the hour, it cost Notes fifty dollars to bribe the one person now in front of him. It nearly cost him his front teeth when he had urged the huge woman currently using the phone to hurry up. She had frowned at him the first time he had asked. The second time he had asked, she swung a round house right at him that had barely missed. Five minutes before the hour a hundred dollar bill had convinced the woman to get off the phone, although she still had uncomplimentary things to say regarding Notes' manhood.

Within seconds of the hour, the phone rang and Slick answered, "I understand you are missing sixty million dollars."

"I don't know what you are talking about," said a voice.

"I have someone here that will explain, but first listen to this," said Slick. He played the tape of the last conversation between Wilson and Misota. When it was over he put Notes on the line. Notes explained it all and passed the phone back to Slick.

"As I said, I understand you are missing sixty million bucks."

"I guess I am. Do you know where I can find it?"

"In Misota's account if we can come to terms."

"Here's the terms, you give me back my sixty and you get to live. I do know who you are and who Jaw is. I also know you both have families," said the voice."

"Let's look at the numbers logically. You don't have sixty million. Let's assume it's for a drug deal. The sixty will probably bring you back a hundred plus the sixty invested. That is a total loss of over two hundred million. Big money even in your circles, not to mention the loss of confidence by a cartel or two," Slick reasoned.

"What do you propose?"

"There's such a thing as a finder's fee. It's usually twenty percent."

"That's twelve million I have to make up!" said the voice.

"I really don't expect twelve, but do keep in mind that that is a bit less than you tried to take from us. A greedy man always ends up dead, or broke. I'd like to propose this. What if I send you back fifty-five million and tell you how to turn it into sixty million the same day?"

"What do you get out of it?"

"Five million."

"Okay bright boy, how is that going to happen?"

"Here's what we propose. I have your word that there will be no reprisals of any kind against the Wilson family, or against my family. You also let Notes and his family off the hook, with no reprisals of any kind, if I do everything I say and if everybody else does what they are supposed to do."

"You make it sound like a lot of people are involved," said the voice.

"I guess it does. Only two actions are necessary, ours and one other party."

"What happens if someone doesn't come through?" asked the voice.

"If it is Jaw and I, the no reprisal deal is off and we are fair game. If someone else reneges, you have at him. Believe me, sixty million we can't spend is not what I want to die for. I'd much rather have the five million and send you back the fifty-five" explained Slick.

"You said the full sixty."

"No sir, I didn't. I said I could show you how to turn it into sixty."

"I will end up with sixty million, or have a piece of who don't come through on the last five million. Is that right?"

"Yes sir." said Slick.

"I'll be back to you in ten minutes or less."

Seven minutes later the phone rang. Slick picked up, "Yes sir."

"Explain this deal to me," said a new voice.

Slick went over the whole thing again.

"When do I find out about the last five million?" asked the new voice

"When you tell me we have a deal sir."

"Carlos was a good friend. I think he may have underestimated you and your organization. His ranting does not become a man in his position. I will accept your terms and give you my word as a man of honor. What about you Lloyd Miller, are you a man of honor?"

"Sir, when I first heard your voice, I pictured in my mind a man of honor just as Mr. Misota is. I too am a man of my word and have nothing more precious. I am negotiating this deal based on the incident at hand. I purposely did not include anything beyond this incident to show that I never again want to negotiate for my life. When you say you accept this deal, I know you are being extremely forgiving of this incident. I do not want to try your patience."

"The last five million will be transferred to your account by Notes. He has assured me that before the close of the day, he can come up with five million eight hundred thousand. He betrayed us, but he also gave us much needed help in the past. Our rules are not like yours. I would leave him with something for his family," answered Slick.

"You speak well, Lloyd Miller. Even though that was a lot of bull shit, it was necessary. I would like to know where Notes got the five million, but I'll have mine so I'm comfortable," said the voice, just before the line went dead.

With a loud sigh Slick said, "It's over. Notes you heard the deal. Get the hell out of my sight and you better pay up."

"Thanks Slick, I owe you," said Notes turning to leave.

"Don't even think I want to collect," yelled Slick as he dialed another number. "Jimmy, Slick here. Send the fifty-five back to Misota's account."

Later standing outside the entrance of the Beverly, Slick and Zipper shook hands with the Wilsons. Slick and Jaw stood

242

looking deep into each other's eyes for a long moment before Jaw said, "It's all yours Slick. I'm taking my wife, my kid and my fat ass the hell out of Dodge."

"I guess it's time," said Slick. "After all these years you finally got what you gave to so many of us, your Second Last Chance. Go for the gold big time, you deserve it."

Slick walked with the Wilsons to the waiting limousine. Everyone got in except for Jaw.

"One last thing," said Jaw. "I located your father a few months back. I called him while you were negotiating for our lives. He's standing over there." Jaw pointed to a man standing about forty feet away. When Slick looked over, Jaw climbed into the cabin and slammed the door. As the limousine began to roll forward, Slick yelled, "You son of a bitch!"

The limousine slowed, a window came down and Jarvis Alvin Wilson stuck his hand out and let his finger do the talking.

Slick did a double take from the limousine to his father and back. Slick and his father squared off, facing each other as if about to re-create the gunfight at the OK Corral. Almost at the same time, both men began walking toward each other with fists clenched and arms arched at their sides.

About The Author

Bill Wiktorek has been writing for over 20 years. As a former Marine Officer and a bit of a "rounder" in his younger days, Bill is no stranger to the rougher side of life. In his current position as an apartment manager he is exposed daily to the ups and downs of life through the residents that pass through his complex. Bill's unique understanding of human nature led naturally to his creating, **"2ⁿᵈ Last Chance."** When he isn't talking tough, he enjoys traveling and relaxing with his wife Marie. They fondly call Charlotte, North Carolina their home.